PRAISE FOR
THE
LOST
MAGICIAN

A *Times*, *Sunday Times*, *Observer*, *I Newspaper*,
Sunday Express and *New Statesman*
BOOK OF THE YEAR

'Piers Torday has an unrelenting imagination,
cleverly mixing nostalgia and modernity. After reading this
you will never look at a bookmark in the same way'
The Times – Books of the Year 2018

'Masterly storytelling, both entertaining and profound'
The Sunday Times – Children's Books of the Year 2018

'A major new voice'
Observer – Best Children's Books of 2018

'A lustrously lovely ode to libraries, to imagination, and to the magic of a wonderful story, if any book has the power to separate children from their screens, it's this'

'A wonderful tribute to Narnia, CS Lewis and the magic of books and reading'

'Artistically daring … it is as much about storytelling as about creating an enjoyable story'

'A phenomenal adventure story'

'Expertly handled, and written with charm, passion and fervour'

THE
LOST
MAGICIAN

Also by Piers Torday

The Last Wild
The Dark Wild
The Wild Beyond

There May Be
A Castle

With Paul Torday

The Death of an Owl

Plays

The Box of Delights
(based on the novel by
John Masefield)

PIERS TORDAY

THE LOST MAGICIAN

Quercus

QUERCUS CHILDREN'S BOOKS

First published in Great Britain in 2018 by Hodder and Stoughton

This paperback edition published in 2019

3 5 7 9 10 8 6 4

A CIP catalogue record for this book
is available from the British Library.

ISBN 978 1 78429 450 2

Printed and bound in Great Britain by CPI Group (UK) Ltd, Croydon, CR0 4YY

The paper and board used in this book are made from
wood from responsible sources.

Quercus Children's Books
An imprint of Hachette Children's Group
Part of Hodder and Stoughton
Carmelite House
50 Victoria Embankment
London EC4Y 0DZ

An Hachette UK Company
www.hachette.co.uk

www.hachettechildrens.co.uk

To Ruby, a Reader

'Many a man lives a burden to the earth; but a good book is the precious lifeblood of a master spirit, embalmed and treasured up on purpose to a life beyond life.'

John Milton, *Areopagitica* (1644)

INTRODUCTION

Inside this archive you will find more classified
government files that have just been released.
They concern the now notorious 'Magician Project'
(KV 1/1567-1 & 3) run at the end of the Second
World War by a small group of idealistic but
controversial scientists working out of the War
Ministry's secret research unit at Porton Down
in Salisbury.

Led by Professor Diana Kelly (KV 3/1567-1), the
Magician Project's aims and methods are still
shrouded in secrecy, as many documents relating
to the affair have since been destroyed. However,
Professor Kelly was quoted on the record as saying
that the aim was, simply, 'to end human conflict,
once and for all, for ever'.

These newly released files prove beyond all doubt
what had until now been merely rumoured – that
children, some as young as 8, were used as guinea

pigs for the very controversial experiments. And, despite repeated official denials to the contrary, these files show that the Magician Project remains the first and last ever instance of the British government attempting to use *magic*.

Not just any magic. The most powerful magic there is...

CHAPTER 1
Larry Goes into a Library

This is a story about four children called Simon, Patricia, Evelyn and Larry. After the war was over, their parents sent them away from London, because their home had been damaged in a bombing raid, and they needed to find a new one.

'But don't worry,' said their father, who had been very brave in the war, with a strip of medals as long as your arm, 'we're at peace now. This is a new beginning for all of us, you'll see. For the whole world.'

Then he saw them off on a very crowded train, waving and waving his hat like a victory flag, until the line of carriages rounded a bend coming out of Waterloo, and the children could see him no longer. The train rattled along to Salisbury station in Wiltshire, near Stonehenge.

Here they were met by a woman with a very upright posture and a kind smile, who helped them with their bags. They clambered into the back of her car. This was an Armstrong Siddeley Lancaster and it looked like a cross between a Rolls Royce and a tank. Larry's eyes widened as he sprawled on to the burgundy leather seat, as he was only eight, and had never seen an Armstrong Siddeley Lancaster before.

'Comes with the job,' said the woman, shutting the doors. 'Don't gawp, Larry, it makes you look like a frog.'

'Look!' whispered Evelyn (who was ten). 'There's an escape hatch in the ceiling.'

'It's called a sun roof actually,' said Simon, because he was fourteen and permanently lived in a world of new excitements that his younger siblings could not even begin to understand.

'What is it you do again, Professor?' asked Patricia, pushing her glasses back up her nose to admire the handsome bank of instruments in the dashboard. As the oldest girl, at thirteen, she felt she could take the lead on conversation with grown-ups.

'Sorry, can't hear you!' said Professor Diana Kelly, as she started the very loud engine. Then she drove them out of Salisbury, driving so fast that they all had to grab the seat to stop themselves sliding off. The car shot across

4

the plain, past Stonehenge, shadowed and lonely in the afternoon July sun, and through the cooling shade of a beech wood.

Then the Professor suddenly turned off the road at such speed that Larry's bear fell clean off his lap on to the floor. The Armstrong Siddeley Lancaster roared down a gravel track, sheltered by neat rows of lime trees on either side. When the house came into view, it was dazzling.

It was a kind of manor house, of which there are many in that part of the world, and to the children it just looked very old and very smart. The stone was honey coloured, blazing in the afternoon sun, and there were roses clambering up the side. They twisted over windows so full of sunlight that the children couldn't see into the house at all. It felt more like the house was looking out at them.

'Welcome to Barfield Hall,' said Professor Kelly, applying the brake expertly, which made a satisfying hiss. 'Very old, even older than me. Also comes with the job.'

The children made faces at each other. They didn't know what the Professor's job was. All they knew was they were to stay here for the summer while their mother searched for a new home in London. The Professor was a friend of *her* mother, although the exact nature of that connection was shrouded in mystery.

'Mrs Martin, the housekeeper, will serve you some tea in the drawing room at four,' called out the Professor, already disappearing through the open front door. 'Feel free to explore, but the top floor is out of bounds. It's not . . .'

The rest of her words were lost as she melted into a shadowy corridor, and faded from view.

They all sat for a moment in the hot car, listening to the engine tick down, and some bees buzzing over the two lavender bushes that stood like sentries either side of the arched main entrance. Then Simon grabbed Larry's bear off the car floor and was out and off, racing across the gravel towards the garden.

'Last one to catch me is It! No sudden moves or the bear's a goner!'

Then they were all racing and laughing, bags and coats clean forgotten about, sprinting along terraces of cracked flagstones, ducking in and out of little box hedgerows arranged in a sort of maze. Somewhere between a lopsided oak tree and a dank pond full of flies, Larry retrieved his bear, and led the march indoors, clutching him proudly like a trophy of war.

Inside the house, everything was shaded and cooler, smelling of beeswax and leather. Now they trod softly, on heavy carpets, looking about in wonder at oil paintings the size of walls, of naval battles raging on tempestuous seas, or panting hounds surrounded by their kill of dead pheasants and hares.

Evelyn made a face. 'I am definitely going to be a vegetarian when I'm grown up,' she said.

'Hark at her,' said Simon. 'Are you going to wear sandals too and live on a boat?'

'Just ignore him, Evie,' said Patricia, punching her older brother on the arm. 'He's being a beast. As usual.' Then she pulled Simon away by the elbow, hissing something in his ear as they walked in lockstep down the corridor.

Evie shrugged, staring at the bloodied animals so hard that she thought she could smell them. Then she didn't want to look at the picture any more, especially not at any more blood. *Not ever again*, she thought. They had all seen enough blood to last them for a very long time indeed. She could feel the darkness pinching in at her mind, bringing with it the memory that never went away, the nightmare she could never shake.

That day on Maguire Street – the water from the jets, the sirens caterwauling, someone – a teacher, or a fireman, she wasn't sure – putting a blanket over her shoulders, and there, there in the middle of the road, right in front of her . . . something that should never be in the middle of the road, or anywhere for that matter.

Something she never wanted to see again.

'Come on, Evie!' called Simon from an open doorway somewhere, trying to sound cheering. 'Look what we've found.'

'We're guessing this is the drawing room,' said Patricia, already sprawled over a sofa that her mother might have described as 'very French'.

It was a long room full of mirrors, and very different kinds of paintings to those in the hall. There were no ships or slavering hounds, just lots of wonderful colours, in so many different shapes. One was nothing but exploding blues and fluorescent yellows, in hexagons, circles and squares. All of it overlaid with ridged sprays of multicoloured paint. Evie didn't know what it was about at all, only that she preferred the bright, cheering colours to the bloodied animals in the corridor.

Simon was poking around at a tall wiry sculpture on a plinth. It looked more like a radio transmitter mast than a piece of art, he thought. 'This your kind of thing is it, E? I bet this one was made by a *vegetarian*.'

Patricia shot Simon one of her looks, the kind that made him flush with shame, and much to his annoyance, he did.

'Anyhow, I don't think much of the service in this place.' He glanced at his watch. 'It's nearly quarter past four already. I wonder where that tea's got to.'

His sister sat up, in that way people do when they suddenly remember important things. 'That's not all we're missing. Does anyone remember what we did with Larry?'

Simon waved a hand airily. 'Probably still making teddy bear picnics in the garden.' He picked up a magazine from a pile on a low silk ottoman. It was very plain, in exercise book blue, with no pictures but lists of names on the front. All the names seemed to be Professors or Doctors of something. He flicked through a few densely typed pages of equations and diagrams and then tossed it aside. There were drawings of the skull and the brain, covered in arrows.

'Very brainy . . . Far too brainy to actually read, unfortunately.' Then he swapped the magazine for a pack of playing cards from the ottoman. 'Right, you two. If we aren't to have our tea, then we are jolly well going to have some gin rummy.'

And he began to shuffle.

Larry was not making teddy bear picnics in the garden. He was standing halfway up a broad oak staircase, gazing in awe at a stained-glass window, which rained down pretty colours upon him and Grey Bear.

'It's very beautiful, isn't it, Grey Bear?'

Grey Bear nodded, with the help of Larry's hand.

Then Larry continued up the stairs, Grey Bear bumping behind him. There were more paintings and things, and soft lamps on tables with curved legs, and it was all rather boring, he thought. Most of the doors were locked, or had nothing behind them, except for beds made up with crisp sheets that smelt of lavender.

Back in London, he had explored so many houses over the last few years, he had lost count. Houses without doors, walls or even roofs. You weren't meant to, but often he and his friends played in the bricky ruins of obliterated terraces. He had found so many useful things – balls, telescopes, spare gas masks – and of course Grey Bear himself.

The dust from the bombed-out street had coated the bear quite grey, and no amount of scrubbing by his mother made any difference. Larry knew he must belong to someone else, but promised to everyone that he was only minding Grey Bear until the owner's safe return. Even though Evie had yelled at him that he was cruel, how *could* he, how did he presume to know what had happened to its owner – the bear had never left his side since that day.

Now he opened yet another heavy door on to yet another

silent room, with nothing but a gilded dressing table mirror staring back at him, and sighed. Since the Allies had won the war in Europe, all the grown-ups did was bang on about how good it would be when things returned to normal. But if normal was silent houses full of furniture, rather than blown up ones full of treasure, he was not sure how good that was.

He was losing count of how many floors he had been up now. He paused at the foot of a final flight of stairs, much narrower than the others. It was bare and rickety as a bunk-bed ladder. The old woman who called him a frog had also said something about a housekeeper and tea, and his stomach was beginning to rumble. What else had she said?

'Do you think the others will shout when there's cake, Grey Bear?'

Grey Bear looked at him impassively. It wasn't a yes, exactly, but neither was it a no.

They began to mount the stairs to the top floor of the house.

Here was a short corridor, narrower than on the other floors, squeezed right into the roof, so the walls sloped on either side. There was no expensive carpet, but a bare scrap of a rug that hardly covered the weathered timbers. Even though it was a summer afternoon, the corridor felt

11

very cool and the sunlight that leached through the dirt-blotched windows at the end felt softer and weaker than it had out in the garden.

Larry took a step. A floorboard creaked so accusingly that he almost went straight back down the stairs again.

Grey Bear shook slightly in his grip.

He took another few steps. This floor looked like it was going to be the most boring of all. There weren't even any doors, just some peeling brown paper. A few flies buzzing fruitlessly in the window.

He sighed.

Then there was a noise behind him. A kind of riffling sound, such as a fan or propellor might make. He felt a shift in the air, a change in the pressure on his bare skin. He turned around, but there was nobody there.

Grey Bear gave his usual reassuring smile.

And now, turning back, the strangest thing.

There was a door after all. He could have sworn there hadn't been one before. How could he have missed it? Perhaps the sunlight, filled with rotating tunnels of dust, had blinded him. Either way, there was most definitely a door, about halfway down the corridor.

A very old-looking one, of solid wood.

He ran his fingers over the surface, which was divided

into carved panels. Larry had never seen anything so beautiful. Around the edges there were garlands and trumpets, wreathes of leaves, scrolls bound with ribbon, pillars and geometrical patterns. And in the centre of each panel there were characters or scenes. The wood was so dark – almost black – and so old, cracked and faded that it was hard to see everything. But there was a very ancient-looking man with a long beard, standing in a forest, it seemed. Some monks bent over their illuminated manuscripts, holding great quills. Someone looking at themself in the mirror. A very large goat, walking upright on two legs.

It certainly looked like a very interesting door, so Larry gave it a push.

To his amazement, it opened.

He stepped inside.

The door softly closed behind him, but Larry didn't even notice. If he had looked like a frog gawping at the Armstrong Siddeley Lancaster, who knew what bug-eyed monster he looked like now? He couldn't stop staring – at the brass chandeliers, burning with candles above his head. It was hard to tell more about the kind of room it was, because the light from the chandeliers was so fierce and dazzling, but it looked like there was a domed ceiling beyond them, a gallery of diamond windows glittering. Beneath his feet there were floorboards, as dark and old as the door. Then he saw what lay ahead and all around: the stacks of narrow shelves, running on into infinity, packed with books of every kind.

And he knew exactly what kind of room it was.

A library.

CHAPTER 2
The Land of the Reads

How Professor Kelly could fit such a large room into her roof space was quite beyond him. Then again, Larry supposed, she was a Professor and so was bound to know lots of things he didn't. In all the libraries he had been to before, there was always a librarian, whom you had to ask where books were shelved, and take the books you borrowed to get stamped. The librarian often sat behind a tall desk and wore glasses on the end of their nose. Sometimes they were working in a side room and you had to ring a bell to get their attention. But in this one there was no desk, and no librarian, and no bell.

There were only three aisles of shelves, each with a sign hanging above them. And again, this library was different to the libraries in London. They had signs which said

things like 'Geography', 'Music' or 'History'. These three signs seemed far less helpful:

1. READ

2. UNREAD

3. NEVER READ

Grey Bear looked blank.

'Don't worry, Grey Bear,' said Larry. 'It's a library, remember.' He thought for a moment, and then decided that he would start by exploring the 'Read' aisle of books. He didn't know if it meant 'Read' as in 'You should *read* these books' or 'All these books have been *read*', but 'Unread' sounded like hard work, and 'Never Read' was a warning if ever he heard one. So, he wandered down the aisle marked 'Read', and his head began to buzz with excitement.

There were so many stories here that he had already read – *Swallows and Amazons*, *The Wind in the Willows*, *The Sword in the Stone* . . . The more he walked the cleverer he felt. He wasn't counting, but if he had been, he must have walked past hundreds of books. And he seemed to recognise all of them. Larry felt better about his reading already. Often teachers told him he needed to read more, but somehow, even though he didn't read as much as he probably should (he preferred making up his own adventures), he still seemed to know lots of stories.

Finally, he saw a book that he thought he would like to read. It was almost half his height, richly bound in leather and embossed with gold. It looked so magnificent and heavy that he wondered whether he was allowed to even pull it down off the shelf. But then he read the title again.

THE GOLDEN FAIRY TALE TREASURY

Larry felt sure that he must be allowed to read that. Everyone was allowed to read fairy tales. He stretched on his tiptoes, reached out his hand and grasped the spine.

He sat down on the floor, leaned against the wall of shelves and opened the book.

But he never got so far as the first fairy tale.

Because as he turned the page, he felt something very cold and very sharp press into his wrist, right across the vein.

And a voice hissed in his ear:

'Move one more muscle, dear Reader, and that shall be the last book you ever touch.'

Larry froze and, daring to glance down, saw that the speaker was a tiny man, not much bigger than his thumb. With one hand, he was clinging to the cover of the fairy tale volume, and with another, he was holding a sword, digging it into the boy's wrist.

He didn't know what else to do, so he dropped the book.

With a muffled scream, the man disappeared.

And then reappeared almost immediately, this time by Larry's neck. He hovered in the air, pressing the sword now against his jugular artery. Larry saw the man could do this because he was riding a butterfly – with the same colouring as a tiger – who fluttered just in front of Larry's chin.

'I'm not joking, Reader!' snarled the little man.

Larry looked down his nose, and could see the man more clearly. His face was pale, his eyes sharp and his mouth pursed. He wore a hat that looked like an upside-down acorn, with sprigs of green oak leaf sticking out either side. His shirt was even more extraordinary, being spun entirely out of cobwebs. The legs that clasped the tigerish butterfly were dressed in very thin whorls of apple skin, and his feet were tucked inside the tiniest, furriest slippers, with sharp spurs on the heels. Everything about him was strange, apart from the fact that he was identical to a picture in a book Larry had once read.

'You look like Tom Thumb,' he said.

'That's maybe because I am,' snapped the tiny knight, sheathing his sword before doffing his acorn hat. 'The smallest ever fairy knight, at your service. The question is, which Reader are you?'

'I'm Larry Hastings,' said Larry. 'And this is Grey Bear.'

Tom Thumb glared at him, uncomprehending.

'We couldn't wipe the bomb dust off,' the boy added. 'Why don't you have wings, though, if you're a fairy?'

'Why do I need wings, when I have Majesty?' The butterfly reared, and Thumb swum about on her in front of Larry's eyes. 'So called because she is the queen of her kind. Isn't she marvellous?'

'Yes, very,' said Larry, blinking as the butterfly flapped her wings at him. Then Thumb reined her in, and he was no longer smiling.

'Now come! You are meant to read stories, not appear in them. If you want to live, I insist you follow me, this very moment.'

'Was I not allowed in the library?'

The fairy didn't reply, which was when Larry felt a soft summer breeze upon his face. He started: they were at the foot of a huge oak tree, in the centre of an empty field. Larry picked up the book, shook it, flicked through the pages and then looked around for a door to the library, or a shelf, or a chandelier.

'You truly have no idea how books work, do you?' said Tom Thumb, who was now also glancing anxiously around him, even though the large field was completely empty and surrounded by trees on all sides. 'Now climb, dear Reader Larry. For we shall never be safe until you do.'

Larry peered up at the trunk, and the spreading branches forming a leafy dome over their heads. Even if he strained his head right back, he couldn't see the top.

'Come, come, follow me!' said Thumb.

The fairy knight surged ahead on his butterfly, hovering close to the very wrinkled bark of the tree. Larry wondered how old it was. Older than all the kings and queens of England, he reckoned. Laying the heavy book of fairy tales down on the grass, and stuffing Grey Bear down the front of his shirt, so only his head poked out, Larry scrambled up the trunk, shimmying as best he could with his hands and knees.

'You're not looking, Reader!' calle

circling back above them.

Now hot and bothered, Larry pause

look at the tree. To his amazement, he

wasn't just wrinkled. It was carved with ~~miniature foot and~~

handholds, each one decorated with an acorn like the one

Tom Thumb wore upon his head. So he began to grip

those, and made much swifter progress, following the holds

as they wound up the tree in a loose spiral.

'At last,' called down a voice from the branch above.

'Your tea is getting cold.'

It was only five minutes later, but Larry felt a world

away from his terrifying climb. He was sitting in an

armchair woven out of willow and ash striplings. It was a

bit small for an eight-year-old boy, but it was a seat. Grey

Bear sat happily in a large upturned acorn shell.

They were in a treehouse, with a floor of rough planks

and the walls made from the branches of the oak tree,

bound together with reed.

Majesty perched graciously on a twig, supping honey

from a tin bottle top. The knight himself was busy at a

small stove that was right out of a doll's house, brewing

a mixture in a saucepan. 'Is rose-hip cordial all right? Or

you prefer something a little stronger? It is past on, after all. There might be some dandelion wine left in the ice box . . .'

'Rose-hip . . . thing is fine, thank you, er, Mister Thumb,' squeaked Larry, wondering where his voice had got to. The tiny treehouse was packed with all sorts of strange things – a velvet top hat dangling from a coat hook, and rows of shoes, piled up on top of one another. Boots, slippers, dancing shoes – so many, and all made from the most unexpected materials. The dancing shoes glittered as if they were actually made from fish scales.

'Oh please, just call me Thumb, my dear,' said the knight, pressing a minute but delicious thimble of rose-hip cordial into Larry's hand. 'Everyone else does.'

Tom Thumb smiled, and Larry thought it was a very polite smile, if a little strained. 'Now, dear Reader Larry. I apologise for all the cloak and dagger shenanigans back there . . . but we must be cautious.'

'Cloak and dagger?' This was very confusing. Larry shivered, and wished he was wearing a cloak over his shirt and shorts.

'She has spies everywhere.'

Larry looked baffled.

22

'Oh, come come,' said Thumb. 'I am sure you are very intelligent, my dear . . . but as a Reader of the Library you don't seem to know very much.'

'I hadn't been there before . . . the door just appeared. We're all staying with the Professor. We haven't got a home any more.'

'Then you will know how we feel.'

'We?'

'Do you know anything at all?'

'Not really,' said Larry, who leaned as far back in his woven armchair as he dared, and promptly tipped right over. The fairy knight stuck his his sharp little thumbs into the waistband of his apple-skin trousers, peering at his guest in total astonishment.

'*Not really*? What do they teach in your schools?'

'Grammar, mainly,' said Larry, squeezing back into his seat.

Thumb tapped his mouse-skin-slippered foot on the floor, and took a deep breath. 'I'll start again. Are you sitting comfortably?'

Larry looked down at his tiny willow armchair. It was beginning to be very, very painful in his sides. He could hardly breathe. 'Yes, thank you very much,' he said.

'Larry the Reader, and his Grey Bear – I formally

welcome you, on behalf of stories and characters everywhere, to the Land of the Reads. And before you ask, that's Reads as in reds or beds.'

'Not as in reeds or tweeds?' said Larry.

'Precisely.'

'What about leads?'

'Now you're being difficult.'

'But what is it?' asked Larry.

'It is,' said Tom Thumb, 'quite simply, the place where stories go to live when they have been read.'

Larry sat up, difficult though that was to do. 'What – *every* story?'

'*Every* story. You are in Fairytale Valley, which has been my home for so many years, but there are many stories, aren't there? Nursery rhymes, plays, novels, poems, stories from history, fables, parables – you name it. They are all here, in different lands of this Library, a world known to those who dwell within its shelves as Folio.'

'Folio?' puzzled Larry.

'Yes, it's an old word for page. Which is about the only thing every story here has in common. They have all been on one, at some point. If you want to know more, look it up in a dictionary.' Larry chewed his lip. 'Now, if we climbed down this tree, in minutes, I could show you the giants and witches and dwarves who are my neighbours, or take you along the river to meet the many talking animals who live down there. Then round the lake to meet the myths . . . and so on, and so on.'

His guest nodded and chewed his bottom lip some more. 'You're saying . . . that stories are real?'

'Well . . . of course they are!' The little knight scrambled up the wall of shelves in the corner that were stuffed with piles of yellowing paper, leaking ink pots and jars of crow feather quills. He pulled out a long, tea-coloured scroll that was nearly twice the size of himself, and unrolled it on the floor, only just managing to stop the rolled ends from snapping back and knocking him flat.

'Here we are, dear Reader Larry. Look. These are the ancient Library rules, drawn up many thousands of opening hours ago.'

'I know the library rules!' said Larry hotly. 'No talking, no boiled sweets, no whistling.'

Thumb shook his head. 'You don't know *this* Library's rules.' And he pointed to the words on the sheet of paper, which were as beautifully written as a manuscript illustrated by medieval monks. The first line read:

Rule 1:

If you can imagine it, it must exist.

Somewhere.

Larry's eyes widened. Then he looked down at the rest of the scroll, which was as blank as a winter day. He turned it over. The other side was completely blank too. He scratched his head. 'What are the other rules?'

'They really don't teach you anything at all, do they? Why would a Library need any other rules apart from that one?'

'Well—' began Larry, doubtfully.

'Exactly!' cried Tom Thumb, snapping his fingers. 'I mean, there have been rumours about other rules, but who needs them? In Folio, if you can imagine it, it exists somewhere. The most incredible stories, the most unbelievable facts – you will find them all here somewhere.'

'Hmm,' said Larry. 'If the Land of the Reads is where stories live, what about facts?'

Tom Thumb beckoned Larry to the leaf-draped walls of his house. Heaving with both his arms, he pushed up enough fronds for him to peek through. Larry could see the canopy of the forest and, beyond, lush green valleys, dotted with pretty villages and wandering rivers.

'The Land of the Reads. Isn't it heaven?' said Thumb. 'Now follow my finger, and look over there, beyond the Plain of Meaning.'

Larry strained his eyes, and could just see, beyond a mighty and vast plain, the outline of strange tall structures, like giant fairground helter skelters, twisting up through the mist on the horizon. He shuddered, as if someone had just placed a cold hand on his back.

'That, my new friend, is where facts and information live. Many that have yet to be discovered. The City of the *Unreads*.'

'And what are they all about?' enquired Larry nervously.

'What they are all about,' said Thumb, slowly lowering the curtain of leaves, 'is nothing other than our total extermination.'

CHAPTER 3
Evelyn and the Painting

'Well, this is queer,' said Simon, stifling a yawn. 'No tea to speak of and you two have absolutely thrashed me three rounds flat.'

'You weren't even trying,' said Evelyn. 'Can I go and read my book now?'

Simon ruffled her hair, and leaped up from the sofa. 'You are a perfect pip, Evie,' he said. 'Don't ever change, please. That's an order.' He stretched. 'I wonder what mischief Larry is getting up to.'

Patricia laid down her cards on the ottoman and also stood up, moving to the window. She looked outside. The sun had moved to the other side of the house, and now everything was cloaked in an ominous purple shadow. The trees, the maze, the little row of statues, they looked

monotone and one dimensional, as if they if were cut-outs in a toy theatre. She put her hand to the bottom of her neck, in the way she had noticed her mother do when she was thinking. It made her feel closer to her, in a way.

'It's getting darker. He can't be outside any longer. Do you think we should go and look for him?'

She turned to Evie and cocked her head, meaningfully. Evie threw her cards down and stomped towards the door, muttering.

'Don't sulk! It doesn't suit you.'

'Not in the same way it does you,' muttered Simon under his breath.

'I heard that,' Patricia said.

But Evie never got to the door, because just as she reached it, Larry burst through, nearly tumbling over Grey Bear in his excitement.

'There's a Library! A magic one, upstairs, only it's not really magic, except sort of and anyway, you have to come and help, because you read a book and then you're in the story and it's real, everything exists somewhere, and oh please, listen, we HAVE to help him because all the Unreads are coming to kill the Reads, and if they win, there won't be any more stories left in Folio or the world EVER—'

Larry stopped, frowning at the wave of sheer disbelief now surging towards him over the parquet flooring. He sat down with a thump on a blue velvet chair with an angular, diamond-shaped back. It was very modern and almost as uncomfortable as Thumb's willow seat.

'But I'm not lying! I was there for the whole afternoon. He made me nettle soup for tea with nut bread. It was like being in a doll's house.'

'Here we go.' Simon lay back with his hands behind his head and stared at the ceiling. 'I thought Father had spoken to you about telling tales. Could you not just lay off with the fairies and witches for once? Otherwise this is going to be a very long summer indeed.'

'It's true! You're all being beastly!' shouted Larry, clutching Grey Bear to his chest. Grey Bear looked squashed and indifferent as usual.

'Now now, Lall,' said Patricia, squeezing next to him and putting her arm around his shoulder. 'I think some tea would do you some good, you know. Perhaps we should try and discover a kitchen, or a housekeeper?'

He wriggled away from her like a restless puppy. 'Why aren't you listening to me? Folio is a real place. We must go and help them, or they're all going to die! There's this woman who runs the Unreads, who are facts, and when she

gets control of the Reads, she's going to obliterate them.
There won't be any more stories left, they'll all be gone!'
He collapsed again, this time on the rug, at Simon's feet.
'There won't be any more stories for anyone and it will be
all my fault. Because he made me promise. I promised I
would help him. Look.'

Larry unfurled his hot pink hand, and there clutched
inside was a ring. It was made for tiny fairy hands and
too small even for his fingers, carved from wood and
polished so fine that it was as smooth as bone. Wrapped
around it was a delicate wreath of oak leaves, sewn and
cut together by a tiny hand. Simon peered over his
shoulder, frowning.

'I say, Lall, did you make that? You have been busy.
Let's have a look.'

Before Larry could protest, he had scooped the ring out
of his brother's hand, holding it up to the honey-coloured
light that streamed through the old mullioned windows.

'Is there some kind of writing on the inside?' Simon
squinted, staring at it with one eye screwed up. He looked
like a jeweller examining a rare gem. 'Well, blow me – there
is. These letters are so miniature – how the blazes did you
manage this? Have you been going to woodwork club on
the sly? Now I know I'm not the world's best reader, but I

can just make the words out . . . Here we go. *If . . . you . . . can imagine it . . .'*

'*It must exist. Somewhere.* And that's mine!'

Larry snatched for the ring, but Simon danced out of reach, teasing.

'Not so fast, little man. What a curious thing to put on a ring, as a poet would say.'

He exchanged a glance with Patricia, who shrugged. 'Maybe we should go and have a look at this Library after all?'

'Yes!' Larry leaped up, all tears gone. 'I'll show you, it's right at the top of the house.'

'Lall, you heard the Professor. We aren't allowed up there.'

Larry stamped his foot, turned and ran back out of the drawing room, leaving the others to gawp at one another as they listened to Grey Bear thudding up the stairs behind their little brother.

'That's torn it,' said Simon.

'Come on. We can't let him run around up there on his own, or we'll all be for the high jump. And besides, I'd like to see the rest of the house if we aren't to have our tea.' So saying, Patricia pulled Simon out of the room behind her.

This left Evelyn, who had remained silent during

Larry's return. Slowly, straightening her skirt, she rose, and looked at herself in the glass of the large abstract painting. The dying sun caught it in such a way that she could almost see her reflection. Not like in a mirror, but like a darker, shadowier version of herself. And she noticed now that the painting had a title, written – by the artist, she presumed – in the margin of the picture.

MEDITATION ON THE IMPOSSIBILITY OF IMAGINING THE FUTURE (IV)

That was all a bit grown-up and gobbledygook, but at least it was different to . . . what she was used to. Then she looked at the title again, and breathed on the glass, covering up each word one at a time. And she remembered what Larry had said.

'If you can imagine it, it must exist. Somewhere.'

Evelyn did not smile very often, because so far life had given her very little to smile about, but she smiled at this.

Then she ran up the stairs after the others.

Evelyn found them standing at the top of the house, in a dingy little corridor, with lots of flies buzzing around the dust-smeared window at the end. She had to climb up some very wobbly steps to get there. Immediately she noticed how much colder the temperature was, given how boiling it was outside. Who cared though? Wandering through the empty corridors as easily as a ghost, the way the noises of the day – a low hum of traffic in the distance, a lawnmower somewhere, the buzzing of a plane – had faded to nothing, the climb up the unsteady stairs, the faint memory of the Professor's warning, all of these things gave her a tingling at the back of her neck.

This was out of bounds. This was not allowed. This was grown-ups-only territory. And Evelyn Hastings liked nothing better than to be invading grown-ups-only territory. Her pleasure was diminished slightly by the sight of her younger brother, half sitting on the floor, half fighting with Simon, who tried to pull him up, tears now freely flowing down the younger boy's cheeks.

'But it was here! I swear! I'm not lying.'

Patricia crouched down to his level. 'Come on, Lall,' she said gently.

'It was here! It was here!' He clutched his bear to his chest defiantly.

Patricia straightened up again, shaking her head. 'It is a lovely painting, though, thank you for showing it to us.'

Evelyn now saw that, directly above Larry's head, was

not a wooden door into a magical Library but a dusty oil painting of a house. A country manor house. Getting closer, she could spot a hedge maze at the front, the pillars of the doorway . . . and the top floor where they now stood.

'Is it this house?' she said. 'Barfield?'

'Top marks, Evie,' said Simon, standing back to admire it with her. 'I'll give you another point if you can tell me when it was painted?'

Evie scrunched up her nose, thinking. The colours were very old-looking, dull greens and browns. And there was no car parked at the front. She sighed. 'A hundred years ago?'

'Come on, brain bean,' he said. 'You can do better than that.'

She scanned the canvas, looking for clues, while Larry noisily sucked his thumb beneath her, smothering his toy to his chest. Were those some windmills in the background? There was no sign of them near the house now. And now, come to think of it, there were other things in the painting that were different to the present day. An old wooden cart tipped on one end in front of the door, with some cows nosing about – they weren't here now. Peering even closer, she could spot more details, like candles burning in the downstairs room through the mullioned glass, rather than electric light or gas lamps. Was that even a tiny figure in one of the windows, a bearded man, wearing a ruff around his neck, like Shakespeare? Yes, it was! And—

'Hello,' she said. 'That's peculiar.'

'This whole thing is damned peculiar, if you ask me,' said Simon. 'Come on, I want a date.'

'I don't know the date, because I don't know when people did such stupid things.'

'Like what?'

'Keeping farm animals in the house. Disgusting.'

Simon now wrinkled his nose up. 'What animals, bright eyes?'

Evie pointed. 'That goat. Standing behind the window.'

'A goat? Have you been raiding the same pill cabinet as Larry?'

'Yes! Why do you never believe a word I say? That goat, there. The one standing on two legs.'

She could see it, as clear as her own pointing hand. Little dabs of oil – a pair of curling horns, a bearded chin – it was a goat, no doubt about it. Simon shook his head with a snort of derision.

'Sorry, Evie, I must need a new pair of specs.'

Evelyn turned to glower at him. But when she turned back . . . it had gone. There was no goat. Just light glinting

36

on the upper windows. Her stomach roiled. Had she imagined it?

'Anyhow, you lose. It was a bit of a trick question. The answer is 1595.'

'How do you know?'

'Whoever painted this wrote the date in the bottom right-hand corner – look. Over three hundred years ago! How about that?'

Evie stared at the number. It was strange how you could see something that wasn't in a painting, and so easily miss something that was, she thought.

'Right, you lot,' said Simon, clapping his hands. 'Enough of these japes. Let's go and track down our absent hostess or this mysterious housekeeper and see what's going on with tea. I could eat a horse, and all its nearest relatives.'

Oh, bore off, thought Evelyn to herself, as Simon and Patricia trooped off down the stairs, half dragging a reluctant Larry with them. *I was last up here, and I shall be last to leave.* She was enjoying looking at the 1595 painting of Barfield, with or without a goat. Tracing her finger over the rough surface of the oil, she thought how amazing it was that paint – all on its own – could make a climbing rose look as prickly as one in real life, or a cloud as fluffy.

Then a noise made her start and turn around.

A strange noise, like someone had turned an overhead fan on and off again. But there was no one there. Just an empty grey corridor, feeling colder and darker than ever before, the sun setting through the window at the end.

What was there, as she turned back to face the painting – which had quite disappeared – was a large, carved wooden door.

CHAPTER 4

More than Anything in the World

As usual, Evie hadn't believed a word of Larry's tall tale downstairs. He was always telling so many, demanding everyone pay attention, as if they were vital news reports rather than the endless far-fetched fantasies which repeatedly spewed out of his mouth. There was a troll under his bed, a witch in the wardrobe, fairies at the bottom of the garden, and now – a magic Library in the attic.

But now, there *was* a Library in the attic, a Library which had mysteriously appeared where before there had only been quite a mysterious picture. So something was going on. Whatever it was, Evelyn was quite sure there was a rational, sensible explanation for it. Before the war, the Russians had been our enemies because they were Communist, then during the war they had been friends,

because the Germans were worse enemies, and we needed the Russians' help to defeat them. Her father had patiently explained it all one bedtime. Everything he said had come to pass. Now Hitler, who everyone had been so scared of for years, had shot himself behind a closed door for that was what bad people who committed awful crimes always did – because they were so ashamed.

Those explanations seemed easy to her. Too easy, perhaps, like the first couple of sums in a maths exam. Some things were much harder to explain. Like that day in Maguire Street. After the bomb, what she saw lying in the road in front of her. What she saw again and again, every night, in her nightmares.

What could explain that? What could ever make that right?

She was determined to find out. *Even if it takes me my whole life*, she had promised, kneeling by her bed afterwards, trying to ignore the layer of dust over everything. First she had prayed, asking God to stop doing such horrible things to people . . . and to her friends, and then she had also made God a promise. She, Evelyn Hastings, was going to find out why he let people drop bombs on schools, when they were just doing their lessons and hadn't done anything wrong. And if she found out that it was God's fault for letting it happen, then she was never going to pray to him EVER AGAIN.

Anyhow, what better place to start finding answers to some of these questions than in a library? Mysterious or not, here it was, and looking just like a library should do (in her opinion) – clean, quiet and neatly labelled. There were three aisles of shelves, marked 'Read', 'Unread' and 'Never Read'. There was no librarian to be seen anywhere, bossing people around with a stamp and shushing noises, which was good. She could read whatever she wanted without being told a book was 'unsuitable' or that she 'wasn't old enough'. (Such a silly thing to say, especially when the book in question had been a biology textbook.)

Evie considered her options. What had Larry been yammering on about downstairs? Something to do with the Reads or the Unreads? Whatever it was, he was only eight. She would decide things for herself. The first decision was easy. The Read aisle was not for her. Who wanted to read stories which had already been read? That sounded boring.

No, she was going to go for the Never Read shelves.

In her experience, if a parent or a teacher told you not to do something, it was imperative to do it. Just to find out why you weren't meant to. Except this sign wasn't from a

41

parent or a teacher, it was from the librarian – wherever he or she was. Although, Evie supposed, a librarian was kind of halfway between a parent and teacher.

So it was the same thing.

She advanced towards the 'Never Read' aisle of shelves.

They looked very dark. Perhaps there were some lights somewhere?

Then, just as she got there, she stopped.

There was that noise again. A kind of riffling of the air, a disturbance in the pressure, that made her step back. Along with a very strange smell coming from the darkness ahead. Evie had been in a very old library once, part of a museum, with her father, and she liked the dusty smell of glue and the old days which the books had. This wasn't a nice dusty smell. It was more the smell of a farmyard. A dirty farmyard.

She wrinkled her nose. Maybe these books were never to be read because they were filthy and rotten? Shaking her head, Evie marched away, and without hesitation into the 'Unread' aisle.

Straight away, she knew she had made the right decision. There were lights here, and no barn smell, just rows of the most perfect books. Volumes on science, geography and maths. Then there were dictionaries, periodic tables and maps – so many maps! And engineering manuals, which really were her favourite.

Diagrams of aeroplanes. Even what a space rocket might look like. Evie, much more so than either of her brothers, loved reading about space rockets. She was quite addicted to comics that told her about tentacular monsters from other planets, and new human colonies on Mars. One day, she had decided, she would like to do more than read about rockets firing into space.

She would like to fly on one herself, burning through the atmosphere, into starlit infinity beyond. Her normal world, London, felt so tired and battle weary, grimy and grey. Evie wanted to leave it all behind, and jet into the first technicolour universe she could find.

The first girl into space. Maybe even the first girl on the moon!

Stacked in tidy piles, there were also bound copies of the magazines like the ones the Professor had downstairs. Each one overflowing with articles on everything from how to harness the energy of the sun, or how to prevent the spread of cholera. There was so much information that Evie's eyes widened as she walked along, like she wanted to drink it all in in one gulp of a read. Running her finger down the spines, she wondered, was it possible to read all the books in the world? And if not, then what was the point of them all being written? Surely one day somebody would write the definitive book which answered all the questions for good.

Then her eye alighted on a book, which looked like it might at least answer one question.

EXPLAINING THE FUTURE

The title reminded her of the strange modern painting downstairs. Explaining, imagining, what was the difference, really? On the dust jacket, there was a picture of a strange-looking city which looked more like a factory, full of curling pipes and bubbling vats. The people in the city wore space helmets and silver diving suits, and the sun was bright red. A flying car hovered above some palm trees. In the flyleaf, a caption explained that the picture was:

An artist's impression of Britain in 2020.

It didn't say anywhere who the artist was, but that didn't matter. The pictures had hooked her.

Still walking, she opened the covers and began to read.

As she read, the Library began to grow warmer and

warmer. And a strong dry wind began to blow on her face. She looked up, and to her surprise found that the walls and shelves of the Library had melted into thin air.

At first, setting down the book, Evie had to shield her face behind her arm from the hot wind and specks of grit that stung her skin. But when she finally dared lower her arm, and wiped away the dust from her eyes to see where she was, she was glad she had. For she was standing on a wall, and beyond the wall was quite simply the most magnificent city she had ever seen.

Evie knew it was a city, because there were lights and buildings and avenues, through which ran a fast-moving stream of vehicles and inhabitants. But in no other regard did it resemble the city she had grown up in. There were no grimy streets, or omnibuses or queues outside butchers' and grocers'. There weren't even any shops that she could see. The houses weren't like the houses she knew. Instead of little streets of homes with roofs, windows and doors, there were towering structures that looked like twisting helixes of sapphire. There were no museums or cathedrals, but huge shimmering pyramids, encased in bars of coloured light. A harsh orange sun glowered over the horizon, and swaying palm trees lined the avenues.

It appeared to Evie that people here didn't travel around

by foot or motorcar or even horse, but in strange machines – cars without wheels, that hovered and dived in the air. They filled the sky, and their headlights were like red bug eyes. She was used to years of darkness – blackouts at night, not even a single torch allowed in bed to read by, and every surface covered in a layer of thick permanent soot, or obscured by smog during the day.

In this city, everything was bright. Light of an intensity and brilliance such as Evie had never seen, burst from the centres of buildings, as if they burned with some eternal fire within. Lines of coloured dots raced along the avenues in such a blur that it made her dizzy just to try and look at them.

But most of all, the people were the strangest. Everyone in London seemed old and tired. Here, though, as Evie strained on her tiptoes and leaned over the concrete balustrade to get a closer look at the crowds below, she could see that they seemed to be glowing. They were not normal people. There were men, women and children, all wearing the same kind of modern-looking clothes. Every inch of them made of shining metal.

A silver crowd that emanated not just a glow, but strangeness, to her eyes. A glowing crowd, in fact, that seemed to be all looking up at where she was standing.

'Have no fear, child,' said a voice behind her. 'They are not looking at you. They are waiting for me.'

Evie turned around to see a tall and slender woman watching her. Her skin seemed to be made of glass, only it wasn't hard and polished, but soft and undulating. And beneath her flexible glass skin, she also shone like the crowds below. Now, closer up, Evie could see what was making her so radiant.

Numbers.

Hundreds and thousands of numbers, in columns of brilliant light. Numbers that changed all the time. There were numbers behind her eyes, behind her face and mouth. In a way, it was frightening, because it was so inhuman, but in another way, there was something soothing about the rippling digits under the fluid glass. They poured straight and steady, as in a waterfall shot through with moonlight.

The glass head on the long neck bent and regarded her, swanlike.

'Hello,' said Evie. 'I'm sorry – I was in the Library, and then I wasn't . . . am I not allowed to be here?'

'The Library?' said the glass head. When she spoke, her lips chattered and moved in opposite directions. Again, this was disconcerting, but also mesmerising. Her voice sounded like nothing Evie had ever heard, apart from possibly a piano. A beautiful and eerie piano.

'That is a rare privilege indeed. Tell me who you are, child, and why you were in . . . the Library.'

'My name is Evelyn Hastings,' Evie said, 'and I want to read all the books in the world.'

'Then you are a Reader?' said the glass woman, and her numbers lurched around under her skin. Evelyn could almost hear them squeaking.

'Yes, absolutely! I love reading, that's why I went into the Library in the first place.'

The glass woman began to hiss, like a goose guarding its young, her long neck swerving about. She seemed to grow taller, and steam rose off her skin into the night air. Her eyes flashed. 'And do you have any siblings, Reader Evelyn?'

'Yes. And please, call me Evie. That's what they all do.' Evie groaned. She had forgotten her family briefly and it had been a relief. 'There's Simon, who's a prig. Patti, thirteen going on sixty, and then little baby Larry. He was telling some story about coming here and meeting a fairy called Tom Thumb . . .'

'He has been to the Reads!' Her interrogator's eyes looked on fire. 'A younger Reader!'

'Well, he said he has, but no one believed him, he's always telling tales.'

The woman swerved in the unsettling way she had, the numbers under her skin jumping about like iron filings pulled by a magnet, muttering to herself. Eventually, she raised a long glass arm, and for a moment Evie thought she was going to strike her, but the arm came down softly, and the glass face softened.

'You are welcome, Reader Evie,' said the woman, with a kind of chattering smile. 'For you are in Folio, and this is the City of the Unreads.' She gestured to the city beyond, with a wave of her illuminated glass hand, at the flying cars, the sparkling helixes that twisted into the sky, the crowds of silver people in the square below. 'These are my subjects, and I am Jana, Secretary of the Unreads.'

Evie's mother was a secretary, in the War Office. She worked very hard, typing letters, often to tell people that a son or a husband had died, and it made her quite unhappy, although she was proud of her work. She knew how to stretch rations into a treat, and never showed her children when she was scared. But she never had crowds gathering outside her window and pointing up at her.

'What are . . . Unreads?'

'The Unreads are everything that we are yet to discover

about this world. They are the hidden facts and figures which make us who we are, which can make us more than we are. Unreads are never foolish fairy tales or fantastical adventures.' The impression of a nose on her face wrinkled with disgust at the very thought. 'No, the Unreads are the very opposite of such made-up nonsense. We are information, books of cold, hard and irrefutable data!' Jana pointed into the air, above their heads. 'Now, child, look up into the sky. Tell me what you see?'

Evie peered into the clouds drifting across the skyscraper spires, and there, as well as a sun, was a moon – a spellbinding sphere in the sky. It had a soft fringed glow, and if you stared very hard, the faint traces of a kindly face. Or so it seemed to her. At any rate, it probably never got bombed, or burned, or worse . . . and she was thankful for that.

'A beautiful, peaceful place.'

'Indeed. Would you like to go there?'

Evie turned to her, eyes blazing. 'More than anything in the world!'

'Then I will help you. In fact, I have teams working on that very Unread possibility as we speak.'

'Do you promise?' Evie took the Secretary's hands. They were hard and cold.

'Child, I am the Secretary of the Unreads. I do not need to make promises.' She turned away for a moment, and leaned over the balcony, giving a little wave to the crowds below. A deafening cheer rang out. Then she turned back to Evie, numbers rippling. 'But I can offer you something much better.'

'What's that?'

'A deal.'

CHAPTER 5
The Professor's Study

The Library was much cooler than the City of the Unreads, and Evie was glad to feel the polished floorboards under her feet once more, rather than hard concrete. She was worried about how long she had been away, not because she cared what the others would think (she never cared what the others thought), but because her stomach was roaring and she really did not want to miss supper. After the Secretary had left her to go and make a speech, Evie just picked up the book on the future, which was where she had left it, splayed open on the ground. Then, without meaning to, she closed the book, and found herself back in the Library, in the Unreads aisle.

So there it was. It was that simple. If you read a book in this Library, you entered Folio. If you stopped reading,

it disappeared. Evie walked back up the aisle. She could see the old oak door ahead of her, the chandeliers glowing in the ceiling, the windows glittering. Such a quiet and peaceful space. Except she could hear someone – or something – outside, snuffling.

'Hello?' said Evie.

'Who is it?' came back a voice, thick with tears.

'Larry?' said Evie, and opened the door back into the house. To her surprise, as soon as she closed it behind her, there was that riffling noise again, and the door disappeared, vanishing into the wall. All she could now see was her younger brother, sitting in the middle of the dusty corridor, clutching his toy bear.

'What are you doing here?'

'You mean what are *you* doing in *there*? Folio was my discovery. I keep trying to find the door again, but I can't make it appear. The others don't believe me.'

Evie sat down next to him and took his free hand, which was hot and warm. Counting to five, she put on a friendly face and softened her voice.

'I believe you though, Lall. Look, here I am.'

He sniffed again, so loudly, that Evie was glad for a moment that it wasn't a real library.

'Did you find Tom Thumb? I promised we'd help him.

I promised!'

She twisted his small hand in hers, holding it tight, trying not to crush it.

'I found something much better than a silly old fairy.'

He looked up at her, his big wet eyes full of a feeling that she couldn't quite place. Was it hope? Or fear? Perhaps simply a mixture of both.

'What?'

Evie opened her mouth, and then shut it again very quickly. She remembered her deal with the Secretary, and how she had promised to tell no one.

'Now, come on, why don't you ask Grey Bear to dry your tears, and we'll go and find the others. Then, perhaps more importantly, find out exactly what is going on in this house.'

The Professor's study was right at the other end of the hall, and then up a very crooked set of steps. It felt like she was leading Larry up the spiral staircase of a castle turret, and that maybe she should have her sword ready to meet any guards defending their quarters. Except she knew that wouldn't happen, because she could smell bacon – which seemed unlikely – and hear her older brother talking loudly. As usual.

'Oh, there you are, Evarola. We were getting ready to send out a search party.' He stuffed something into his mouth.

'Dripping?' said Patricia, offering them both a plate of some toast smeared with something that smelt like bacon but which, alas, wasn't bacon. It very rarely was, these days.

Even in the half-lit gloom of her study, the Professor must have seen Evie's face fall. 'I'm afraid so. Even Professors working for the Ministry of War are subject to rationing. Despite what you may read in the papers,' she added, in a mutter. 'But Mrs Martin does her best!'

Evie took a piece of toast – a very small, thin and stale piece, and offered the last remaining slice to Larry, who buttoned his mouth shut and shook his head.

'Don't be silly, Lall,' Patricia said. 'Not eating won't help find your fairy.'

Sighing, Larry took the toast, and bit into it with a very loud sulky crunch. Evie looked around the room. It was very old, with wood panelling so dark it was almost black. There was only one window: a pointed arch of diamond panes, which let in hardly any light.

Then a thought struck her. Was that the window she had seen the goat on two legs behind, in the painting of

Barfield, the one that had appeared and then disappeared?

'Professor—' she started, but Simon shushed her with a wave of his hand.

'Not now, Evie. Professor Kelly was telling us something interesting about this old pile if you'd only listen for a second.'

Evie glared at him, while Patricia took her hand silently in the gloom, giving it a welcome squeeze.

'Well,' said the Professor kindly, 'I think your brother might be overstating my case a little. It is a very old and magnificent house, as I am sure you have discovered. But as I am only a temporary guest, while I complete my work for the Ministry, there is still much I have to learn. Indeed, it seems to me that nearly every time I turn a corner or go down a corridor, I discover something that I could have sworn wasn't there before.'

Was that a twinkle in her eye as she said that? Evie smelt a game in the offing, and there was nothing she liked more than a game.

'How old is this house?' she asked, looking carefully at her feet.

'A good question. No one quite knows, but we believe that there has been some kind of dwelling place on this site since at least the thirteenth century. Many people have lived here over the years, but the one I find the most interesting is a man called Nicholas Crowne, who moved here in 1580. He made many improvements to the house, including building this study we are now in, enlarging the gardens, making the kitchen bigger, and so on, but perhaps the most remarkable addition he made was his—'

'Library,' said Evie, now looking her host directly in the eye, who looked her directly back.

'Quite so. How perceptive of you, my dear. But why was his Library so important, can you tell me that?'

'Because it had fairy knights in it?' said Larry.

'Lall! The Professor isn't interested in your nonsense.' Simon bopped his brother lightly on the head with his bear. 'And neither am I, come to mention it. Not a huge fan of libraries, as a rule, Prof.'

An unwelcome flush suddenly started to creep up his neck. Simon hoped it wasn't visible in the gloom. It wasn't his fault. The words jumping about on the page like Mexican beans on a hot plate. What to others was clear as day was like deciphering hieroglyphics to him.

Everyone had their curse, Father said, and that was his. 'Stick to your hands, my boy,' he had said, clapping Simon round the neck. 'They'll see you all right. Leave the books to your sisters, that's my advice.'

So he had. And at school, too. He made up excuses about why he didn't want to read out loud in class, he copied friends' work, he guessed things rather than understood them – and sometimes even got them right. It didn't matter either way. His teachers had given up on him long ago.

If the Professor had noticed his blushing, she didn't show it. 'But what was so special and amazing about Nicholas Crowne's Library was not so much what was in it, but its size. His personal collection of books was the biggest known such archive in the world at the time.' She paused and took a sip of cooling tea from her cup. 'In fact, it is believed that Nicholas Crowne was the first person ever, and quite possibly the last, to own a copy of every book in the world – something that just wouldn't be possible any more.'

Patricia let out a low whistle. 'Had he read them *all*?'

'Entirely possible. Crowne was a very wealthy and intelligent man, with no need to work and plenty of time in which to read. But some of the stories told about him are very strange indeed.'

'I like strange people,' said Evie. 'Did he wear a ruff?'

'Yes, Evie, he did. But that was quite normal for certain men of his time. What was more strange were the experiments.'

'Like a scientist, you mean? Is that why you're interested in the house?' asked Patricia.

'Not like a scientist, at least, not like you or I would understand the word. Much more like a . . . well, I suppose you could call him a magician.'

'A wizard!' said Larry, cheering up.

'I wouldn't use that word. Wizard sounds . . . friendly somehow. A flowing white beard, a staff perhaps, a Merlin-like figure. There was nothing friendly about Nicholas Crowne. He was secretive, a total recluse, and yet . . . one of the most powerful and mysterious men who ever lived.'

'What happened to him in the end, then?' said Evie, who was growing bored of this game.

'Now, children, it's turned rather dark!' said the Professor brightly. It was unclear whether she meant the evening or the conversation. 'Shall we go back downstairs and see if we can find a board game to play before bed?'

Nobody moved. The unanswered question hung in the air.

'What do you do for the Ministry, Miss?' said Larry, his mouth still full of dripping and toast.

'You can't ask that!' hissed Patricia. 'It's top secret.'

Larry shrugged. Everything grown-up was top secret.

If you didn't ask, you would never find out.

'It's quite all right, my dear,' said the Professor. 'Take a look around and tell me what you think I do?'

So he did, peering about in the semi-darkness. Peeling ocean charts, diagrams of the brain and maps of the galaxy were fixed to the walls with brass pins. There were piles of very old-looking books, with waxy black covers, split down the spine, and rough-edged pages. Scrolls stuffed in glass jars like dead flowers, quills and ink . . . a typewriter and printers' blocks, scattered about like dice. The narrow desk was a mess of crumpled maps and hastily scribbled notes. But what caught his eye most of all was hanging on the far wall – a small portrait in a heavy frame. It was of a man, with very pale cheeks, a strong widow's peak of dark hair and a pointed beard. His eyes seemed to stare straight through Larry, and an almost invisible smile played around his lips.

Larry thought for a moment, and then said, 'Are you a magician, like Nicholas . . . the man who used to live here?'

The Professor laughed, a light tinkling laugh, and shook her grey hair. 'I suppose I am . . . but in a very modern way. I am trying to use what we have learned about the world more recently – about time, space, physics, chemistry, that kind of thing – to see if we can understand how the so-called magic Nicholas Crowne was famous for actually worked.' She fidgeted at her desk, moving papers around, as if she didn't want to discuss the matter any further.

'But why?' asked Larry, refusing to give up.

'Because his magic was said to be very powerful, the most powerful in the world. And the government wants to understand how it works – or worked, rather.'

'Why does the government want to do magic, though?' said Larry again, now ignoring the sharp jab in his ribs from his elder brother.

'Because,' said the Professor, 'now that awful, horrid, evil war is over, the people I work for are determined to do anything to make sure that human beings never do anything like that to each other ever again.'

'What happened to him, then?' demanded Evie again. Larry's persistence had emboldened her. 'You have to tell us. Now.'

'Evie!' said Patricia, who hated being embarrassed by her brothers and sister perhaps more than anything else in the world. 'Don't be so rude!'

'It's all right, my dear,' said the Professor, with a kindly smile. 'You have a right to know. You are staying in his house, after all.' Professor Kelly took off her glasses, and

61

rubbed either side of her nose between her fingers. In the half light of her desk lamp, Evie thought how very old she suddenly looked. 'Once Nicholas Crowne had collected – and read – all the books in the world, the strangest thing happened. This man was wealthy, powerful and extremely intelligent. Then one day—'

'The Queen cut his head off?' said Larry hopefully.

But she didn't smile. Not even half a smile. In fact, there was a very great sadness in her eyes. 'No, she didn't, my child. Something far worse. Much, much worse for him, and for all of us. He . . . disappeared. Completely vanished without trace, off the face of the earth. No sightings, no letters – he simply went into his Library one day . . . and never came out again.'

In the gathering darkness, the children felt a chill settle upon their skin.

'How can disappearing be worse than getting your head cut off?' said Larry.

'Did they ever find his body?' said Patricia.

'Now,' said the Professor, sitting up straight. 'Look at me, talking on and on about goodness knows what, while you poor darlings sit here without any proper supper. It is way past your bedtime, and I fear I shall get into terrible trouble with your mother and father if I send you back even skinnier than when you arrived. Why don't we go and see what Mrs Martin can forage for us in the kitchen?'

And ignoring all the children's further questions and protests, she swept out of the study and into the night.

For now, the matter was closed.

The Magician Project – Extract 8a

(KV 1/1567-7)

REPORT

1st Intelligence, Surveillance and Reconnaissance
Brigade

HQ Company, Ashford

13th July 1945

Author: REDACTED/CLASSIFIED

2 p.m. Professor Kelly leaves Barfield Hall for
Salisbury station. She collects the four Hastings
children (2.43 p.m.) off the 12.31 departure from
Waterloo station.

3.39 p.m. Professor Kelly arrives back at Barfield
Hall.

The children are observed. Playing. Professor
Kelly has a way of making herself invisible in
the house. She cannot be viewed through any

windows or picked up by the listening devices we have installed. (NOTE FOR COMMS, can we look at this? More radios?)

4 p.m. Reconnaissance mission completed. Property has multiple entrances, driveway accessed from Winchester Road (heading south) but there are various footpaths leading into garden from surrounding farmland (SEE MAP, APPENDIX 6B). There appears to be a maze.

Weather conditions: Fair.

Temperature: 24 degrees Celsius.

RECOMMENDATION: Further observation requested.

CHAPTER 6
A Summer Holiday

The next day arrived with a glorious dawn that slid in over the tops of the curtains of Patricia's bedroom and called her awake long before anyone else in the house. The air was already heavy with heat, and it wasn't even breakfast.

'It really is the summer holidays after all,' she said to herself with great satisfaction, as she peered through the curtains at the hazy blue sky, the shimmering drops of dew on the lawn trembling with anticipation. Somehow, the strangeness of their arrival, Larry and Evie's obsession with the Library, the unsettling conversation with their host the night before, all now seemed like a distant dream.

In fact, for a moment, it *all* felt like a dream. The old house, the golden cornfields, the cloudless horizon, they made the experience of the last six years feel terribly

far away. Gathering by the radio, dry-lipped, waiting for news. The expression in her parents' eyes that she had never seen before, and didn't recognise. Although she knew what it was now, of course.

Fear.

She also knew what real fear felt like. Lying in bed, the coverlet pulled up to her nose, staring at the ceiling, the electric light in the ceiling rose that shook as the bombs thumped down here, there, here again . . . Wondering if next time it might be near enough to go to the shelter. And often it was. Or when they waved Father off from the front step, on a day like this one, not knowing if they would ever see him again. Or if they did, whether he would still look and behave like their father.

Patricia rubbed her eyes. No, she decided. It wasn't a dream. It had all been horribly, horribly real. And the proof was her. How she felt, how she now thought, spoke and acted.

Like a grown-up.

She pulled on her lightest summer dress, and walked barefoot downstairs.

Unbolting the front door, she stepped outside and spread her arms wide, luxuriating in both the stretch and the sun on her face. Bees were hard at work on the lavender by the steps. Patricia took in a deep breath of all the scents in the garden, and—

'Now this is more like it, don't you think, Patti?' There was Simon, startling her, his stale breath in her ear.

'I thought staying in the countryside meant I might get the odd moment to myself,' she said, rolling her eyes at him. 'How wrong I was.'

'Beautiful old place, isn't it?' Her brother looked around, hand over his brow, taking in the fast-ascending sun, soaring up over serried rows of burnished wheat on the horizon. Suddenly, he hated it. The sun, the fields, the healthy, golden perfection of it all. It was a lie. Life wasn't golden or perfect, he knew that now. You could be the fastest runner in the school, like him, but no one could run fast or far away enough to escape a war. War was a smoking monster, which steamrollered over everything, crushing the world you knew. Even when it was over, and you thought you had survived, you felt a pain in your chest, and there was the monster incubating inside, slowly crushing your heart in its claws, and wringing out every hope and dream you ever had. He shook his head, trying to shake the horror out, as if it were only dust. 'Hard to think of some creepy Shakespearean spook getting up to rum things, isn't it? What was his name again?'

'Crowne,' said Patricia. 'Nicholas Crowne.'

'That was it. Can't say I made head or tail of what she was on about.'

'Me neither, but . . . Si?'

'Yes, sister dearest?'

'Lall and Evie . . . this secret Library of theirs . . . I don't believe the Professor thought they *were* making it up.'

Simon heaved a huge sigh. 'I know. She'd be the most marvellous headmistress somewhere, don't you think? Very comforting.'

'But what if—'

He turned to her, half his face submerged in shadow, an ancient mask in a museum. 'What if what? You worry too much. Come on, remember what Father said – everything is getting back to normal. The sun's out, we've got this whole house to ourselves, and all the Germans are buried under rubble or dangling from a rope, so—'

Patricia's lip trembled. She didn't know whether to slap him or cry. 'How could you say such a thing? Why must you always be so beastly?' She unfolded herself in a single bound and marched back indoors. Shutting her ears to his cries – 'What? What did I say . . . Come back!' – she slammed the door, making the medieval windows wince.

'I was only going to say,' Simon muttered to his absent and oversensitive (it always seemed to him) sister, 'why don't we persuade that trout of a housekeeper to make us a picnic, and we go and explore those woods? There must be a river somewhere for splashing about in.'

Yes, he hated the Germans. He was glad lots of them were dead. So what if not every one was a Nazi? The war was still their fault. Making his family frightened and angry, crying all the time. Even father, inexplicably, sitting by the fire with his pipe, tears sliding down his cheeks when he thought no one was looking. Someone had to be strong. Someone had to be the man of the family.

Besides, he was blown if he was going to let some childish chatter about spooky libraries spoil his stay here. It was, after all, not just the end of the war, not just some pile they were knocking around in for a week or two, not just the beginning of the rest of their lives, but the summer holidays! In 1945! Sometimes he felt like boxing his siblings around the ears, and saying, 'Come on, why the long face? We won!'

But later, after much commotion and to his great satisfaction, splashing about in the river was precisely how the rest of the day was spent. And not just that day, but several days after. They only ever returned when the light had all but gone, trudging barefoot and still wet back through the long grass, towels and dripping bathing suits slung over their shoulders.

When they weren't swimming, Simon liked to explore the old sheds and outbuildings around Barfield. One afternoon, he uncovered a rusty croquet set buried under a stack of mouldy deckchairs. Dragging it out, he unevenly pegged the hoops into the long lawn that flanked the side of the house and took great joy in thrashing Patricia and Evie repeatedly (Larry preferred to sit and watch with Grey Bear). Sometimes, he thought, whacking the ball to victory for the eighteenth time, there were perks to being the only real boy in the family.

Simon had spent such a long time finding his siblings incomprehensible, but being so far away from their old lives somehow made him feel closer to them.

From the funny leathery smell of the Professor's car, to the secret diving spot he had discovered in the river and their shared disgust at Mrs Martin's noxious cooking attempts with rations, the holidays piled up with stories he couldn't wait to make everyone laugh about when he got back home.

Yet in many other ways, the children had never been

further apart. When thunder clouds bloomed in the distance and the summer rain slid down the windows in relentless stripes, the four felt trapped, and found it unbearable to be together in the same room. Evie lay on her bed, head in her hands, staring at the same page in a book on jet propulsion engines till she felt she had read it a thousand times. How could you read the same words so many times, she wondered, and yet not take a single one of them in?

Simon escaped to the woods, and could be found drenched, with mud spotted over his face, as he crouched under a tree, whittling a branch with his penknife. At first, it might have been into the point of a spear. Then an arrow. Or just a sword, a knife ... then ... He whittled furiously, eyes set, driving the raw, sandy shavings on to the dark wet ground until there was nothing left in his hands but dashes of mulch.

He looked at the mess he had made with grim satisfaction. Well – what of it? Everything else had been destroyed. Houses, schools, churches. Even Tube lines blown up. The whole world on fire, night after night.

Still, the fires hadn't got him. He was a survivor. Even if the Russians turned nasty again, and came for them, he would hide out and survive in the woods like Robinson Crusoe. It wouldn't matter that he couldn't read as well as the others. One day he would be as brave a soldier as Father and then he would show them. He would show them all.

Patricia sat at a silvery desk in the strange, modern drawing room, attending to her diary. She always began with such good intentions, writing in her tidy, narrow hand in neat, sloping strokes.

Yesterday we walked down the lane to the village, and there was a fair on the green. They put up a large tent, and inside it smelt of flowers. There were so many kinds of jam and a dog tried to bite the vicar's trousers which sent Larry into a fit. And we all got a cup of tea from an urn and then . . .

Then she woke up, after what felt like hours later, the dusk falling outside as she awoke from the deepest and most dreamless sleep, her head resting on the open page, the ink blurred.

Larry used the rainy days to sneak up to the top floor. He peered up at the painting of Barfield. He got Grey Bear to keep guard while he drilled a small hole in the wall with a compass – to see if the Library was still there, behind everything – but he found only flaky white plaster and stopped drilling, in case he got into trouble. He cried and sulked, sometimes hiding in his room with the curtains drawn while the others – it seemed to him – did nothing but laugh and chatter loudly.

At night, he dreamed about Folio and the Land of the Reads. He tossed and turned in his unfamiliar bed, his head full of a brave tiny fairy knight, his land under siege. He tucked the polished oak ring under his pillow, checking throughout each sleepless hour that it was still there. A ring given to him by a knight, just like in the stories.

A knight that Larry had let down.

Evie would not admit it but, when she wasn't confining herself to her room, was exactly the same. She gave up checking the corridor after she saw the mess Larry had made of the wall. That was such a boy thing to do. So physical, practical and mindlessly literal. She tried other experiments, like saying 'The Library!' to herself, while she was alone.

In a cool tiled bathroom, sinking below the soapy water, squinting at the bright high sun that blinded even through the dust-filled skylight. Alone in the dining room, with the empty plates she had promised to clear. But no Library appeared, and even thinking of it gave her a headache ... until she remembered, with a startling precision, what she had seen.

The sapphire skyscrapers that glowed at night. The flying cars. A woman made of numbers.

Six weeks, more or less, passed in this fashion. It was late August now, the dog days of summer. The sun fading just that bit earlier, the rays just noticeably cooler on the shoulders while they swam in the river after tea.

Simon was pretending to be a long-lost river serpent, swerving about under the surface grabbing everyone's legs, and then emerging from the water with a roar, weeds plastered over his head. Larry took a run-up from the bank on his short legs, yelling, 'Look at me, look at me, I'm a dam buster!' before showering them all with spray as he splashed in. Evie didn't like even the vaguest jokes about bombs, but she got her own back minutes later by doing exactly the same thing.

Patricia was getting some rays, stretched out on a large boulder they had christened the 'Diving Rock'. As the shouts and squeals of the others washed over her, she remembered how it used to be like this all the time, Simon leading them from one lark to the next – playful, foolish and fun. The war had changed them all, she could see that. Larry had disappeared into the stories in his head. Evie was isolated, locked inside her awful memories. She herself felt older, more responsible, even if she didn't want to be. But Simon had become so hard, so bitter. Whether it was the fact their father had rescued people at Dunkirk, while he was too young to join him, or the endless worries of the last few years, or just something at school she didn't know about, it was impossible to say. There was no escaping the facts though. Her boisterous and doting older brother was becoming a different person. It wasn't a person she liked.

But then Simon was at the rock, hauling himself half out, his hair dripping water all over her. Shivering, she sat up, and wanted to scold him, but he looked so happy, and golden and sleek. The way his mop of hair was slicked back, he suddenly reminded her of a seal. A big, grinning seal.

'You look like a—' she tried to say, collapsing into fits of giggles before getting the word out.

'A river god?'

This only made her laugh more. But she still couldn't say it. 'No – a . . .' Only all she could do was collapse in further gales of hooting laughter as he flicked water at her furiously. Then the others were crowding around, bobbing in the rust-coloured water.

'What did you call him, Patti?'

'I thought she said a heel!'

'Go on, tell us, please!'

Then Simon the Seal snatched her towel, sinking back into the water with it, which was clearly a declaration of war.

'Right,' said Patricia, and rolled up her non-existent sleeves before diving in after him.

The sopping towel was retrieved, rolled into a ball and passed from sun-kissed hand to hand as they jumped and swam and laughed, until the light finally bleached away beneath the horizon, flies dancing across the glossy surface of the river. Gathering their things, they walked back to the house.

They weren't talking of much, if anything all.

Evie had a sandal dangling from her hand, and Patricia had tied her damp white towel around her waist, like a waiter's apron. Larry was seeing how many dried grass seed heads he could send flying into the hazy air by running Grey Bear through them at speed.

It was Simon – marching ahead as usual, in exaggerated strides like a drill sergeant, just as their father had taught him – who heard it first.

Then they all saw it.

A truck, skidding across the gravel, in front of the hall. A truck full of soldiers.

CHAPTER 7
Unexpected Visitors

The truck doors slammed open, booted feet jumping out, and angry shouts.

The children didn't know whether to run or hide, so at first they just watched through some large bushes. They saw the soldiers, wearing distinctive berets, as deep green as the rhododendrons they hid behind. Soldiers who were also brandishing revolvers.

'I thought the war was over!' said Patricia.

'It doesn't make sense,' said Evie. 'Why would British soldiers be carrying guns here?'

Simon, who wanted to join the army one day, like their father, and knew about these things, pointed discreetly at their berets and badges. A rich red rose, garlanded with leaves. 'These aren't regular soldiers, Evie.

They're military police. Intelligence corps.'

'But why here?' said Patricia, feeling like her mother once more as she gave Simon one of those looks that said, *What in blazes is going on?*

He could only shrug.

A partial answer soon followed. The children crouched lower, making themselves as hidden as possible, as the soldiers piled into the house – not even ringing the doorbell but kicking the door down, the ancient wood splintering under their boots and gun butts.

Behind the bush, they all looked at each other, their throats too tight to speak. Larry tucked Grey Bear extra snug under his arm, which was still damp from the river.

Somewhere, in the wilting summer wood behind them, an owl hooted.

Then, they heard the gunshots.

Three loud, clear, unmistakeable gunshots, fired not quickly, but in a calm, well spaced and deliberate order. Three gunshots and a scream.

There was no time to discuss anything. Simon picked Larry and his bear up – as if his eight-year-old brother now weighed no more than a cushion – and started to run as silently as he could, through the woods, to the other side of the house. Patricia, equally silently, nearly had to drag Evie away – who was rooted to the spot, staring at the gaping hole in the door of Barfield Hall.

The war was over. She was not meant to see horrid things again. Maguire Street was behind them. This was the countryside. The Professor was wise and kind. It was the summer holidays. Yet here they were. British soldiers in one of the oldest houses in their own country, smashing things and firing guns.

She yielded, and ran after Patricia.

Simon checked the coast was clear, lying flat behind a box hedge on the back lawn facing the other side of the house, and then scurrying across to the nearest window, bent low, beckoning the others on behind him. As the others caught up, now cold and shivering from their wet towels and bathing suits, he prised open the chipped and peeling frame. He did so as slowly and as quietly as he could.

'What are you doing?' hissed Patricia, crouching down next to him, wishing that the ferny wisteria clambering up the wall could have hidden them more than it did.

Simon mimed going through the window.

'Inside? But so are the soldiers!'

'Exactly,' he whispered, with a crafty smile. He had

watched enough war movies; he knew what to do. 'I've seen it in the pictures, Patti. Hide in plain sight. The last place they'll look. Trust me.'

Shaking her head, Patricia began to wonder how many other things Simon thought he knew about.

The window squeaked open, just far enough for them to squeeze through. One by one Simon beckoned the others in, and they clambered through, scattering flaky white splinters of paint on the floor, while he kept a nervy lookout.

Then they were inside a small shadowy room, with the lingering perfume of lavender water, piles of sheets either sitting rumpled in baskets or crisply folded on a sideboard, waiting to be distributed around the house. The laundry. For a moment, Evie looked longingly in the half light at the large stained porcelain sink with gleaming taps, the steam iron and the stacks of linen, and took a deep breath.

The order. Everything in here was organised, and tidy, and under control. Unlike inside her head.

Simon opened the door a crack, and peered through.

In fearful, automatic response, conditioned by years of nightly bombing raids, the children began to wordlessly dress for imminent departure, discarding their towels and wet things, Patricia even grabbing one of Simon's crisp shirts from the pile on the ironing board.

81

At his signal, they crept out along a dusk-darkened passage, wincing at the slightest creak from the polished floorboards. Then, on the corner, by a large leather armchair pushed back against the wall, he gestured at them to freeze.

There were more shouts. A woman sobbing, who didn't sound like the Professor. The housekeeper, Mrs Martin. The military police hadn't left yet. They were opening drawers, cupboards, pulling books out of cases, smashing and ripping things.

'They're searching the house,' Simon muttered.

'Where do we go now?' said Patricia.

'There's only one place we can go,' said Evie, and then surprised herself by saying it so quickly and calmly. 'The Library.'

Her two elder siblings stared at her.

'This is no time for a game, Evie,' said Patricia.

'It isn't a game!' said Larry. 'Come on, we'll show you. It will be there this time, I know it will!'

And he took her hand, and led them all up the back stairs to the dusty corridor in the attic.

The four of them clustered at the top of the rickety steps, hesitant to take a step further. It was quite dark outside now, nothing visible but an inky blue through the window at the end. They didn't even dare turn the light switch on.

'Does it look like the painting is still there?' whispered Patricia.

No one could tell. There were just shadows and edges and corners that could have been anything.

Someone clomped up on to the floor beneath them in heavy boots. 'There's more rooms up here, Sarge,' a voice yelled out.

'Then keep searching! They have to be here somewhere,' came the reply from down below. 'How hard can it be to find some flaming . . .'

But the word was lost as the speaker moved out of earshot. Whatever the soldiers were after, there wasn't time to ask now.

'Well, go on then! What are we meant to do now?' said Patricia, clenching and unclenching her fists so her nails dug into her palms.

'You had better not be fooling,' warned Simon.

'We're not,' protested Evie. 'We just walked down this corridor . . .'

Which she now did, followed by Larry and Grey Bear.

'. . . and there it was . . .' said Larry.

'The Library!' they chorused in unison.

Because there it was. A golden light that squeezed

through the hinge of the door, around and underneath it. The carvings of gods and oak leaves and animals that they could reach out and touch.

'I'll be blown,' whistled Simon, placing his hands on Larry's shoulders, who flushed with pride.

'Is it safe . . . I mean can we just go in?' Patricia looked at the door with suspicion.

Before anyone could reply, they heard someone begin to climb the rickety steps up to the corridor. Which, in a way, was the only answer they needed.

Without another word, Larry stuck his hand out, pushing the Library door open. It swung easily in, revealing the polished floor and burning chandeliers. The Hastings children stepped in through the doorway, their heads so full of wonder that they did not even hear the angry cries and gunshots as the Library door shut firmly behind them.

Once inside, the children did not dare stop to catch their breath. Looking wildly around, they searched for a way out, or someone to help them. But there was still no librarian to be seen, just the three large signs – 'Read', 'Unread' and 'Never Read', hanging under the chandeliers and the domed glass ceiling.

'It's not like any library I've ever been in before,' said Patricia.

'That's because it's not just a library,' Evie started to explain, 'at least, not . . .'

Her words faltered as she realised that Larry, in typical Larry fashion, had already marched on ahead straight down the Read aisle, Grey Bear bouncing along behind him on the floor as the others followed.

'This way!' he shouted as he was swallowed up by the shadows between the shelves. 'The book we need is on this shelf. You'll see.'

Simon snorted with laughter at his younger brother's determination, and looked at the others.

'Oh why not!' he said, and marched after Larry.

Patricia shook her head and followed him.

'Wait!' said Evie. 'You don't understand!'

But no one was listening. They had gone.

She stood for a moment, and looked at the Unread aisle. Closing her eyes, Evie could almost feel the hot air of the future city blowing on her face. Then she remembered what the Secretary had said to her, the deal they had made. And pulled herself together.

As she sprinted after her brothers and sister down the Read aisle, she could spy them at the far end, clustering

85

around Larry as he slowly opened the pages of a large, leather-bound volume.

'Wait for me!' she cried, and hurtled towards the readers and the book, as together they began to tremble with light.

Once more, Larry found himself standing in the same field where he had first met Thumb, a summer breeze upon his face. Only this time, his brother and sisters were with him. They looked up from the book, marvelling at the new world around them.

But Larry wasn't marvelling at all.

'There's something wrong.'

He put down the collection of fairy tales to go and take a closer look. The other children, who hadn't even believed him that the Land of Reads existed, had to agree. For where the great, spreading oak tree had stood, with the beautiful treehouse perched on top, Larry found himself now peering at just a blackened, smouldering stump, as stark and ugly as a severed wrist jutting out of the earth.

'So much for fairy-tale land,' said Simon, trying not to choke on the acrid fumes. 'I always knew those stories were a load of rubbish.'

He could see what this was all about. It was another war. And that meant fighting, not lying around reading. Simon allowed himself a half smile. Perhaps he was going to see some action after all. He may have been too young for the war at home, but he wasn't too young for this one. Fighting story characters! He couldn't wait to see the glow on Father's face when he told him.

'They've chopped down his tree,' said Larry, because just describing what he saw was all he could manage. He knew if he tried to say any more, he might cry. Thumb had been so friendly to him. And to Grey Bear too, who dangled forlornly at his side, looking anything but happy. The former meadow of tussocks, dandelions and daisies had been churned up by heavy wheels. He clutched the oak ring tight in his pocket and said a little prayer in his head.

Patricia looked at the muddy gouges in the ground, the rutted tracks, and tried very hard not to think of the newsreel films of tanks in France. But she found that was all she could think of.

Evie kicked at the still burning ash, scattered around the base of the stump in a fiery wreath. 'Wherever I go, things seem to get burned down,' she muttered to herself. As Thumb's tree had been felled, the children could not climb to the top as Larry had done, and see the valleys, rivers and villages of the Reads. But just standing there, by the smoking tree and the cratered earth, they could see what was happening.

'Is that a flying car?' said Simon, pointing to one carving blackly through the sky in the distance, like a monstrous bat.

'Yes,' said Evie, who could not keep the mounting joy out of her voice, her fingers crossed tightly behind her back. 'They are from the City of the Unreads.'

Then she smelt the smoke from the tree stump again, and a memory blitzed through her brain. It felt like a moment lasting an hour, but perhaps it was only seconds. It was Maguire Street all over again. Evie thought that there was nothing worse in the world than what had happened that day. What she had seen. What – who – she had stepped over to get down the stairs, reduced as it was to a frame standing alone in rubble.

Now it was a fairy's treehouse burning in front of her.

She knew who had done it too. But somehow this was different, wasn't it?

It wasn't a school full of innocent children that had been burned down, but a tree. With one fairy living in it. Who probably was still living for all she knew, but had just flown off somewhere. That was all fairies did, in any case, wasn't it? Fly about.

It wasn't horrid Nazis in bombers who had destroyed the tree, either. The flying cars were full of beautiful machines. Jana's silver robots, from a land where, Evie knew, even on her very brief acquaintance, she could thrive.

A place of facts and information.

Where being a girl was not going to stop her doing what she wanted. Women could be leaders speaking to crowds in squares, not having their hair mussed by stupid elder brothers, never taken seriously, never listened to. She would show them.

Evie would take them all to the City of the Unreads, and show them that she was not stupid or silly little Evie. These magnificent robots alone would be enough to persuade anyone, surely? When she could command machines such as these, perhaps even build them herself, who would be laughing at her then? She would use them to make sure no one ever dropped bombs on anyone ever again. No headmaster would ever have to weep, as they read each name on the register and no replies came back. Not with her Silver Soldiers in charge.

That was worth one burned-out tree, surely?

Larry whirled around to face her, tears streaming down his hot cheeks. 'And they're murderers! I hate them! Look at what they've done.'

'Hang on, Lall,' said Patricia, 'we don't know the full facts yet—'

'They aren't murderers,' said Evie. 'They're wonderful and clever. They know so much—'

'I hate them! It was special here! I promised to help Tom Thumb and now . . .'

Evie shook her head at her brother. 'Calm down, Larry. He's just a fairy tale. He's not even real. But those flying cars, on the other hand, they're . . .'

'Landing just over there,' said Simon.

The Magician Project – Extract 10a
(KV 1/1567-8)

On Saturday 25 August 1945, Professor Diana Kelly
wrote in her diary:

'So after all the thinking, the meetings, the
planning – it has finally begun. I just hope the
children are up to what we are asking of them.
The war has made them older than their years,
but there is a tremendous innocence too. They
could be straight out of an Enid Blyton story,
bless their hearts! XXXXXXXX [REDACTED] insists
we are doing the right thing, for the country
etc, but that will be no comfort for their parents
if we have made a fatal miscalculation.'

CHAPTER 8
A Flying Car

The children turned and looked. At the far end of Thumb's field, one of the flying cars was indeed now landing, as gracefully as a giant metallic dragonfly, the glittering wings folding in upon themselves as the airborne machine once more became a landbound one. It sped towards them, bumping over the field in sprays of dry earth.

No one moved. They waited, and watched, as the car that had been a plane got closer and closer. It stopped just beyond the stump of the oak tree. They watched the metal doors open with hydraulic formality, through the wisps of black smoke. Some soldiers climbed out. Men and women of silver, with blank silver eyes and moulded silver lips, who hovered lightly above the ground. Their helmets and boots joined to their bodies, fashioned out

of the same block of precious metal.

'Silver Soldiers!' breathed Larry, half in fear, half in excitement.

As the soldiers drew nearer, it was possible to see that black lines snaked over every inch of their silver skin, like tattoos. Tattoos that were columns of numbers, moving and changing, in a constant stream. The first one, who appeared to be the leader, stopped a few yards away and scanned them in a jerky way, his head cocking like a bird's.

'Read or Unread?' he asked, in a voice as brittle and metallic as his body.

Patricia stepped forward. She was shaking, but she knew she had to say something, as the most responsible member of the family.

'Neither, actually,' was what came out of her mouth.

The lines of numbers rippled angrily over the soldier's face. He didn't move.

'Read or Unread?' he said again.

'Now listen,' said Simon. 'You heard my sister. We're neither—'

He stopped, as three tiny people, all with pointed ears and equally pointed hats, dressed in leaf-like rags, dashed out from a bush behind, carrying a small log between them. With a high-pitched roar, they charged at the lower leg of Simon's interrogator, battering his shiny calf.

'Look, more fairies like Thumb!' said Larry.

'Aren't they more like pixies?' said Patricia, peering over her glasses.

It didn't matter what they were, because the soldier just calmly extended his silver arm, pointing it at the little people. The tiny creatures jumped up and down, furiously shaking their fists and yelling in high-pitched voices, while preparing for another charge.

Black lines of moving tattoos along the soldier's arm fizzed and jumped, and then – making the children stumble back in shock – a stream of fiery numbers spat out from his outstretched finger. They shot through the air in a jet of burning, numerical flame, and devoured the pixies in a ball of fire.

All the children watched in horror as the little creatures disappeared in an explosion of inky letters, spraying into the air. As the smoke subsided, all that remained of the tiny attackers was a few sheets of paper falling softly through the air, until they landed on the scorched earth.

The Captain of the Silver Soldiers studied the ink spats and paper briefly, without comment, and then turned to face Simon again. His face was as cold and as impassive as before.

'They were Reads,' said the soldier. 'So I ask you again. Reads or Unreads?'

Not normally lost for words, Simon stammered. Evie was about to explain to the Captain how she had actually met the Secretary, and was thoroughly on their side really, when there was a whistling over their heads.

Larry looked up, clutching his bear, and just caught sight of what looked like a large honey pot flying through the air, before it exploded into the flying car in shooting flames. The Silver Soldiers standing by the car jerked around like puppets, their automated limbs flailing uselessly, melting in the heat. The Captain retreated as swiftly and silently as he had arrived, to the remains of his men and his vehicle.

Then there was a crashing sound, like the remains of a house's roof finally caving in, and Evie cried, 'Look out!'

Whatever had thrown the honey pot had burst through some bushes, and was running towards them, a giant beast that snuffled and roared at the same time. The children ran in the opposite direction, only to be met by another one, bounding towards them from the undergrowth on the other side of the field.

'Bears!' said Larry, and held up Grey Bear, as if to say *I like bears!* but the real bears did not seem to care.

In fact, as the children ran for their lives, tripping over their own feet, Simon decided that teddy bears ought to be done for false pretences. Teddy bears were soft and fluffy. These things were all teeth and claw, and enormous too, now towering either side of them on their hind legs. He had charmed his way out of scrapes before, but you couldn't charm a giant bear. Every move felt unpredictable, every noise they made was unexpected and bone-rattling. And the stink was something else – he had once stuck his nose into a fox hole, and that was like a rose garden compared to this.

'Hold hands,' ordered Patricia, and everyone was just grateful to be given something concrete to do. 'Form a circle,' she said, and had no idea why, but an image of Roman army battle formations with shields had flashed into her head, which was better than nothing. They all held hands and shuffled together in a circle, as the bears fell on to all fours with a thump, and stalked towards them, sniffing the air as if they wanted to inhale the whole day right down their throats.

Then another bear came racing up behind them, a much smaller one – a baby bear. He hid behind his parents. Growling, the older male bear stalked towards the children, who began to shiver as the animal drew closer. They could see all too clearly the oily shine of the fur, the worn claws and the uneven, stained teeth.

'Who are you, and why are you here?' he growled. His voice was as dark as the burnt tree.

'We're looking for Tom Thumb,' said Larry, who was more used to talking to bears than the others.

The bear rounded on him, and Larry shrank into his elder sister's side. 'Who sent you to look for Thumb?' the bear snarled. 'Was it her?'

'Please, sir,' said Patricia, 'we mean no harm. We were in a Library, and we opened a book, and then we were here.'

For the first time since his arrival, the bear stopped moving. There was even a trace of surprise in his deep eyes. 'Opening a book is always a serious matter,' he said.

His mate ambled up behind him. 'My love,' she said. 'Did you hear that? They're Readers. They're really here.'

'I hate Readers,' said her cub, bouncing around the edge of the circle, trying to catch a fly. 'Reading is boring and Readers are even worse.'

'Shush, little one,' said his mother. 'This is serious.'

A frown creased his father's face as he studied the children. 'Then you are in danger. You will need our protection.'

'From those metal monsters in the flying car?' ventured

Simon, almost immediately regretting his words, as the bear's muzzle was straight in his face. He was so fast for such a large creature, and his head was three times the size of Simon's.

'Yes,' he said, studying Simon intently. 'What do you know about them?'

'Nothing. We just saw the car land, and then . . .'

'They are the army of the Unreads, sweet child,' said Mother Bear firmly. 'They are trying to destroy all our stories. They will kill you or anyone who stands in their way.'

'But what if they actually wanted to help us?' muttered Evie in a low sullen voice.

'Trust me, help is the last thing we will get from them.' Mother Bear looked down her snout at Grey Bear, singed, but still tucked under Larry's arm. 'Goodness – what on earth is that?' she enquired. 'Is it alive?'

'It's Grey Bear,' snapped Larry.

'Still none the wiser,' she said, shaking her big head. 'I suppose you want him to come with you as well?'

'Come where?' said Patricia, standing protectively in front of her brother.

Mother Bear's face softened as much as her bear face could. 'Out of the open and into safety, of course! Or do you all want to end up the same way as those pixies?'

Then before things could get any more complicated, the Bears instructed the children to sit on their backs, two a piece, and they ran at great speed through the forest until the stench of the burning Silver Soldiers had long faded behind them.

'A house?' said Simon behind his hand to Patricia as they approached through the forest. 'I may have missed something at school, but don't bears live in caves?'

Although it was only a house of sorts.

A poorly thatched roof hung shaggily over crooked stone walls, with low windows. Thistles, nettles and brambles had invaded from the surrounding fields, and now jostled for space in the front garden, while trails of ivy devoured what remained of a picket fence. A rotted, empty chicken coop lay drunkenly tipped to one side.

Patricia's heart did a funny twirl as she caught herself remembering their old home, before the raid. Peeling window frames, the glass taped up against bombs, the coal fire in the front room that seemed to make everything too hot and damp at the same time, shivering upstairs while she washed with the jug and basin . . . But in the end the tape on the windows hadn't stopped a nearby bomb putting a great crack through their walls so it wasn't safe to live in.

'I think we lost them,' said Father Bear, bowling up an uneven path. With a claw, he carefully parted the fur on his head to reveal an iron key nestling on his scalp. He turned it in the stiff wooden door and ushered his guests inside quickly. 'Hurry, hurry. If they discover us, we're done for.'

'You poor things, you must be starving,' said Mother Bear. 'I'll put some porridge on.' As she began to bustle around a dusty stove, Patricia wandered around the low-beamed kitchen, looking at everything. There were three rickety kitchen chairs around the table, two quite large and one rather small. There was something about the house and its occupants that seemed oddly familiar, but she couldn't quite place it.

Evie explored further, mounting the spiral staircase that led to the upper floor. She found a bathroom, with three different-sized towels hanging on the rail. Pushing at another door, she found three beds, again of three different sizes, from very large down to small. But then, how peculiar, there was a dress lying on Baby Bear's bed – the kind of thing she might have worn to a party when she was Larry's age. Yet this Baby Bear was a boy, and she didn't know much about baby boy bears, but she was pretty sure they didn't wear party dresses.

The door was closed firmly before her eyes by a large paw.

'Oh dear,' said Mother Bear, smiling but with a steely glint in her eye, 'what a mess we've left the house in. We never normally have visitors, you see.'

She led Evie back downstairs, ignoring her many questions, where the others were all sat around the table. At length the porridge was cooked up, mixed with cream and served with a heavy sprinkling of brown sugar. The children's eyes went as wide as the broad bowls it was served in. They had not tasted such deliciousness for years, and Larry ate his so quickly, Patricia was worried he might be sick.

The Bears watched them as they ate.

'Are you not hungry?' said Simon, scraping the last dollop of porridge out with his spoon.

'We have already eaten,' said Father Bear, his arms folded. 'But thank you.'

Simon licked his spoon clean, which his mother always told him off for, but she wasn't here. Then he regarded his hosts again. 'This is going to sound very peculiar,' he said, 'but I feel like we may have met before.'

Patricia smiled in disbelief. 'A talking bear? You're as bad as Larry.'

Mother Bear inclined her head softly. 'Your brother may have met us . . . in another form.'

Larry looked up from his porridge, and blinked once, and then twice. 'Wait. I know who you are!'

'Quite the detective,' muttered Baby Bear to himself.

'You're the Three Bears . . . and Goldilocks!'

CHAPTER 9
What Always Happens

There was an uncomfortable silence in the room, with only the sound of Evie pointedly scraping her bowl clean. She was thinking about the dress upstairs, the one she had seen on the bed. Larry blushed a deep scarlet as if he had made a terrible mistake. But Father Bear nodded in polite acknowledgement. So Larry pressed on, hotly.

'You're much scarier than you are in the story. You've got really sharp teeth too. What's happened to Goldilocks? And why are you attacking the Silver Soldiers—'

'Larry!' Patricia smiled at the Bears, hoping they wouldn't do anything rash. 'It's really very rude to ask so many questions.'

Father Bear coughed. 'I can see we owe you an explanation—'

'Not at all,' said Patricia. 'You saved our lives. Though it is all a bit . . .'

'Odd,' said Simon. 'Very odd indeed. You didn't eat the porridge. Are you going to eat us instead?' It sounded like a joke, but he wasn't smiling.

'Eat a Reader? Never!' said Father Bear.

'I'll make a fresh pot of tea, shall I?' said Mother Bear. And she heaved herself up, bustling around the dirty sink and stove. Once the kettle had boiled and the pot had brewed, they all sat down again, warming their hands around chipped cups.

'We never wanted this war with the Unreads,' she said. 'They started it. We have been fighting for years, but they have never attacked like this before. Their leader Jana – the coldest and cruellest machine you could ever meet – won't rest until she and her silver minions have taken everything.'

'It was very impressive how you saw off those silver devils back there,' said Simon, swigging his tea down. 'Was that a honey pot you threw at them?'

'Naturally!' said Father Bear, who looked surprised. 'What else would you expect a talking bear to use as a weapon?'

'We didn't expect any of this.' Simon tried to forget

about the soldiers they had narrowly escaped back at
Barfield, or guessing what had happened to the Professor.
He pondered again what they had been looking for, what
the Professor could possibly be hiding that involved British
soldiers kicking doors down and firing guns.

'A Reader should know better,' the bear snorted,
wiping a drop of tea off his chin with a chequered napkin.
Larry laughed at the sight of a bear using a napkin, but
when his host twitched and stared at him, his smile
soon fell away.

'But please, sir, what happened to those pixies?'

Father Bear glanced at Mother Bear. Then they
looked together at Baby Bear, who was noisily licking his
spoon clean.

'Don't mind me,' he said. 'I know anyway.'

Mother Bear grunted. 'Those vile machines have found
a way to return us to where we came from.'

Then it dawned upon the children. The ink. The sheets
of paper. 'You mean, the pages of a book?' said Larry,
who liked things to be logical.

'Exactly!' said Father Bear, thumping the table, making
everyone jump. 'Their souls have returned to their original
form, leaving nothing behind but their inky pages. They
simply become . . . forgotten.'

'Where do forgotten stories go, then?' asked Simon.

'Anyway!' said Mother Bear, with a grimace. 'Anyone for more tea?'

'But,' said Patricia, 'who exactly are the Unreads and what do they want?'

'And what have they done with Thumb?' added Larry in a small voice. 'Has he been forgotten too? I haven't forgotten him.'

Father Bear set down his cup. Baby Bear looked up from his, and froze.

'The Unreads are everything we are not,' said Father Bear. 'We are stories, the tales of the past already read and known to Readers such as yourselves. Every kind of Read story lives in Folio – be they myth or legend – and you are in one of its many kingdoms, in Fairytale Valley. For thousands of years we have lived together in these beautiful green dales. All we ever did was follow the path our story had laid out for us. We were each very different – from bears who eat porridge to tiny fairy knights – but we all got along, because we knew our place on the shelf.'

Baby Bear poured himself another cup of tea, filling his cup right up to the top, letting the tea overflow and slosh on to the saucer, which he then began to slurp clean. 'Except I hate fairies.'

'Shush, my little one,' tutted Mother Bear. 'At least, most of us got along well enough, until the Librarian disappeared.'

Now it was the children's turn to look at one another.

'We noticed there wasn't a . . . librarian . . . in the Library,' said Patricia, choosing her words carefully.

'That Library, the one you entered our land through,' said Father Bear, 'is a magic Library, a series of doors into other worlds, like Folio. You would never have seen the Librarian there.'

'I bet I would have,' said Baby Bear.

'No you wouldn't, my love,' said Mother Bear. 'The truth is, no one has ever seen the Librarian who created this collection of stories and lives and facts, all living next to each other.'

'A magic Library,' mused Patricia to herself.

'Then how do you know he exists?' demanded Simon.

'We don't, for sure. We only know that he has kept our world in peace and order since time began. Until . . . something terrible happened.'

'You ran out of porridge?' said Baby Bear.

'Far worse than that, my son,' said Father Bear. 'He disappeared into one of his own lands, and was never seen again.' He set his cup down and stared at it for a while.

'The most dangerous land in all of Folio.'

The children followed his gaze through the grimy windows. They looked out through the thistles and nettles, out across the overgrown lawn, past the wild woods beyond, to a line of black peaks, sharp against the morning sky. The dark mountains were swathed in mist, and seemed very far away, yet every single one of the children felt cold as they looked at them, as if they were suddenly there, on the distant slopes, breathing in the fierce, icy air.

'A kingdom that wasn't anything like ours,' said Mother Bear grimly.

'The Unreads?' said Patricia.

'I wish! The Unreads are more like us than they think, just the different side of the same coin. That is why this war is so stupid and dangerous! There is a far greater enemy out there, an enemy we must face together.'

Patricia was beginning to understand. At least, so she thought. 'There was another shelf we saw in the Library . . . it stank something rotten. The Never R—'

Mother Bear flew at her, a note of desperation in her voice, sending her empty bowl clattering on to the floor. 'Never say that name!'

The lamps on the wall flickered, and outside the sky

darkened imperceptibly. Patricia felt cold and clammy, and when she next spoke, her voice was quieter than she intended.

'Why not?'

'Because of what you might summon.'

Simon leaned back in his chair, his arm dangling over the side. These animals couldn't possibly know what they were doing. But once he made them understand that he knew more about warfare than they ever would, surely they would ask him to take charge. It would be like running a unit for the British army, just like his father had. Deliberately, he let a note of superiority slide into his voice. It gave him a funny feeling inside, even as he saw his sisters wince. 'So let me get this straight. You've lost your Librarian in this Land of the Never—'

'Don't say it!' warned Father Bear. 'But yes, we have – and until he returns, we are all at the mercy of those silver robots.'

'What have they got against you in the first place?'

'They are a race not of stories, but of information. They call themselves the Unreads because, unlike us, they only like discovering new things. Facts, figures and formulas!'

'And what is so wrong with facts and figures?' interjected Evie, who had kept her head lowered for this whole exchange, sitting on her hands to keep herself calm. Father Bear growled so loudly that Patricia couldn't help edging her chair away from him.

'They want to take over all of Folio!' he thundered. 'Jana wants to answer all the questions in the world. Well, she might be able to explain what makes a car fly, but can she explain why lying is wrong? No! But Pinocchio can. Those are the sort of questions that stories have been answering perfectly well for centuries, thank you very much. And who needs flying cars anyway?'

The talking bear picked up a large slice of toast covered in marmalade in his claw, and devoured it whole, in one bite. Larry sat, gripping his seat, barely able to take his eyes off the bears. Not only had he never seen someone eat a slice of toast whole before, but for the first time he had met some people who made more sense than his parents. He knew stories were best. Making things up was always better than real life, it just was. You could make the world what you wanted in a story. You could imagine that there were fairies at the bottom of the garden, even if there weren't. But when he had seen a scientist in the newspaper, analysing some photographs to demonstrate – conclusively – that there were no fairies at the bottom of the garden, Larry felt two things. He felt sad, and he felt angry. When something was the truth, what was it, after all? You couldn't believe in the truth, you just had to accept it, like a rainy day that made playing outside much less appealing. Human beings needed stories more than stupid facts, he was sure of it.

'I don't understand,' said Patricia next to him, breaking his line of thought. 'Can't you have stories *and* information? Reads and Unreads? I mean, they're two different things, aren't they? Our libraries at home have both and they aren't full of people trying to kill each other.'

Mother Bear shook her huge grizzly head sorrowfully. 'Jana doesn't want there to be both in Folio. She thinks stories are silly, old fashioned and made up. Only facts matter to that robot. Only facts are the truth for her. But here we are!'

'And we are made up, aren't we my darling?' said Father Bear, placing a large paw over his wife's, staring fondly into her eyes.

'Completely!' she said, looking with equal adoration into his.

'Is that what you really believe?' said Simon, with a look of utter incredulity at the heavy bears bulging out over their tiny wooden chairs. 'You look pretty real to me, if you don't mind me saying so.'

'Oh, we're real now, all right,' said Father Bear. 'As real as this lovely little house, perfect for a bear family of three—'

'But what happened to Goldilocks in your story?' interjected Evie. 'I saw a dress—'

'Do you know, I really can't remember, little girl,' said Father Bear with a growl. 'The point is, it's the first rule of Folio.'

The bears all stood up and chanted slowly: 'If you can imagine it, it must exist. Somewhere.'

'I saw that, in Thumb's treehouse!' said Larry, proudly.

'He's another fine example,' said Mother Bear. 'Small and irritating though he was. If you can imagine a fairy the size of your thumb, then he exists somewhere. Somebody – an old lady, a poet, a child in the school yard, who knows – made us up one day, and we have been living our story in this happy valley ever since.'

She stood up, and with a great bear sigh, gathered up all the empty bowls and plates and spoons and knives, hauling them to the sink, while Father Bear and Baby Bear sat on and watched, cleaning their teeth with their long claws.

For a moment, there was just the sound of Mother Bear running water, gently brushing and scrubbing, while she hummed a low tune to herself. Outside in the rambling garden, a blackbird hopped about on a bare patch of grass, pulling out worms with his beak. Patricia stood up and went to the window. She watched the bird, and wondered what story it was from. Mother Bear noticed her looking and tutted, shaking her head fondly.

'They will just keep on escaping from that pie, won't they!'

Then Larry couldn't bear it any longer. He felt the blood rising in his cheeks and, clutching Grey Bear to his chest, stood up as well.

'But what about Thumb! Do you think the Unreads . . . killed him?' he said in a quavering voice.

'He should be so lucky,' said Father Bear. 'Jana has probably taken him back to her palace for processing.'

'Processing into what?' said Patricia, still staring out at the bird.

'You don't want to know.'

Simon joined his sister by the window. 'Well, are we just going to sit here? Can't we do something? I mean, I don't fancy trying my arm against the Silver Soldiers . . . but how about the Librarian? If he can sort it out, then why haven't you gone after him already . . . Couldn't you persuade him to return?'

The Bears stared at him blankly. 'You really don't know anything, do you?'

'What now,' said Simon, 'another Library rule I'm supposed to have swotted up on? Not a big fan of libraries as a rule, I'm afraid. Too warm, you always fall asleep, and you can't sing songs or make jokes.'

Father Bear stamped his foot. 'No! This is far more central than any rule. This is just common sense. Something everyone should know.'

'The reason we thought you were here,' said Mother Bear.

'The reason we *hoped* you were here,' said Father Bear.

'Although I don't want you here,' said Baby Bear.

'You're Readers, aren't you?' said Father Bear. 'You entered through a Library, after all?'

'Well, kind of . . .' said Simon.

'But don't you see? Every inhabitant of Folio knows; it is inscribed into the core of our being . . .'

'. . . that peace and happiness shall never return to our world, until the Readers rule,' said Mother Bear, finishing her husband's sentence for him, dabbing at her eyes with the corner of her apron.

'Until the Readers rule,' repeated Father Bear and Baby Bear.

Standing in the gloomy kitchen, the story characters stared at the children, and the children stared back. A solemn hush fell over them.

Then Patricia grabbed Simon's arm.

'Hang on,' she said, 'where's Evie?'

CHAPTER 10
The Secretary's Residence

Evie didn't care that she should have been wearing a coat, or at least a cardigan, as she walked, rather than the thin shirt and shorts she had been wearing at Barfield. So, shivering through the cool woods, she strode on in the direction the flying car had come from, away from the Bears.

Ha! She snorted and kicked a big pile of old leaves with her boot. She knew *their* story, all right, one she had been told many times at bath and bedtime. Only the real life version didn't feel like a bedtime story at all. The story of a little girl called Goldilocks – who was only looking for something to eat, somewhere to sit, a bed to lie in – and fate led her to the house of those Three Bears. Perhaps she shouldn't have eaten all their porridge, but what had

happened to Goldilocks? Why wouldn't the Bears tell her? In some versions of the story, the Bears came home and discovered her. Then in other tellings, she was thrown out of a window. Evie had even heard a version in which the little girl got eaten alive. She wondered which version of the story these bears were from.

There had been that dress on the bed, after all. A dress far too small for Mother Bear. They couldn't fool her with bowls of porridge and mugs of tea. Their cottage was run-down and creepy. It was clear they were only trying to act like good, ordinary human beings when in fact they were thieving, murderous wild bears. So what if they had 'rescued' them from the Silver Soldiers?

Evie liked the Silver Soldiers. She *adored* the Silver Soldiers. A shudder of excitement ran down her spine just thinking about them. They were beautiful, and perfect. She had no idea how they worked on the inside. But she knew one thing. If they had been in her school, in Maguire Street, on that day, then maybe – just maybe . . . With a toss of her hair, she put the terrible memories out of her head for the thousandth time.

The woods gave way to fields and then, hopping over a stile, a winding country lane. Everywhere there was the smell of burning. Palls of smoke rose into the sky from the blackened shards of burnt-out homes. Evie picked her way along the twisting road, strewn with items of clothing, that either the fleeing Reads had dropped in their haste to escape the Secretary's army . . . or worse, was all that remained of them. A glass slipper, a golden fleece . . . and a rather fetching red cape.

That would do nicely, Evie thought to herself. It was much finer than her miserable duffle coat at home, full of holes and held together by Mother's sewn-on patches. She picked it up, and found the cloak a perfect fit. Best of all, it twirled in the wind as she marched on down the ink- and paper-strewn track, towards the alien towers of the future in the distance.

The journey towards the City of the Unreads was a lot harder than Evie had expected. For one thing, although the wood had been cool, the open sky was entirely without clouds or mercy. Evie felt the beams of the sun drilling into her neck, as if a ray gun from a space adventure had been trained on it. The Bears' breakfast felt a long time ago. Others passed her on their way – an old woman and her children, dragging the most enormous old shoe behind them, followed by a young girl with so much blonde hair to carry that she had piled it up into a bundle on top of her head, and a poor shivering middle-aged man, who appeared to have lost *all* his clothes, apart from a large golden crown. They seemed so weary and worn, as if they had been marching for ever.

Refugees, thought Evie. The tottery line of people with their belongings, searching for a new home, was very familiar to her. She had seen them before. The children in the railway stations in their shapeless overcoats, with labels dangling from the collar, brown paper parcels tucked under their arm. People from so many different countries, and of so many different colours. Even the tribes of soldiers who looked English at first glance, but turned out to be from Czechoslovakia, she had been told, when they raised their glasses at the table outside the pub and called a toast. Britain wasn't their home either, but they were fighting for it. It was strange that a few people passing in the street cast them crooked glances, frowning at their accents.

Evie pulled the red cape tighter. Was she now a refugee too, she wondered? Where could she call home in this strange land? She had hoped that the magical world through the Library door would be different to her own one. It was a little disappointing that it appeared to be the same, if not worse. Then Evie remembered the deal she had done with the Secretary, and walked a little faster.

Together they were going to make the world a better place.

The Secretary's house stood some way back from the city centre, behind a high iron gate, which slid noiselessly open as Evie approached. A fragrant scent of jasmine greeted her as she walked up an immaculate drive, past freshly mown lawns as perfect as village bowling greens, shimmering ponds dotted with lilies, and tall sheaves of bamboo that wafted in the breeze.

At the end of the drive, the Secretarial residence looked quite unlike what Evie was expecting. A long slab of concrete roof angled up into the sky, like a ramp, supported on walls made entirely of glass. As she drew closer, she could see that beyond the glass, elegant pillars of golden wood also held up the roof, in formation. They reminded her of the pillars of a church, forming a nave with aisles on either side.

'Oh!' Evie drew back as the glass wall she was peering through suddenly slid across, creating an opening.

Inside the house, everything was soft and light, and quiet apart from the faint humming of a distant machine. *Perhaps she isn't at home*, said Evie to herself, but she went in anyway. They had an arrangement; she was sure not to get into trouble for it.

Then, turning a corner, she drew a sharp breath.

Standing on a plinth beneath a bright spotlight, his sword raised in eternal combat, was a tiny fairy. He had an acorn for a hat, a shirt of cobwebs, and was completely frozen. Evie knew who it must be. Tom Thumb, the knight who Larry had first encountered in the Library. Now, something awful had happened to him.

Involuntarily, her hand went to her mouth.

'She's turned him into a statue!' she exclaimed.

'*She* has done nothing of the kind,' said a voice behind her. 'I have no idea how to turn anyone into a statue, and even if I could, why would I? A precious waste of resources.'

Jana stepped out of the shadows towards her, making almost no noise as her glass feet appeared to glide over the floor. She cocked her head at Evie, blinking. Instantly Tom Thumb brought down his sword, with a grin, finishing the move with a flamboyant flourish.

'Ha! Fooled you! Tom Thumb, at your service,' he said, doffing his acorn hat.

'But, I thought . . . Larry said . . . the Unreads were your enemy. He wanted to – that is, he wanted all of us – to come and rescue you.'

'My intention exactly,' said Thumb, leaping on to the Secretary's shoulder, where he perched elegantly. 'Once I knew that Readers had entered Folio through the Library, well . . . I had to draw you in somehow.'

'You mean you were on Jana's side all along?' said Evie.

'Let's just say, as a tiny knight, I've learned to survive in life by playing all the angles,' said Thumb. 'I'm afraid I had enough of the Reads. All of them so smug, with their enchanted castles and pretty princesses. None of whom ever so much as cast a glance at a tiny fairy like me, I might add.'

'Thumb saw the writing on the wall, didn't you? The old stories of the past have had their day. The future awaits – a glorious future of fact-filled information! More knowledge than you can possibly imagine.'

Evie nodded, half listening, but her eye was drawn further down the corridor by some flashing lights on a wall.

Twinkling blue lights, like stars at night, darted up and down across a giant black screen. As Evie watched, the lights settled and drew shapes. Tall blocks of graphs. Flashing pie charts. And even words, streaming across.

The average dwarf can work in a mine non-stop for fourteen hours a day! was a typical example. By the side of the black screen, a smart bronze label read:

SNOW WHITE AND THE SEVEN DWARFS
Data Processed

What was that the Bears had said about processing? 'And how about the other Unreads,' said Evie, feeling more uncomfortable by the minute. 'The ones you captured, what have you done with them?'

'As you can see, I haven't turned them into statues either.'

'Then what have you done?' She remembered the Silver Soldier blasting the pixies, the cloud of inky letters, the pages flapping to the ground. 'Have you returned them to where they came from?'

'Some of them, the more useless ones, for sure. As for the others, I have . . . well, a higher purpose. Think of it as a reinvention.' She gave one of her chattering smiles, and Evie was reminded of a neighbour's cat that used to sit for hours, perched on a hedge, waiting to pounce. 'I have turned them into Information. Useless, made-up stories, are now data with which we can explore and conquer the world.'

Her eyes boggling, Evie followed the Secretary down another corridor. A door was marked 'Giant Killer Research'. She stood on her toes and peered in through a round window. Lying on a trolley in the middle of the room was a boy, whom Evie presumed was Jack the Giant Slayer. He looked fast asleep, and had wires sticking out of his head, which led to a large bleeping machine. Silver Soldiers were studying the bleeps and making notes furiously on their clipboards.

'Jack was a fairy tale that parents read to their children. Now we will study his skills and powers to make a weapon that will help us win a war. So much more useful.'

They walked on. The corridor was growing narrower and darker. She couldn't be sure in the gloom, but it felt like they were headed down a slope, too. Finally, they came to the end, by a door – which was very shabby and scratched compared to the others.

Evie shivered. It was so dark and cold, she wondered if they were underground.

'Where are we?' she asked, trying to sound calm and not at all scared, which she was. Before the Secretary could reply, a low, shuddering groan came from the other side of the door. Evie backed away.

'What is that? Who is in there?'

'Nobody important. Just someone whom I needed to answer a few questions. This is the room where I find out answers to difficult questions, you see. Every library should have one.'

Evie swallowed. 'I came . . . like you asked me to.'

The Secretary's eyes closed to slits, with a gentle whirr. 'On your own! I specifically asked, did I not, for you to bring your brothers and sisters to me? That was the deal. You could come and join our revolution and follow your dreams, but you had to bring me the other Readers in return.'

'Well, yes, but they were being boring and talking ... about finding some Librarian, so I thought I'd just come on my own.'

Jana, the Secretary of the Unreads, went very quiet indeed. Not speaking, not moving, even the streams of number tattoos slowing to a sinister black trickle across her skin. Even Thumb flew away on Majesty, backing off into the shadows.

'They were talking about looking for *whom?*' said the Secretary, spitting out each word like it was a silver bullet.

'The . . . Librarian. I didn't know—'

'But there is no such thing, Reader Evie, do you understand?'

'I'm only telling you what they—'

'*No. Such. Thing.* As the Librarian. And even if there was, he disappeared a long time ago. To a place no one has ever returned from. Do you understand?'

Evie nodded, and she didn't mean to, but all her nerves jangled up inside her and a large tear rolled down her cheek. 'I'm sorry, Secretary, I didn't know . . . can I still be part of your revolution?'

'That all depends,' said the Secretary.

'On what?'

'On how you answer my questions.'

She pressed a switch on the wall, and the door swung open.

'Don't be frightened, child,' whispered Thumb softly in Evie's ear, where he was now hovering on Majesty. But she was. More frightened than she had ever imagined it was possible to be.

The Magician Project – Extract 17

(KV 1/1569-4)

Letter, Professor Diana Kelly to Frank and Edith Hastings (3/9/45)

Barfield Hall

Salisbury

Wilts

Monday 3 September 1945

Dear Mr and Mrs Hastings,

Thank you so much for your letter. The children were thrilled to hear your news. How fortunate you have been to find a spot in such a handsome new estate. It all sounds very modern. I am sorry that because our wretched telephone is down you have not been able to speak to them personally. We hope to get it repaired in the next few days, but you know how things are in this poor country at the moment.

On that note, I know the children were due to return to you later this week, as agreed, but as the glorious summer weather is holding, and we are all having such a jolly time together, they wondered whether they could stay on till next Monday? I know it will involve missing a day of school, but equally it will give you time to properly settle into the new flat. And I am very happy to give the odd maths and English lesson in the evenings until then.

Yours ever,

Diana

CHAPTER 11
The Search Begins

'There is no time to lose!' said Mother Bear, standing up so abruptly that she nearly knocked the teapot on to the floor.

'But I haven't finished my tea,' said Simon.

With a sigh that could have very easily been mistaken for a growl, Father Bear heaved himself upright on to his feet, standing tall on two legs, so his head scraped the low kitchen beams. Simon gulped, trying not to splutter on his last mouthful. The Bears had saved them from the Silver Soldiers, they had taken them in and made cups of tea, but there was no escaping the fact they were also bears.

Father Bear's black lips drew back in a snarl, exposing his large teeth. 'Would your sister betray us?' he said.

'Evie! Not on your life,' said Patricia. 'She is never late for school and always does her chores at home. She isn't a betraying kind of girl.'

'Isn't she?' said Father Bear. 'I'm afraid traitors never look like traitors to begin with.'

Now Simon stood up too, brushing a splodge of porridge off his jersey. 'Where are you going now, then?'

'You were right,' the bear said bitterly. 'Dangerous as it will be, the alternative is even worse. We must try and find the Librarian before it is too late. In . . . the land beyond the mountains.'

Mother Bear pulled a large canvas rucksack out of a dresser drawer, and began to fill it with provisions as Father Bear continued. 'If your sister has betrayed us, the Secretary's soldiers could be here at any minute. We must leave immediately.'

Patricia waved her hands in exasperation. 'Wait, wait. What journey? Where are we going? And what about Evie? She could be terrible danger for all we know!'

Simon was torn. He knew he should go after his little sister . . . but she had already had an adventure at home – terrifying as it was – and now she was off on another, without so much as a by-your-leave. Well, it was his turn now. He could smell excitement and bravery. And this time he was not going to miss out. 'Come on, Patti, she can look after herself. She decided to run off, didn't she?'

'She's ten!' said Patricia with barely concealed fury.

Father Bear looked at Mother Bear, uncertain, but she nodded her approval, her eyes filling with what seemed like genuine concern for her guests. 'Perhaps you are right. You don't have to come with us. Perhaps you should find your sister and go back to your world, it might be safer. Readers you may be, but you are also only young ones, after all.'

Baby Bear clasped his mother, pulling at her apron. Patricia instinctively mirrored them, pulling Larry to her side, who was still clutching Grey Bear. Where was safe for him, or for them all now? Even if they could find a way to get back to Barfield, would the soldiers of the Intelligence Corps still be there? Evie was, at least, still in this world rather than that one. Patricia prayed she knew what she was doing.

'Very well. You saved us from the Silver Soldiers. If you think he will bring peace . . . we will help you find this . . . Librarian.'

'We will?' said Simon, looking surprised.

'Yes, we will,' repeated Patricia.

Father Bear nodded gravely. 'No one has crossed the

mountains for as long as I can remember. We don't know who . . . or what lurks on the other side.' He bent down and pulled a rug away from the floor, to reveal a large wooden trapdoor set amongst the flagstones of the farmhouse kitchen. Noting the children's surprise, he said, 'This was an improvement we made to the property after the war with the Unreads began, many years ago. This tunnel takes us under the river and out into the wood beyond, which should give us some cover while it is still light.'

He saw the children looking at him, hesitating.

'Come on, we have to leave, now!'

Hooking the trapdoor up with one of his claws, he levered it open to reveal a set of stairs leading down into the darkness. And, picking up the lantern between his teeth, the bear dropped to all fours, his family heading after him into the shady passage, grunting as they did.

For a moment, the children stood alone in the cottage. The tunnel smelt damp and fetid. Following three bears into the gloom was the last thing anyone wanted to do. A clock on the fireplace ticked relentlessly, until Simon said, 'Oh, for goodness' sake, you lot,' and sprung after them. By the time Patricia and Larry decided to follow, it was all they could do to keep sight of the Bears' furry backs as they bounced along, gently gleaming in the lantern's glow.

The tunnel was much longer and harder than Larry imagined any tunnel could be. In his imagination, tunnels should always lead to a smugglers' cave, buried treasure or an underground kingdom. But this one just seemed to lead to more and more rocks, which cut his shins when he stumbled against them in the dark.

'We dug this ourselves,' called back Mother Bear proudly, from further up front.

Patricia sighed, but kept on pressing ahead, just in front of him. Larry couldn't help sticking his hand in his pocket, where he felt the small, polished oaken ring that Thumb had given him. He'd promised he would help the tiny knight, and what was he doing here with these scary big bears in this gloomy tunnel? Everything smelt awful, and he didn't feel safe. It was like the air raid shelter in the Underground all over again. The world above shaking as it was pounded, people whimpering in the dark, and everywhere the awful, rank smell of fear.

'But the Bears are meant to be on the same side as Thumb, aren't they?' whispered Larry to Grey Bear, who remained as neutral as ever.

'What was that?' said Patricia, distantly, not quite turning around.

'Nothing!' he called back. Then, again, softly to his bear, 'I'm not sure I want to find the Librarian.'

The librarian Larry remembered from London was friendly and kind and kept suggesting books for him to read. But this Librarian didn't sound that friendly. He sounded powerful and scary, even if he was in trouble. Thumb hadn't said anything about him either.

He had only wanted to save his people and his country.

Then, before he knew it, Larry had stopped, and was all alone in the dark tunnel. Normally, he would have asked Evie what to do. But she was gone, off on an adventure of her own, abandoning him. The others wouldn't listen. They would just boss him about, as usual.

What would Father have done?

He felt very far away right now, farther than he had ever been. Larry concentrated on remembering his smile, his moustache, the sound of his voice. What he had said, when Larry had told him about some boys at school who were being mean, who had taken Grey Bear and refused to give him back, before dropping him in a puddle and calling them both names. Father had looked at him very seriously, and taken his pipe out of his mouth. Then he'd said, 'I am sure you will do the proper thing, Larry.'

He had never explained what the proper thing was, nor had Larry dared to ask any further, so definite had the instruction been. He hadn't done anything, but that didn't work, because the boys kept bullying him.

A pansy.

That was the most horrid word. When he told his father this, there had been a frosty sense of disapproval. But now, growing in his heart, like a real, beautiful pansy on a windowsill, yearning towards the light, Larry felt a very clear sense of what to do.

Tom Thumb had been nice to him. Tom Thumb hadn't smeared Grey Bear in shoe polish. He had offered him a chair and rose-hip cordial. And now his home was in ruins and he had disappeared. Larry couldn't explain exactly why he had turned around, and was heading back to the Bears' empty farmhouse, only that he knew it was the proper thing to do.

'No,' said Patricia. 'No, no, NO!'

She was sitting on a moss-covered rock in a glade dappled with sunshine, the entrance to the tunnel at her feet. If she could have faced looking around, she would have seen it was a truly beautiful place, the forest floor curling with delicate fronds of bracken, a furry caterpillar idly crawling along a log without a care in the world. But she couldn't look at anything. 'We have to go back.'

'There isn't time,' said Father Bear, growling. 'The Silver Soldiers will be here any minute.'

'No!'

'I will not let you endanger us or my cub. Finding the Librarian is the only way—' Father Bear stood up to his full height, casting her into shadow.

Now Patricia looked scared rather than cross. But still she persisted.

'And I will not let you endanger my sister and my brother! They could be anywhere by now, in who knows what sort of trouble. Silver robots, talking bears, tiny fairies – they've never experienced anything like this before. I mean, we come from Bethnal Green!'

'Where?' said Mother Bear, looking very confused.

'Come on, sis, Lall will be all right,' said Simon, patting her shoulder. 'He's got that daft toy bear to keep him company. And we survived the Blitz, didn't we?'

'The what?' said Baby Bear.

Simon thought he might explode. These bears didn't know anything about real war! The discipline, the sacrifice, the honour . . . night after night he had sat opposite his father in the parlour listening to his wisdom, the hero who faced down the whole German army in a sailing boat. If only Simon could have been with him! But he was too young, and at school. Now he was finally going to make his father proud, and teach these bears a thing or two. He would find this Librarian, and drag him back by the scruff of his neck if he had to.

'We've been through so much,' Patricia choked out, 'spending every day not knowing what the night would bring. Nobody telling us anything so we didn't get scared, which only made it worse. Never enough food or money, nothing working properly half the time. The fighting. Every day in the newspapers, the cinema, grown-ups talking, nothing but shooting and bombs and tanks and so much—'

She broke off, overwhelmed by the sobs that shook her entire body.

'Don't you see, Bears? We fought for our freedom. We didn't need a Librarian. British men and women gave up their lives. And when the war in our world ended, we thought it was all finished,' said Simon. 'That everything was settled. No more change for a very long time.'

'But then we got sent away from home to that strange house, those soldiers broke in with their guns, and now we've lost Larry and Evie too.'

Patricia stood up and walked away a little into the wood. She didn't say anything for a moment. Her thoughts were an angry spiral of crows, and she stared hard at a beetle hanging upside down from a branch, trying to settle her fevered mind. The others waited in silence, while she stared so hard that the beetle scuttled shamefully away under a leaf, as if it was all his fault.

Which it truly wasn't.

At length, the crows in her mind settled into a line. She took a breath, and brushed down her clothes, returning to the rock. It had been summer when the children arrived in Folio, but, moment by moment, the season seemed to be changing. A sky the colour of a bruised plum, leaves falling, and now a cold wind that snatched and pinched at her skin. Yet the freezing air sharpened her wit, and her nerve.

Patricia wiped her eyes on her sleeve, and tried to smile through her tears. 'Now we're left just with you. You may only be stories, but you're all we've got.'

'So let's find this wretched Librarian of yours,' said Simon. 'And fast.'

CHAPTER 12
Silver Man, Green Man

Evie, on the other hand, had nowhere to run to. She was standing at the end of an underground corridor in the Unreads, and now in front of her stood the Captain of the Silver Soldiers they had met by Thumb's tree. As he watched her, his jaw worked slowly up and down noiselessly, like a praying mantis considering its prey.

Jana introduced him, as you might a guest at a party. 'Child, this is Captain MAG R-1, the leader of my secret robot police. I believe you may have met before?'

Evie nodded, not daring to speak.

'It's a very useful facility, being able to terrorise people on sight. I have found that when you are leading a revolution, such as I am, sometimes people are reluctant to come forward with answers to questions, in case they

don't fit. But the Captain is very persistent in his questions.'

Captain MAG R-1 stepped forward, his eyes glowing.

'Where are the other Readers?' he said, in his monotone.

'I don't know,' lied Evie.

The Captain glittered in the shadows, his head twitching from side to side.

'Where are the Readers?' he repeated.

Evie shook her head. This normally worked with her parents or teachers. 'I don't know!'

Then the soldier lowered his arm, and spewed a shot of numbers at the floor out of his silver finger. Evie watched as the numbers tore into the concrete slab, like a horde of ants consuming their prey. With a jolt, the Captain sucked them back into his arm, leaving only a void in the floor. Not a hole in the concrete, not a gap showing the earth below, or even the air outside – just a void.

Nothing.

Jana appeared amused by Evie's horror. 'Stories are made of letters and paper. It's very easy to deal with them. But did you know that everything else is made of numbers?'

Evie shook her head, still too terrified to speak.

'Numbers. The secret ingredient of the universe, the single ingredient to which everything can be reduced. From the cells inside your body to the circuitry inside mine, to the molecular composition of that concrete floor – everything we see and touch, and much that we can't, can be reduced to a number, changed by a number, or even . . . as you see . . . destroyed by a number, if there are enough of them, in the right order.'

Evie nodded, even though some of what the Secretary was saying did not make sense to her. It didn't matter. She had seen the evidence for herself. She believed what she was told.

'Next time, it will be your foot or your hand,' added the Secretary.

'Where are the Readers?' repeated the Captain, moving his arm so it was pointed at her feet.

'I keep telling you, I don't know!' she stammered. She stammered, she knew, not just out of fear from what the Captain of the Silver Soldiers might do to her, but what fate awaited her brothers and sister if she did. Evie had been cross at them, and the Bears, for being so smug about old stories when, surely, what the world needed now more than ever was new ones?

But perhaps she shouldn't have run away without telling them where she was going.

Perhaps she had run straight into a trap.

More than anything right now, she wanted to give Larry

a squeeze of a hug, and bop him on the head with that rotten bear of his. His hair that always smelt lightly of soap, no matter how filthy the rest of him got.

Instead, she found herself peering into the insect eyes of the robot queen, her reflection endlessly refracted darkly within them.

'I only ask these questions because I am a wellspring of maternal concern, child. If your siblings have fallen in with the Reads, they may be filling their heads with all kinds of nonsense, which will need correcting, of course.'

'Who does the correcting?' said Evie, although she knew the answer.

'Enough questions from you!' snapped the Secretary. 'I want some answers!'

The Captain's arm began to glow, and numbers started to stream through the air from his pointing finger towards Evie's foot. They tumbled in the air, tiny black figures propelled by a jet stream, forming a buzzing cloud at the bottom of her leg. And she felt them begin to chew, and bite, and—

'No! Please! I'll tell you!'

Later, much later, she would find herself considering how quickly she had betrayed the others, and wondering why. It wasn't a real betrayal, more an act of self-preservation. Who wouldn't have done the same? And besides, she had stalled for long enough now. The Secretary had made her a deal. The others would understand once they saw how magnificent the City of the Unreads was, she was quite sure of it. Even Simon. Patricia could even work alongside her, as one of the top scientists.

What's more, who knew what those Bears really had in store for them? She had seen that dress in the bedroom. That poor Goldilocks. How could they be trusted with her brothers and sister? That was it. It wasn't just her self-preservation; it was their well-being she had foremost in her mind. What else would any of them do with this silver monster trying to devour her? Her mother would be proud; she was sure of it.

So, that was all it took, a moment.

'The Bears!' she blurted. 'They're with the Bears, who are awful, forcing everyone to eat porridge—'

The Captain lowered his arm, and the numbers disappeared back inside their glass prison, seething and frustrated. Evie leaned down and touched her foot. It was sore, but still there.

'You see, these saboteurs will stop at nothing,' said Jana. 'The Bears? Didn't they steal that house from a little girl?'

'I don't think that's quite what happened in the story—'

143

'Of course they did! The Reads have stolen everything! The fertile land, the rich forests, the sparkling water! This city is surrounded by desert, thanks to them. They have even stolen our rain and our sunshine on occasion. They cannot be reasoned with. Nothing ever changes. It is just in their nature, the same stories destined to be repeated over and over again until the end of time. Which is why they must be destroyed, so the glory of our new age can rise! The age of the Unreads!'

Alone and scared as she was, Evie still felt a flush of excitement. A new age. Glory. That was what everyone wanted and longed for, wasn't it? Not just in Folio, but at home too. Perhaps she could take Jana there as well . . .

'The age of the Unreads!' she echoed, and it came out even more fiercely than she had intended. She looked up at the Secretary, suddenly eager for some kind of approval in the whirring glass face. Her words tumbled out in a gush. 'I think I understand . . . This is the future, isn't it?'

Much to Evie's surprise, the Secretary embraced her. It was only then that she noticed how icy cold her cheeks were. Releasing her at last, and chattering with pride, the Secretary began to issue instructions.

'Captain! Take a squadron of your soldiers to the Bears'

house. Raze it to the ground. Bring any survivors in for questioning.'

The Captain clicked to attention, before gliding back off into the shadows.

'Any survivors?' said Evie. 'But—'

'All will be well, my child. Trust in the revolution. The Unreads have spoken!' Now she turned to Thumb, who had not said a word during her speech but remained hovering on Majesty, at her shoulder.

'Thumb! See to it that my Statecraft is prepared immediately. If those foolish Reads are tempted to search for this magical Librarian, they may be capable of anything. But thanks to this hero, Reader Evie, we have the advantage of surprise.'

Thumb nodded curtly, and sailed away up the corridor.

Evie noticed that he had not said a word in reply to the Secretary's vision of a new glorious age, but kept her thoughts to herself.

'What will happen to me now?'

Jana clasped her hands.

'You will be decorated! As a national hero, forevermore known as Assistant Secretary Evie! The very first Reader to be so garlanded, I can add.'

Evie flushed with pride and looked at her feet.

'And you will join me in my airship. You will have a ringside seat.'

She locked her arm into Evie's, and they began to stride back up the corridor, towards the light.

'What will I be watching?'

'The most wonderful thing anyone can witness. The destruction of the old and the birth of the new.'

Unaware of their sister's betrayal, and the Secretary's plans, Simon and Patricia continued their journey towards the mountains of the Never Reads, one riding Mother Bear, the other Father Bear. They had no idea of the destruction that was planned, but the sense of foreboding was impossible to escape. The dark clouds which had begun to gather in the woods by the Bears' house were now unmistakeably black. Fierce gusts of wind rushed through the trees, shaking them so hard that they seemed to groan, dropping sharp showers of leaves on the travellers as they hurried beneath. Then, further ahead, a branch fell just to the side of them with a resounding crack. Patricia flinched.

'Do not be afraid, Reader,' said Father Bear as he neatly sidestepped it, 'but we must hurry now.'

'Because of the storm?' said Patricia.

'No, because the storm from the east means something

is stirring beyond the mountains. Something we should all fear, Reads and Unreads alike.'

Patricia did not reply but noted how the woods around them were changing. The trees were growing older, the path more blocked by twisting brambles. Giant scarlet toadstools bloomed under them, faded and spotted. Every shadow across the path looked like it might grow horns at any moment. The undergrowth was so dense that even the Bears had to slow their pace, and Baby Bear went ahead, slashing at the briars with his paws.

'Woods,' he said. 'I hate woods. One day someone is going to invent a way for bears to buy honey in a shop.'

Was it possible, Patricia thought as they moved between twisted oaks, that some of the trees he slashed around even had carvings on their trunks? It was hard to make out what they were in the dim, deep green light. And beyond them, in the overgrown twilight avenues, was that something moving? Misty shapes floating, like ghosts . . . perhaps it was nothing. She took off her glasses and gave them a good rub with the corner of her shirt tail.

'Where are we?' she asked.

'This is the Forgotten Forest,' replied Mother Bear.

'I can see that,' said Simon, carefully unhooking a dogwood rose which had snared a thorn in his cuff. 'The gardener hasn't been round for months!' he added, but no one laughed.

The trees grew taller around them. They were old and forgotten trees, as warped and striped as fossilised bones, more moss than bark, their leaves dry and withered but black enough to block out the day. A low mist hung around the ground, painting broken ferns and rambling bushes into sinister shadows. It swept and hissed between their legs.

'What happens in the Forgotten Forest?' asked Patricia, although she had half-guessed the answer.

There was silence from the Bears, as if they, too, did not want to discuss the subject any further, until Baby Bear, romping ahead and biting the heads off thistles, said, 'I can't remember!'

'When a story is returned, when they are just ink and paper again, and no longer live in the imagination,' said Father Bear, 'when they are forgotten, this is where they go.'

'What kind of stories do you mean?' said Simon. 'Do you mean like the ones we saw before you rescued us . . . the little chaps . . . oh, what were they called again, Patti?'

Patricia thought, and then frowned. 'Oh! How frustrating. It's on the tip of my tongue.'

'That's just it . . . I can't remember either!' said Father

Bear with a rueful chuckle, looking down at the grey mist that wound about their legs.

'The Fog of Forgetfulness has found us,' said Mother Bear. 'We should be careful.'

'Why?' asked Patricia.

'I can't quite remember but I know that we should . . . you know,' she said, and they walked on.

A few paces later, Simon said, 'What was that you just said?'

'Did I say something?' said Mother Bear, looking around in surprise.

'Who said that?' said Father Bear, and he looked at Mother Bear with great suspicion. 'Who are you?'

There was a long pause while she stared back at him, then said, 'Who are you, for that matter?'

They had now stopped in a small clearing, where the air smelt as stale and foul as the rotten mulch which covered the floor. It reminded Patricia of the way that city she knew smelt after people dropped those things on it, a while ago. The Bears huddled together, looking around with fear at the gloomy shadows around them. Baby Bear clung to his mother.

'I have no idea who you are,' he said, 'but I know I want to do this.'

'Who are we?' wondered Mother Bear aloud. 'Why are we here?'

Which is often what people wonder when there are no stories to give them the answer.

But in fact, the Forgotten Forest was full of stories. It was just that no one could remember them. And it was one of these stories that they approached now, the Bears beginning to strain as they lumbered up a slope that wound higher and higher through the thinning trees, until upon a mound flooded with moonlight they came upon an ancient oak standing all by itself, wreathed in clouds of green.

Simon watched the tree in the soft light, and gave a little gasp as a ghostly shape, with groans and cracks, detached itself from the trunk, walking towards them. A figure cloaked in sleeves of green, atop which a wrinkled, bearded circle of a face peered out at them, almost as if it had been consumed by the tree itself.

The Bears growled, but stood their ground.

As the figure drew near, still half swathed in shadow, a long treelike arm unfurled and, with a flick of its stick fingers, threw a flame into the ground, which burned into fire, a kind of lime-green phosphorescence.

Now it was Patricia's turn to gasp.

For there, as the full figure now came into view, was a

man – it seemed – either made from or imprisoned by the forest around them. Rustling leaves were his hair, a nest of twigs his beard, and tangled creepers the veins which burst out from his cheeks. The head cocked to one side, studying them for a moment, and in the whorl black of the eye sockets, two beady emerald eyes sparkled with amusement.

Then he spoke. His voice was like the scraping and sanding of bark.

'What would you,' he said slowly, 'with the Green Man?' And as he bowed his head, they could hear the creak of wood that had lived a thousand years or more.

CHAPTER 13
The Half-Finished Story

While Evie was preparing to board the Secretary's airship, and Patricia and Simon faced the Green Man, Larry was focused on rescuing his friend, tiny Tom Thumb.

He thought that if he could find the Bears' trail it would lead him from their cottage, through the woods, back to the charred remains of Thumb's tree. Then perhaps he could find some clues as to where he had gone. Perhaps he might find *The Golden Fairy Tale Treasury* again – which had been clean forgotten about when the Silver Soldiers turned up. He could use the book to get back to Barfield . . . but then the real British soldiers might still be there. And running away wouldn't help save Thumb.

Larry tried hard not to think too much about his elder brother and sister, because he already knew leaving them in

the tunnel with the Bears was going to get him into hot water, sooner or later. He was always striking out on his own, and getting a clipped ear for it. Larry just couldn't help it. He would start doing something completely innocent, like trying to lift up a bomb-damaged manhole cover to see what lived under the road or taking apart a wireless to see where the voices came from, and before he knew it, he had been missing for hours and everyone was furious.

As for Evie, well, he knew she could take care of herself. The Germans had dropped a bomb on her head and it had only made her even more difficult than before.

He had to tip his cap to that.

In the end, though, this was why he preferred playing with Grey Bear, because Grey Bear never told him to 'snap out of it' but always just went along with whatever dream world he happened to be in.

Grey Bear was typically uncomplaining as Larry swung him harder and harder through the thorns and thistles in the woods around the Bears' house. The boy gave a cry of frustration. He hated it when there were no easy choices. Why did everything have to be so complicated all the time? He was so focused he almost didn't hear the guttural throttle of the flying car roaring overhead.

The two hid behind a tree stump as they watched the flying car descend on to the lawn in front of the Bears' cottage, like an angry wasp. The soldiers climbed out, their great metal skulls rotating from side to side. Then their leader nodded and it began. Grey Bear remained mute as Larry gripped him tighter and tighter. If Grey Bear had been able to look up, he would have seen Larry's eyes as wide as they ever were, and, burning in their glossy reflection, the crumbling beams and smouldering walls of the Bears' house as they disappeared under a barrage of number rays.

Then one of the intruders twisted his silver head towards them, his bright eyes narrowing, digits glistening under his skin. He blinked, and then began to stride in jerky lengths towards the boy and the bear, the others following in the same way.

'Come on, Grey Bear,' whispered Larry. 'How fast do you think you can run?'

The bear didn't answer, but he did not complain either as Larry shoved him in the waistband of his shorts and began to hurtle through the woods, pursued by the robot intruders.

Larry had taken part in two Sports Days, and won one egg-and-spoon race, but he had never run as fast as this. He no longer cared how fast his heart was beating, whether his feet were landing in cold streams or on dry earth. He jumped over whole logs spanning the path – something he didn't even know he could do – and swerved and dived, trying to shake the soldiers off. His knees were cut, his shins bruised, his breaths choked and painful, but he did not dare turn around, in case he saw a flash of silver skull.

Until at last (because he had to), Larry stopped running, just as he found himself by the edge of a winding river, where a shaggy horse stood quarter deep in the fly-covered shallows, slurping. He stood and watched him for a while, bent over, hands on his thighs, heaving for breath. His eyes were having difficulty focusing and his thoughts were too many and too fast to make sense. It seemed hard to believe that this horse was all the colours of the rainbow, for example, but that was what he appeared to be.

There was something familiar about the scene too, that he could not place, which only added to the general sea of confusion in his head. But slowly, as his breath subsided in his parched throat, an idea began to float to the surface of his mind's muddied waters, until it was so clear and persistent that he could no longer ignore it. If the Bears could talk, then . . .

Larry inched down the bank, snatching at bunches of cow parsley to keep his balance. 'Hello . . . I say . . . excuse me!'

The rainbow-coloured horse turned around and Larry saw the horn.

That was also when he nearly fell in.

'A unicorn!' he said in surprise. 'A rainbow unicorn!'

'Good afternoon,' said the rainbow unicorn, in a slow and ancient voice.

'My bear and I . . . we were just running away from some Silver Soldiers' – at this, the unicorn snorted, and Larry thought it was a snort of contempt – 'and now we need to find my friend Tom Thumb . . . and rescue him.'

The unicorn sighed. 'Rescue him. Fight that. Attack this. It's blooming nonstop round here. I don't know.' And he returned to drinking from the river.

Larry frowned, and dared go a bit closer. He could see the unicorn looked, as unicorns go, quite beaten up and muddy. The rainbow stripes which made up his coat were encrusted with mud, the odd tick and dappled with raw patches of mange.

'So you won't help me?'

'Did I say that?'

'No, but . . .'

'I am a *unicorn* you know!' he snapped. 'And unicorns got rights, just the same as everyone else.'

Larry rolled up his trousers and, taking deep breaths because of the cold and the sharp pebbles, tiptoed into the water. Somehow, he felt he knew the answer, but he asked anyway. 'What rights are those?'

The unicorn turned around in the water to face him. His eyes were bloodshot and red-rimmed. A battered pair of gold pince-nez were delicately balanced over his nostrils. 'First off, the right to be a unicorn. We are not just horses with horns, got that?'

'No, absolutely,' said Larry. 'What are the other differences, by the way?'

'There's no need to take that kind of tone,' said the unicorn.

'Sorry,' said Larry, although he wasn't quite sure what tone he had taken.

'Loads of differences, actually. For a start, I'm called Roderick, and there are no horses called Roderick.'

Roderick. Where had he heard that name before?

'You know that for a fact? No horses at all, ever?'

'For a fact. No horses at all, ever.' Roderick stared at him levelly, not blinking once. 'Furthermore, unicorns are good at maths, whereas horses are terrible.'

'Very well,' said Larry, thinking furiously. 'What's two plus—'

'Four,' said Roderick. 'See, told you. Now ask a horse the same question.'

Larry looked around, up and down the river, but no horse could he see. 'I can't—'

'Told you again,' said Roderick. 'Different. I've got a horn, I'm called Roderick, I'm good at maths and . . . oh, what's the other one?'

'You've got magical powers?' said Larry, hopefully.

'Don't talk daft,' said Roderick, frowning at his reflection in the brown water. 'Oh yes! I know, I've got these.'

Larry stumbled back as two gorgeous wings of off-white feathers, dripping with water, unfurled out of the river and into the evening air.

'You can fly?'

At this, the wings sank back into the water, and Roderick looked away. 'That's just it. No, I can't.'

'I'm sorry,' Larry said. 'But why can't you fly?'

'Who knows? Why can't *you* fly?' snapped Roderick.

'Because I haven't got wings. Unlike you. So, come on, why can't you fly?'

Roderick grew even more subdued. 'Because I don't know how to. My story—'

'What is your story? I know about Thumb, and the Three Bears, but I can't remember any fairy tales about rainbow unicorns. At least, I don't think so . . .'

'And your point is? Did you wade out here just to make me feel bad? Little boys should know better.'

'I'm not making a point; I just want to know your story!'

'It's unfinished,' explained the unicorn. 'I am a half-finished fairy tale. Written down in a book somewhere, or told around a campfire, and then never completed. Whoever wrote me only got to the bit where I stand in the river looking at my reflection, and so here I stand. Who knows what was meant to happen next? Was there some river worm lurking in the depths about to swallow me whole?'

Larry looked at the dark water rippling around his knees nervously and hoped there wasn't.

'Or did a sorcerer teach me how to fly? Was I transformed into a prince by kissing a beautiful princess? Was I killed by the evil huntsman?' He sighed. 'We will never know. So here I stand.'

Larry thought about this for a moment. He gazed up at the sky for a moment. It was darkening. Clouds were beginning to gather. In fact, not just gather, but prowl about menacingly, like a pack of wolves closing in for the kill. And though he didn't understand how, suddenly Larry knew, beyond all possible doubt, what was going to happen next in this story.

Something bad was about to happen.

The Magician Project – Extract 23
(KV 1/1570-7)

INTRODUCTION – CLASSIFIED

BY PROFESSOR DIANA KELLY

13th September 1945

Humanity stands on the brink of a brave new dawn. We have acquired, through the atomic bomb, godlike powers of destruction and death. But we have also discovered antibiotics which could eradicate some diseases from the face of the earth for ever.

We have not, alas, learned how to stop fighting. In this last great war, yet more millions have perished or had their lives altered for ever. Impossible challenges await us as we rebuild our shattered nations.

One thing is for sure. There is so much we do not

yet know about our world as we step into the future. I want to uncover the most fundamental human mystery of them all.

Consciousness. We are beginning to understand how the brain works – controlling speech, nerve reactions and so on. But what is consciousness itself? The power that enables us to turn black marks on a page into a film inside our heads. Or be moved to tears by music. The ability to fall in love, to grieve, to laugh. Our memories, our dreams, who we are. Is that real? Do we really exist? Or are all those sensations merely intricate hallucinations designed to convince us that we do?

It was as a student at Cambridge, some years ago, that I first came across the works of Nicholas Crowne, a feared sixteenth-century magician with a reputation for sorcery and dark arts. His sole crime, it transpired, was to be cleverer than everyone else. He read every book available, and knew all there was to know. He reached the limit of human knowledge in his own time.

In doing so, he discovered the boundaries of

consciousness. A magician? Perhaps. His papers suggest that he found a way to access the mind, the soul, the imagination – whatever you choose to call it – as a physical place. An extraordinary land, that existed in a parallel dimension to our own.

There was just one problem. To access human consciousness, and physically enter into the world of the imagination, Crowne discovered you needed one vital qualification.

You had to be a child.

CHAPTER 14
A Time of Gifts

Simon had heard of the Green Man before. He had seen him on wooden pub signs swinging in the wind. A passing mention in an old book of folk tales his grandmother used to read him before bed. These were the kind of stories he could get behind. Bedtime stories for them all. But they had stopped during the war. Blackouts, raids and nerves had seen to that.

The man's shaggy mane of roots trembled as he spoke, his voice coming, it seemed, deep from within the earth itself. 'I am the guardian of this Forgotten Forest; from whose oak the Library was carved. I am the oldest story that was ever told in this Library, and can never be forgotten, unlike the others who wander in my mist below.' He shot another flaming ball of green into the air, which

exploded mid-trajectory, like a firecracker. In that moment, as the shower of sparks filled the air, they caught a glimpse of the many ancient branches of the tree behind him, twisting into the darkness until they became one.

Father Bear and Mother Bear bowed low. Baby Bear followed suit, whispering, 'If there's one thing I like even less than trees, it's trees that talk.'

Patricia took a careful step forward. She had never spoken to a tree god before – for that was what she assumed he was – but then she had never ridden a talking bear before until earlier that day. And after all, what difference did any of it make? She had never worn a gas mask till six years ago, or helped her dad dig out the garden to build an air raid shelter, or eaten eggs made from powder, or seen . . . things that she would rather forget. Everything changed all the time, didn't it? Just as you thought you were on top of things and knew how the world spun, it started going backwards or upside down.

'Please, sir,' she said. 'Are you the . . . Librarian?'

The Green Man's shiny round face crinkled up, seeds dancing in his throat.

'No, Reader Patricia, I am not the Librarian. Only the mere guardian of his world. The Librarian found this oak behind me here, which gives me life, long ago, in a park from your world. It was a royal tree, a sacred tree protected by divine decree, but such trivial concerns never troubled our creator. For only such a special and sacred tree would do.'

'Do what?' said Simon, who was only really interested in trees that were good for climbing.

The Green Man turned his forest fire eyes upon him, his leafy fringe fluttering in the evening breeze. 'Do all that was commanded! The Librarian cast a spell over me. Every timber, plank and grain of this tree is magic. The wood can form together, at the Librarian's command, to create a shelf, a wall . . .'

'Or a door,' said Patricia, understanding.

'Or indeed, a tree spirit and guardian,' said the Green Man.

'So the Librarian could cast spells—' began Patricia, but Simon interrupted.

'Wait a moment, are you saying that the Librarian invited us here? The doors appeared on purpose? Larry and Evie said that sometimes the door was there, sometimes it wasn't.'

'The Library never admits Readers by chance,' said the Green Man gravely.

'Why us, though?' said Patricia. 'And why now?'

Another thought also began to turn in her mind, a small light in the darkness. How long ago had the Librarian found the tree in a park? But she was very well behaved and never asked more than two questions at the same time.

'No library reveals all its secrets at once. You may be still a child, but you must know that.'

'Then how do we find out?' she said.

The Green Man flung an arm of twisted bough behind the tree, to where, in the distance, a slash of red sky illuminated a range of mountains that looked as ancient as him. 'The only way. Read on,' he said, with a cold smile.

The children made to get back on the Bears, and continue their journey, but the Green Man planted himself in front of them. 'Patience, patience, Readers. For first I am bidden to show you some fruit of the oak.'

'I'm not hungry, thanks,' muttered Simon.

If the Green Man heard this, he ignored it. He clenched his fist, and shook his arm. Some leaves fell to the ground. Then he opened his fist. Sitting in the gnarly palm was a plump and polished acorn, about the size of a small bomb.

He summoned Patricia forward. Examining the oversized nut, she found that the cap unscrewed, like a jar lid. Reaching inside, she found some long threads, all the colours of the rainbow, sewn into a strip of card, from which they dangled like a curtain. It might have been from a headdress, or from a necklace of some kind, or perhaps one of those ritualistic implements she had only previously seen in museums.

Frowning, she laid the threads across her palm, and studied them in the Green Man's light.

'What are they for?'

'When all seems lost,' said the Green Man, 'this will remind you where you were.'

'A map, you mean?'

Patricia peered at the string and the card closely, but could not see any guide or chart of any kind. There were just threads, woven, and a very old bit of stiff paper.

'But I don't understand.'

'The Librarian knows all,' said the Green Man firmly, and with that, the matter was closed.

Next, it was Simon's turn. His acorn contained something more recognisable, but no less mysterious.

A book.

Simon studied it with a mixture of curiosity and disappointment. It was a dark leather volume the size of a pocket Bible.

His hands tightened around the book, and a wave of fear swept up from his gut. For a moment, he was no longer in the Forgotten Forest, but back in the school hall, last term. Heat had prickled his neck as he stepped up to the lectern and smoothed down the pages of the old Bible. And as the text swam before him, the rows and rows of his schoolmates and teachers below him craned their faces up to stare, waiting, watching and listening for the words that never came . . . He shuddered, and snapped out of it, hiding his fear by running a hand through his hair.

'The book may look blank but it will be of use when there is nothing left to read,' said the Green Man. 'You will need it where you're going.'

'Where are we going, anyhow?' said Simon.

'No,' said the Green Man, his voice crackling with urgency, 'where *you're* going.'

Larry had to act fast. He took a good look around where he and Roderick the unicorn were standing – at the river deep and long, the silent forests on either side, and at the mountains fading to blue in the far beyond. Grey Bear took a good look too, but didn't have much to say about it. Larry was sure they both saw the same thing, though.

There was only one possible course of action. The unicorn was so chippy he made him nervous, but he asked him anyway.

'Excuse me, Roderick, but can you be ridden? You know, like a horse?'

'Of course I can ride!' said Roderick. 'I must ask you to desist with these questions. I am fragile at the best of times. I am a unicorn, and along with having a horn, being good at maths and having wings, I am extremely sensitive!'

'So, could you ride us over there?' Larry pointed to the other bank.

'Why on earth would I want to do that?' sneered Roderick. 'I've never even looked over there.'

Larry stuck a hand in his pocket, clutching the small wooden ring he found there, turning it over and over again, until he was sure he had all his words in the right order. 'Because when I first came into your world, I met a tiny fairy knight called Tom Thumb who rode a butterfly called Majesty. He showed me his treehouse, where he made Grey Bear and I tea and told us some of the most amazing stories I've ever heard.' He bowed his head, fiddling with the brush head of a reed between his fingers. 'He didn't think I was silly. He didn't say I was stupid or living in a make-believe land. He was nice to me.' He frowned. 'It was like we were very similar somehow. I made him a promise. That I would help him against the Unreads.'

Roderick snorted but didn't say anything.

'Then when we came back to help him, his house was all burnt down and he was gone.'

'So what am I meant to do about it? I've got enough problems of my own. Why don't you both disappear back to where you came from, and leave me to my maths? I've just thought of a delicious equation that might keep me busy for at least an hour.'

Larry shook his head. 'I'm sorry. I can't. I made Tom Thumb a promise. I promised!' He was beginning to feel hot and bothered.

'I still don't see how I can help.'

'You can help me by getting us to those people over there. Because I think they might be able to help.'

'What people?' said Roderick, and then he stopped thinking about his equation, because – for the first time ever – he cast his gaze across to the far shore. There, beyond a golden bank of sand, arrayed on a vast and grassy plain, was a row of glorious pavilions, in splendid reds and whites and blues. Pennants fluttered from their tops and, wandering in and out of their folds, were warriors. They wore tunics emblazoned with different sigils, over metal armour that winked in the afternoon sun. In their hands, they either clutched parchments – maps or battle plans, perhaps, Larry guessed – or wielded swords. It was an army.

An army that both Roderick and Larry now stood and watched.

These troops, however, were quite unlike any that Larry had seen. The soldiers he had seen in knots on the streets of London, gathered outside a pub or a railway station – tossing their hats in the air, smoking cigarettes, whistling at women – all seemed very much alike. It was even harder to tell them apart on the newsreels, where they were often either tiny distant matchsticks dropping out of planes, or indiscriminate packs of helmets and rifles, pouring out of landing craft.

But here, stretching out before them, were ranks of the fantastical, the mythical and the fairy tale – characters from every story in the land. There were snarling wolves who walked on two legs, iron visors hanging over their jaws. Princesses in crowns conferred with evil-looking queens in high-collared capes. Knights in shining armour, riding under banners that Larry recognised from the books he had read about King Arthur and the Round Table. A toad in a fur coat and goggles driving a car at great speed, followed by a rabble of weasels and stoats brandishing sticks angrily in the air. Above them, a group of children in old-fashioned clothes swooped on a flying carpet, with loud cheers, urged on by a glittering phoenix.

They defied everything Larry had ever been taught at school. They rode over the laws of time and space with a clattering cheer, and turned gravity itself upside down. He knew that all the medieval knights in the world had died hundreds of years ago, and that King Arthur himself might never have actually existed. But what if the Library rule was true? What if things you could imagine really did exist, somewhere?

Larry now realised he should not have run away from Simon and Patricia. The encounter with the Silver Soldiers was close enough. He could not rescue Thumb on his own. But over there were thousands of people who would be on the same side as him, surely. All he needed to do was go up and ask. His home country had won the last war with the Allies, he knew that much. Now here, arrayed in total splendour, were the best allies Larry could ask for.

The army of the Reads.

CHAPTER 15
Something in the Air

What Larry and Roderick couldn't yet see was the Secretary's airship, the Statecraft, as it sped through the sky towards them at a hurtling rate of knots. From the outside, it had looked to Evie like a blimp, one of the silvery barrage balloons that had swayed over London during the war, like giant eyeless fish guarding their rock bed. But, inside, it felt more like she imagined how a space rocket would one day look.

Up at the front, Silver Soldiers busied themselves over decks of instruments, dials spinning, lights flickering up and down in bars, while their operators listened intently to information being delivered via their headphones. Above their heads, a large electric screen, like something out of a war room, displayed the Land of the Reads, marked with

various place names – Fairytale Valley, Monster Marsh, River of Rhymes and the Forgotten Forest – and bright dots streaming out of them in the direction of the Unreads. Periodically, a robotic voice echoed out from loudspeakers concealed in the walls, announcing the speed, temperature and wind factor.

The Secretary and Evie perched opposite one another on silver leather seats, while Thumb darted about on Majesty inspecting the luxurious cabin fittings. Evie drew her red cape in tight, and pressed her face to one of the porthole windows, exhilarated by the force and stream of the air rushing past outside. The light was bright, and she closed her eyes to enjoy feeling it on her face. Then it was just her, travelling faster than she ever imagined possible, the distant roar of the rocket humming in her ears. *If you let go enough*, she thought, *sometimes you could almost be hardly there at all.*

Her reverie was broken by Majesty, gently nibbling at her ear.

'Look, Reader,' Thumb said, pointing out of the porthole. 'It is beginning.'

The white wisps of cloud below gave way, and with the alien structures of the Unreads now behind them, the Statecraft flew over the lush fields and woods of the Reads.

In a large green plain below, the stories were gathering in a babble of rage and energy. Evie saw creatures she had never thought to see outside the pages of a book. Her heart leaped at the sight of actual dragons, breathing fire, monstrous reptiles thundering on their clawed feet behind the other story characters. Just one of them looked big enough to take on the Statecraft, and Evie could count seven at least.

'Finally,' said the Secretary, 'after years of waiting, and pointless skirmishes – the battle to end all battles. At last it will be decided.'

Evie got up and crossed the narrow cabin to the other side. Rubbing away some condensation on the glass, she could see what the Army of Reads was facing. Legion after legion of Silver Soldiers, each one identical, each one as powerful as the next. They swarmed in on flying cars and tanks that hovered above the ground, with shining rockets and bristling guns. When she looked back at the rows of giants, gods and dragons, and witches throwing bolts of fire from their sticks, it did not seem like such an unequal match. But if she was honest, the prospect of any fighting of any kind still made her sick in the pit of her stomach. She wanted change to make things better. She just didn't want anyone to get hurt. Not ever again.

'When are they going to start?' she said to Thumb, after the ship had circled the battlefield several times. 'I want it to be over before it has even begun.'

'So do I,' said Thumb, and to her astonishment, Evie noticed a large tear slide down his elfin cheek. It was large compared to him, but really no more than a pin prick of rain.

'Thumb! You're crying. Why? I thought you were on the side of the Unreads?'

'I am,' said Thumb, his nose pressed against the glass. 'But those people down there, they are my neighbours . . . and friends. They are fighting for my country. I lived there my whole life, as my story decreed, a fairy knight. One of the oldest inhabitants, in fact. I accepted my place in Folio.'

'Then why are you here in the Statecraft?' whispered Evie, her cheeks flushed and eyes wide. 'Fighting for Jana?'

Thumb wiped the tear trail from his cheek, his expression hardening as he stared down.

'Because they never accepted me!' He turned to glare at Evie, burning with hatred. 'Look at them! Giants, dragons, dwarves – have you ever seen such a bunch of freaks! I was living in the Land of the Reads before most of them were imagined, and yet . . . I never felt part of their world. Do you know what that feels like, Reader Evie? To feel that you are always different, never welcome? Unappreciated, invisible, with no part to play?'

Evie nodded. She thought of Simon, laughing and mussing her hair. Patricia telling her not to be silly. Larry being sillier than her and yet somehow what was so annoying in her was sweet in him. Worst of all, just wandering the streets. Dark streets full of smoke and wet spills from the hoses, clogged with dust and fragments of the school. A fireman had told her roughly to get out of the way, but all she could do was stare. 'This is no place for little girls,' he said. 'What can *you* do?'

She would show them. She would show them all.

'So now,' said Thumb, as if he was reading her mind, 'I will get my revenge.'

He tugged Majesty's silken rein of spider web, and the pair fluttered gaily away to the leather chair opposite, where he whispered in Jana's ear. The Secretary nodded, and rose, rippling in the light.

'It is time,' she said, 'to activate the Page Turner.'

The Bears and the children, carrying their gifts like shields, emerged from the Forgotten Forest on to a desolate mountain slope. In the sky above, the storm clouds whirled and spun, spitting out vicious forks of lightning. With each electric crack, a mini avalanche of pebbles and rocks issued down the mountainside, repeatedly forcing the travellers to stop and take cover behind a large boulder or solitary fir.

'They know we are coming,' said Father Bear, pausing for breath, wiping a smear of dirt off his black muzzle. They stood a while, and watched what looked like sprays of hot lava leaping into the air behind the savage peaks ahead.

'I don't think *they* like us very much, Father,' said Baby Bear.

Too tired to even smile, Simon put his arm around Patricia. Their clothes were muddied and torn, he noticed, but somehow he no longer felt the cold. Perhaps it was the lava.

'What do you think Never—' Patricia began, then caught sight of the Bears scowling at her in alarm. She dropped her voice so only her brother could hear. 'I mean, what do you think the land we're going to means? Reads are stories we all know and tell ourselves over and over again. I get that.'

Simon nodded in agreement, whispering back. 'And the Unreads are facts and information, which of course are unread, because we keep discovering new ones all the time . . .'

'So those who live over these mountains are . . .'

'Either stories we should never tell or facts we should never discover?'

'Or perhaps even both.' Patricia shivered again and drew her cardigan tighter. 'I fear there's only one way to find out.'

The Bears led the way. As they approached the summit, all familiar features of the hillside receded into nothing. There were no more trees, or boulders, or landmarks of any kind, only the fearsome peaks ahead, and beneath their feet – endless, sliding, shifting grey dust.

'How much further is it?' asked Simon, wiping sweat from his brow.

'I believe the land we dare not name can only be accessed through a narrow pass up there, which takes you through the peaks and out the other side . . .' Father Bear gestured roughly with his snout. 'I do not know how passable it is. You will have to discover for yourselves.' He turned to face Simon and, in the molten dusk, something in his rich ursine eyes looked utterly alien. Simon saw only deep, black water behind them, and had to turn away.

'We will have to discover for ourselves? You mean you're not coming?'

Father Bear placed a heavy paw on his back, and Simon flinched.

'You surely did not think that we could come with you?'

'Please don't let us do it alone,' said Patricia. 'We're only children, really.'

Mother Bear gave her a spoonful of honey from the pot in her bag. 'There, there, my dear. We will wait down at the Forgotten Forest for your safe return. But only you can cross the mountains . . . and find our Librarian.'

'Why?' said Patricia. 'Why only us?'

'We are mere subjects of this world. We dare not face its creator. The land beyond these peaks is called . . . what it is . . . for a reason.'

'And guess what, it's not a good reason,' piped up Baby Bear.

'You haven't answered my question,' said Patricia. The wind was relentless now, never letting up for a moment, flinging dirt into her hair, her eyes and her mouth. 'Why us?'

'Reader Simon. Reader Patricia. Never forget how you are different to us. Only Readers can ever come close to the power of the Librarian.' Father Bear bent down and scooped up a pawful of the grit that swirled around them. 'What do you think happens to inhabitants of Folio who displease him?'

And the children watched in horror as the grey dust slid

through his claws, borne away and scattered by the mountain wind.

CHAPTER 16
The Page Turner

Far away from the mountainside, up in the sky, in the giant silver airship that hid behind the building storm clouds, Patricia and Simon's sister was staring out of the window, peering through the fog below to see if she could pick out three familiar figures, along with a family of bears. To her relief, she could not see anyone she recognised.

'What does the Page Turner do?' said Evie.

'I'll show you,' said Jana, and, flipping up a lid in the arm rest of her leather seat, pressed a button.

A compartment slid open in the nose of the Statecraft, visible through the huge glass cockpit. Then, shuddering, a mechanical lever raised itself from the clockwork innards concealed beneath.

It looked like a robotic arm, with wires and cables for

sinews and tendons, that held a giant fountain pen. The pen started vibrating, and as it shook, it glowed red hot. On the dashboard, amongst the dials and levers, Tom Thumb was peering at a target, with a cross hairs just off centre. Riding Majesty, he was able to manipulate a joystick, moving the giant pen so the cross hairs aligned over the bullseye.

Dimly, the scene below came into view on the screen.

And Evie realised that the Page Turner wasn't a pen.

'Now, Reader Evie,' said Jana, who had glided over to Thumb's side, 'what's your least favourite story? "The Ugly Duckling"? How ridiculous, that a duckling might turn into a swan! Biologically impossible for one thing. Who on earth would believe that?'

Evie wasn't sure she had ever *believed* 'The Ugly Duckling'. That was a bit different, surely, to enjoying the wonderful ending where the unhappy little bird transforms into a swan? Or even believing what she understood the moral message to be – such as that beauty might be on the inside. But Jana pressed on, studying the assembled Reads below, her teeth chattering faster and faster till the clicking noise made Evie's ears hurt.

'There is the Princess of the Pea, making her servants drag her pile of mattresses along behind her! What nonsense. What privilege... Except, I do so loathe Hansel and Gretel too. Look at them! Why would any right-thinking person go into a witch's house made of sweets? It is illogical and far-fetched. Never mind baked alive, they ought to be taught an even more memorable lesson. Which reminds me, witches in general are the worst of the worst. Look! There are dozens of them down there, floating about on their broomsticks. I do hate witches, don't you?'

Her sharp eyes twinkled, and she gave an electronic cackle.

'They're not very nice,' admitted Evie.

'Not very nice! They're wicked. And if we aren't careful, they'll come for us on their broomsticks and cast a spell, and crash this ship. What do you say to that?'

Evie had nothing to say to that, but Jana carried on as if she did.

'Yes, you are correct. Let us turn the page on a witch or two. Commander Thumb – when you are ready, please.'

They turned and faced the window. In the distance, Evie could see some very dark and sinister-looking mountains, over which purple and black clouds bloomed in the pellucid sky, like drops of ink in water. There were even sparks flying above the jagged peaks. What lay behind? A fiery pit? A volcano?

'Excuse me, Secretary,' said Evie. 'What's that over there?'

'Over where?'

'Those clouds and mountains there?'

Something inside the robot whirred, an engine overheating.

'That is nowhere!' snapped Jana. 'Never ask me about there. Nothing happens there. There is nothing to be afraid of, nothing at all. Why do you even ask?'

It didn't look like nothing to Evie, though. She exchanged glances with Thumb, who then looked away sharply. As if he knew a secret, but didn't dare say what. Jana clapped her glass hands together, which Evie thought looked like they were trembling.

'Now, the Page Turner, please! How many times must I give the order!'

Thumb gave a short sigh, and, with his sword, flicked a couple of switches on the flight deck. Sticking out of the Statecraft, like an angry sting, the Page Turner grew darker and darker, rows of miniature nozzles filling it with a black liquid.

Then it swung around, aimed directly at the witches diving and swooping in the clouds below.

'Wait!' said Evie. 'You're not going to hurt them, are you?'

Jana cackled again. 'Of course I'm going to hurt them! Then send them to a better place. Forgotten for ever!'

Evie couldn't bear it. The whirring drone of the Statecraft, the dark clouds swirling on the horizon, Jana's jaw chattering up and down, Thumb dancing about over the controls – everything was too strange and frightening, and her stomach turned. A gust of turbulence pummelled the craft from below, and the entire cabin lurched to the left. Evie stumbled, clutching at one of the metal struts for support.

With a whine, booster jets righted the airship. The lights flickered off and then on again. Jana remained where she was, balanced and upright.

'Please don't hurt anyone,' said Evie. 'Why do you have to hurt anyone?'

The numbers rippled. 'How else do you change anything in this world?'

'But so many people have already been hurt.'

Not just hurt, she knew, killed. Hundreds. Thousands. Millions. Many of them in her own street. Some in her own school, for heaven's sake. Where did war end? At the door to the Library? It should always end there, surely.

'Reader,' said Jana, and she placed her glass fingers on Evie's shoulders. The grip was so tight it made her gasp for air. 'In the end, you have to decide what you believe in. Do you want a world of fantasy, like the one below, trapped in the same foolish narratives for eternity? Or do you want to build a brave new world, rationally built upon only the hard facts we know, and those we have yet to discover?'

'I just want things to be better, everywhere, for everyone! Can't we have both?'

She was confused. Wasn't the dream of a new world nothing more than just a story anyway? At least, until it became reality – if it ever did.

'That is logically impossible,' said Jana. 'There will always be winners and losers. The question is, which side do you want to be on?'

The air rushed past the windows. They were descending. Just five feet away from her, a Silver Soldier stared intently at a screen, typing. Numbers flowed down through her skin, and Evie caught sight of the charts and graphs on the screen reflected in her face. There was nothing familiar about this moment or this world. There was nothing kind, or cosy, or homely. But although it was hard and cold, it was shining in a way she never thought she would see anything shine again. It made her pulse quicken and an electric charge of excitement shoot down her back. She straightened up and adjusted her blouse.

'Winners,' said Evie, because she had sworn she would never be a loser again. Ever.

'Thank you,' said Jana, removing her hands from Evie's shoulders, and patting her on the head. 'I knew you would see reason. Dry your eyes, child, and turn them to the glass. For you will see that we are writing a new story over the old. A process of creative destruction, if you like. From the rivers of their spilt ink, we will water our fields. From the dust of their ruins, we will build our empire. And in the troubled annals of their history, we will erase their words and write our own. In short, dear Reader Evie, all we need do is turn the page!' She nodded to Thumb. 'Fire at will.'

'Target engaged,' said Thumb.

Beneath their feet, the Page Turner began to fill with inky numbers. A clutch of witches sailed into view, brandishing their wands at the ship as if they now realised how much danger they were in. But it was too late, much too late.

'Target locked,' said Thumb. Then he pressed a button.

The whole ship recoiled. An empty cup slid off a table and smashed into pieces on the floor. Beneath their feet, they could hear storage crates in the hold shift about. And from the nose of the ship, the Page Turner spat out a jet stream of numbers.

Evie could only guess what the force used to push the number stream out at such pressure must have been, but it looked strong and powerful enough to slice through solid steel. It sprayed the clouds aside, and hit the witches full on, enveloping them in a ball of smouldering blackness.

She gasped and looked away, her fingers over her eyes.

When she opened them again, the Page Turner was quiet once more. There were no witches to be seen. And the pink evening sky was full of paper. Sheets and sheets of paper, curled and tossed by the wind. For a moment, they fluttered uselessly in the air, as if borne aloft by one last breath, and then all at once they fell in a shower on the crowds below.

'What on earth – did you see that?' said Simon, pausing on the barren slope and staring into the sunset.

'See what?' said Patricia, who was entirely focused on putting one foot in front of another, and trying not to slide back down five feet for every step she took. But it was hard, the ash was so loose and fine.

'That, over there – like a huge stream of oil or something,

flying through the air . . . almost like a rocket.'

'An oil rocket? Doesn't sound very likely.'

'No. Nor did doodlebugs till they started to land.'

'You don't think . . .' said Patricia, pausing, her hands on her hips.

'Surely not,' said Simon, but the unthinkable had now entered his mind as well. A young girl and a young boy, their own flesh and blood, caught up in the turbulence of a conflict they didn't fully understand. Whatever foolishness Evie was up to or wherever Larry had run off to, they did not deserve to die in some strange foreign land. In the creeping dusk the two elder siblings strained their eyes and tried to make out more, but could only see glimpses of the Reads on the grassy plain with their medieval banners and flags, in all the colours of a stained glass window, and the grey metal Statecraft in the sky above.

'Can't see enough from here. It's the two armies, that much we do know. Fighting like dogs and cats,' said Simon grimly, flicking a pebble into the darkness below.

Patricia shook her head, and sat down, sending a cloud of dust into the air. 'More fighting. Does everything have to be solved with fighting?'

'Looks like it. Either way, this is a real mess we've got ourselves into. What do you make of it?'

Patricia thought for a moment. 'I'm not sure. It is very strange, all this' – she gestured at the battlefield in the distance, their mysterious gifts from the Green Man, the mountain of dust they sat upon – 'but there must be some reason for everything, and I've been trying to work out what it is.'

Simon snorted. He now had a fragment of twig from the Green Man between his thumb and forefinger, twisting it repeatedly. 'Girls! You always think there is a reason for everything!'

'But there is,' said Patricia, and she wasn't smiling. 'Nearly always.'

'Go on then. Try me.'

'Do you remember, at the start of the holiday, when Lall said he had discovered this place, and we didn't believe him? And then we had that jolly strange chat with the Professor in her study?'

'Yes. Whatshisface – who owned the hall to begin with, and his book collection.'

'Nicholas Crowne.'

'What had he done again? Read every book in the world or something? You don't think this is to do with him, do you? Have to say, he gave me the creeps. All her candlelit talk of his magic and experiments, then that odd painting

192

in the corridor . . .' His eyes lit up. 'I see where you're going. Because he disappeared. But he must have died centuries ago, Patti.'

Patricia shook her head. 'Maybe. But look, here we are, in Folio – a world we entered through a Library, from Barfield House, looking for the Librarian who disappeared. Professor Kelly said Crowne added the Library to Barfield. She said that the War Ministry was trying to use his magic to stop a war ever happening again, like the last one.'

Simon pointed to the noise and rage of the battle in the distance. 'Well, if this is her idea of stopping a war, I'd hate to see her start one.'

Even Patricia had to laugh at this. Then she said, 'And what if Nicholas Crowne isn't dead?'

'Please don't tell me you've lost your head as well. Then I shall be all alone on this hellish mountain, the only sane person left in the universe.'

'Don't you see, though? If there are Bears from Goldilocks still alive, hundreds of years after their story was first told, if Tom Thumb is still around, then why not Crowne?'

'How though, sis? He was a real person, not some made-up story character.'

'Yes, I know. But the Professor said he was a magician.'

Simon groaned. 'Do you remember that conjuror we had at Larry's party? You could see where he stuck the cards down his sleeves, and that poor rabbit . . . I wanted to call for a vet.'

Patricia slammed her hands down on her thighs with frustration.

'Not that kind of magician. Look at us! Everything that has happened since we walked through that door. Fairy-tale characters fighting silver robots. Can't you see? This whole world. It's all magic. Is any of this even real?'

Simon bent down and scooped up a handful of the grey ash, letting it slip through his fingers. 'Feels and looks pretty real to me. And besides, what was that first rule of the Library that Larry told us about?'

'If you can imagine it, it exists somewhere . . .'

Her brother stood up. 'I have no idea what that means. But you don't need much imagination to realise we should keep going, if we have any chance of crossing these mountains before it goes completely pitch black.'

He offered Patricia a hand, and hauled her up too.

If anyone had been looking, they would have seen the two small figures clambering up a slope so steep that in places they were almost reduced to crawling on their hands and knees. They would have seen how the further they climbed, the more the grey ash spread over their hands, faces and clothes, until they were quite coated and smeared with dirt. As the light faded, they would have found it harder and harder to make them out, until eventually, already the colour of charcoal, they became swallowed up by the encroaching darkness, sinking beneath the featureless black of the mountain's shade.

CHAPTER 17
The One Who Knows Nothing

At last, Simon and Patricia emerged from the mountain path, and felt the hot, dry air of the new land on their faces. Wiping away dust from her eyes, Patricia found that the place beyond the mountains was not what she had been expecting. Evie had described the skyscrapers and denizens of the Unreads, and she and Simon had seen the terrifying Silver Soldiers in their flying cars for themselves. The Land of the Reads, when the bombs weren't falling, and the refugees weren't marching, had looked like the best summer holiday they could ever wish for, with its endless green forests and sparkling streams.

By contrast, the land they dared not name was a desert.

The top of the mountain they had climbed so hard to reach was a broad plateau of scattered, yellowy-grey

boulders, across which a fierce wind howled, flinging trails of sand into the air, making it hard to see. Above, in the sky, the heavy clouds turned more darkly and angrily than before, fizzing with rage. The showers of spitting sparks appeared to be coming from molten geysers in the ground, which would occasionally erupt with a fiery blast. Everything felt swollen and ready to burst. It was like the land before time began, she thought.

There was no sign of any Librarian – or, indeed, magician – or anywhere you might think to find one.

Simon shouted something in her ear, but the wind was so loud she had to ask him to repeat the question. It was no good. So instead, he jabbed his finger into the sandstorm, and beckoned her to follow. This wasn't a tempting prospect, but, glancing behind her at the shadowy way back, neither was returning. So, pulling her shirt over her head, trying to stop the specks of grit hurtling into her eyes, she hustled after her brother, both of them crouching as low as they could. Soon it became clear what he had spotted. The peaks of the mountain encircled the summit, like a colossal crown, and on one slope there was the mouth of a cave, just visible through the tumbling clouds of sand.

Patricia hesitated. She had no desire to go into a

cave, after a night spent walking through the darkness of the mountains.

Simon tugged at her arm. 'Come on!' he shouted, just audible. 'We need shelter. Then we can . . .' but the rest of his words were lost to the wind. She shook her head, yet followed him all the same, as there was nowhere else to go. Once inside, the air became instantly clearer and sharper, and the pair could hear themselves think. The floor was soft enough to sit on, and the cave smelt dry. A strange, washed-out desert light filtered down from a crack far above their heads.

Patricia leaned back against the steep walls and sighed. She tried to get comfortable, but it was difficult as there was no smooth flat section, and so many ridges. Turning around, on her knees, she decided to search with her hands for a more comfortable section to slump against, but there wasn't one. In fact, she noticed, every inch of the cave walls was more ridged and dimpled than the carved wood of that wretched Library door.

Then she realised.

'Simon . . .' she said, her hand tracing the lines.

He kneeled alongside Patricia as they peered in the fading light at the walls. The carvings stretched from floor to ceiling, and ran deep into the cave. Rows and rows of shapes and symbols.

'Are they hieroglyphics or what?'

'I don't think so,' said Patricia. She wasn't sure herself, but she was sure that she had read more books than Simon. Hieroglyphics tended to be more pictures of things, she thought, like a crouching lion, an outstretched hand or a watchful eye. These were simpler, cruder – stick-like inscriptions. She had seen something like them before, though.

'Runes. I think they're runes.'

'Do you now? And what's a rune when it's at home?'

'Well, they're a very early form of alphabet. Anglo-Saxon, perhaps?'

Simon scratched at the engraved letters, some of which were so thin and tightly packed together it was hard to tell where one letter or word started or ended. He flushed with shame. For this was just like normal reading. For him this was what words and books often looked like. He could never let his sister know that, though – unlike his teachers, Patti hadn't yet wised up to all his tricks and feints. Simon coughed into his hand and sounded stronger than he felt. 'Do you have any idea what any of it means?'

Patricia shook her head. 'The shapes don't give much of a clue, either. I wonder how far they go on for?'

She wandered further into the cave, marvelling at the hours of work it must have taken to carve so many letters into solid rock. 'Look! They cover the ceiling as well.' Up above, the ceiling revealed itself to be in the bell-like shape of a large dome. 'And here's – oh!'

'What on earth?' said Simon.

It was, indeed, like nothing they had seen on earth.

Standing before them, in the centre of the inscribed cave, beneath the vaulted ceiling, was the colossal hexagonal base of a statue. This too was inscribed, but with only one row of very large runes, stretching from top to bottom.

Standing astride this hexagon were the remains of what must have been a huge figure, carved in what looked like very hard rock. There were two great feet planted into the stone, strong legs, draped in a swirling robe, and a pair of hands in which rested an open book. But above all that was gone, the statue sheared clean in half at the waist.

'Some kind of god?' wondered Simon, running his hand along the smooth surface. 'I'll tell you this much. Whoever sculpted this, and whoever put it here would have to be incredibly strong. This stuff is like solid granite. I wonder what happened to the top half?'

Patricia was still looking at the half torso, the robe and the book. 'There's something familiar about it . . . Come here. Look at it with me, from this angle.'

Simon obliged, with the little flourish he often made, which so infuriated and amused her at the same time. 'What am I looking at?'

'His feet.'

They peered in the gloom and saw the statue was wearing an elegantly carved pair of slippers, with a high heel.

Simon shrugged. 'So what? He's wearing fancy slippers. Kind of thing Father might wear with a dinner jacket.'

'Come off it! Not with those buckles. I bet you those are Elizabethan – look at his stockings, for heaven's sake! Even the fur trim to his gown. It's hardly the latest London fashion.'

'Hmm. Very well. Suppose for argument's sake that you're right – and this statue is of this Crowne fellow, who you say is the Librarian, then we are still no nearer discovering where he truly is. The whole idea gives me the shivers. A four-hundred-year-old wizard?'

Simon stuck his fingers in his mouth and eyes, pulling a face, so he looked like some ancient gargoyle.

'I'm serious, Simon! Have you even bothered to notice what he's holding in his hand?'

'Looks like a dictionary of some kind. Or a Bible?'

'Not a Bible, but a book we've seen before. Give me your bag.' A kind of realisation dawning, Simon slowly handed over his bag. Patricia reached in and pulled out the book the Green Man had given him. She held it up to the statue. 'Yes. I am right. The binding. The grain on the cover. Those gilded page edges. They're identical.'

Simon shrugged. 'A book's a book, sis. They all look pretty much the same. Y'know, like *books*.'

Patricia held up the blank book to his face, shaking it. 'What did the Green Man say about this one, though?'

'Some gnomic utterance or other.'

'*What* did he say?'

'He said it would be of use when there was nothing left to read.'

Patricia closed her eyes, clutching the small volume as if it was a prayer book. 'I knew it. Nothing left to read!'

Her brother stared at her blankly.

'Come on, Simon! Where are we now? What are we surrounded by, from floor to ceiling?'

He glanced about. 'In a desert cave surrounded by incomprehensible gobbledygook that we can't . . . oh, I see. How very clever.'

They stood for a moment looking at the blank book.

'How does it work, then?' he asked.

'That's just it, I don't know.' Patricia took the book and turned it over in her hands, carefully examining the cracked leather spine, the cloth covers and tightly bound pages. 'There's nothing. No title, no words, not even a printer's mark. Perhaps—' She broke off, and, crouching low by one of the heavily graffitied walls, held the book open, firmly splayed out against the carved letters.

'Not really sure this is the time for brass rubbing.' Simon's chortles echoed around the cave.

'Oh, do shush! I'm only . . .' She moved the book away, peering at the pages in the half-light, but there was nothing, not even the faint imprint of the letters. Patricia clicked her fingers and rose again. She shook the book, but no pages were stuck together, there was nothing sewn or glued in behind the end papers. Just a big blank book of nothing. Simon peered over her shoulder at it.

'Perhaps it's a sketch book? I could try my hand at some of the landscapes around here, or even a little sketch of you? Might be an improvement on some of the Prof's modern splodges, don't you think?'

Patricia loved her elder brother, of course, that was simply what one did. But his words, his manner, they so often set her teeth on edge that she had to give a little shudder to shake herself free of them.

'Well, have you got a pencil, then, or a pen or something?'

Simon rooted around in his pockets. He turned out some string, a very dirty handkerchief and a couple of pennies. 'Oh – hang on, what's this?' Buried deep in one was a grubby stub of a pencil, as blunt as anything. But it *was* a pencil. Patricia took it, and tried writing her name. She didn't even make it as far as the P. The pencil splintered in her hand, and she threw it away with a little cry.

'That hurt! It was like trying to write on marble.' She snapped the book shut. 'Some help this is turning out to be.'

They stood in near darkness and despondent silence, listening to the desert winds make gritty protest at the cave mouth.

'There is one other thing we could try,' said Simon, with a funny look in his eyes.

Patricia shivered at the night once more closing in around them. 'What?'

He had a queer half smile on his face, his upper lip glistening. 'Hold out your hand.'

'I don't – no, Simon, absolutely not.'

'Hold out your hand.' He wasn't joking now. She held out her hand in the dark.

'This isn't one of your silly secret school societies you

know— Ow! What did you do that for?'

Patricia pulled her hand away, hot blood oozing out of the finger which Simon had pricked with the splintered remains of the pencil. 'Thunderstorms, exploding lava, now this temple place. I don't think our Librarian does things by halves, do you?' He whipped the book under her hand, catching the drops of blood. 'Look!'

Where the blood fell on the open pages, it sizzled, as if on a hot oven plate rather than blank paper. Patricia was amazed, but only for a moment. Taking her pricked finger, she smeared more blood over the book. Then, squinting as hard as she could in the remaining light, she copied out some of the runes in the smear of it with her finger.

The letters flared up. It was like writing in the snow with a hot poker.

Only now they could read them. It took Simon, as ever, a moment or two longer to work out what the words were, but at least the letters were large and clearly spaced out. Patricia squeezed some more blood, and wrote some more, until a complete phrase appeared.

I have read everything

'Now we're getting somewhere!' cheered Simon. 'This

must be Crowne after all. A message for us. Why don't you try that one next?'

He pointed to a different line of runes further down the wall.

Patricia carefully copied them on to a fresh page in the book, in faint, fingerprint-daubed lines of her own blood. Immediately, more words flared into being underneath.

I know all there is to know

'This sounds like our man,' she said. 'Now, if we could just find a clue as to where he has got to . . .'

Another drop of blood, another line of words burning with fire.

And only this I fear

The two children looked at each other.

'Well, go on!' urged Simon. 'What does he fear?'

Patti paused, blotting her finger dry on her shirt. A strange feeling rushed through her, as if she might faint. 'I'm not sure I want to find out.'

'Nonsense!' Simon looked strange too, a kind of light glowing behind his eyes.

'But what if . . .'

'But what if nothing!' He thumped the wall. 'Go on then! What do you fear, Mr Magician? Tell us! If you want a fight, we're ready!'

At first there was nothing, just the unmoving wall and the winds blowing outside. Then, looking down, smoke began to slowly curl up from the pages of the book, the beginnings of a fire. Both gasped in alarm as Patricia flung it to the ground, where the book was consumed by flames. The flames rose higher and higher into the air, and, as they did, the children could see the cave walls properly again.

'The runes . . . they're changing!' said Patricia. 'Something is overwriting them.'

'Impossible,' said Simon. 'They're carved into the stone.'

'They *were*,' she said. 'Look.'

They turned around and around again, as by the glare of the burning book they saw every line, from floor to ceiling, now bore the same phrase. It was only written, and not spoken, yet it seemed to ring in their ears. Simon took his sister's hand. He no longer sounded so bluff or cheery as before.

'What's happening, Patti?'

'Watch.'

The book had landed at the foot of the statue, and cast

its fiercest heat on the inscription that ran around the base. And here, in foot-high letters, the runes had melted into different words. Smouldering and red-hot, here was a phrase that filled them with a new kind of awe – and total dread. The name of the only thing the all-powerful, all-knowledgeable Librarian feared.

The one who knows nothing

CHAPTER 18
See for Yourself

More than anything else, Evie did not want to look weak in front of the Secretary. She turned to the porthole window beside her, as if looking at fresh air would be like breathing it, and gave a little start. Plastered to the round hole was a sheet of paper. Black ink dripped down the page. Then a gust swept the sheet away, leaving only the faintest trace of the ink on the glass.

'You killed them,' she murmured.

'A crude analogy,' said Jana. 'I have simply sent them back into the pages from which they sprung. Hence my clever name – the Page Turner. They are now useless letters and paper, like all stories. The first step in building a world based on numbers and provable theories. Like gravity,' she observed, watching the final few sheets of

witch stories flop feebly to the earth below.

'Could they become Read again?'

Jana eyed her beadily. 'And why would anyone want to do that, Reader Evie?'

Evie steeled herself to eye her back. 'I only wondered, that's all.'

'A little wonder is a dangerous thing.' Jana turned away. 'Thumb, take the craft down. Now we've dispatched their airborne troops, time to take out those on the ground.'

'Yes, ma'am!' The fairy busied himself at the controls as the Statecraft began to sink lower and lower in the sky. Evie braced herself as the crowds of story characters came into focus. The sunset was marred by storm clouds drifting in from the mountains in the far distance, but as the Statecraft reached what Thumb called 'optimum operating height', a shaft of honey-coloured light shot out across the field, like it had been fired from a bow.

For a moment, the scene was as a fantastic tableau from an illustrated history book, medieval swords clutched by Beauty and Beast alike, richly emblazoned shields borne by sailors fighting alongside thieves, woodcutters standing tall with snow queens, the evening sky above their heads thick with enchanted songbirds and ravens. And, everywhere, explosions of letters and paper as the forces of the Unreads ploughed straight through them.

It was wonderful, exciting, terrifying and sad to behold. She did not know which way to turn. But whichever way she did, Evie still saw no sign of the trio she now hungered to see more than anyone else alive. It was with a strange mixture of relief and fear that she saw no trace of her siblings on the battlefield. Whatever was coming, she would have to face it alone.

She was so lost in the battle below that when Thumb called out, 'Steadying the ship,' and the thruster engines wound down to a low hum, he might as well have been speaking underwater. As his words came distantly to her, she found herself wondering why this world of strange and colourful characters had not accepted the fairy knight as one of their own. Such as that pirate with a hook for a hand, in an unlikely alliance with a ticking crocodile, marching in lockstep with children wearing pyjamas. Or over there, a sharp-faced man in a deerstalker hat, puffing on a pipe, scribbling furiously on a notepad while his jovial companion fought off a Silver Soldier with a large black doctor's bag. Not to mention the ranks of hideous trolls, wielding uprooted trees as clubs, roaring as they sunk their weapons into crumpling masses of glistening machines. *And look*, she thought, *there is even a little boy on a unicorn.*

A little boy on a rainbow-coloured unicorn with a teddy bear.

Try as she might, she could not recollect that fairy tale.

Then she looked again, and felt such a tightness in her chest that she could not breathe for a moment, the air clean sucked out of her lungs. The golden light faded sharply, and the roar of the battle returned with a rush.

Larry.

'Secretary, please—'

Jana turned her most ghastly and shimmering smile on her favoured recruit. 'Yes, Reader. What is it to be now? We have already dealt with the witches. Shall we write a spell to send the wizards into oblivion? Or perhaps you want to play Jack and be a giant killer? I propose demolishing those Prince Charmings and their inane, mindless grins.'

'No,' said Evie, struggling to get the words out in any way which made sense, 'you don't understand. There's a boy down there . . . on a unicorn—'

'Now there is a ridiculous creature! A unicorn! They really have no right to exist. Be a horse. Be a deer. But for truth's sake, don't be something in between. Good choice, Reader. The boy on the unicorn it is. What silly tale is that, by the way? It doesn't matter. Thumb! Prepare the Page Turner.'

Before the fairy could get to the controls, Evie threw herself over them. He jabbed at her with his needle sword.

'What are you doing, girl? Out of the way!'

'You can't . . . He's my brother.'

Thumb froze, horror draining his pale face of blood till it looked like ice.

Jana blinked in surprise, and then clapped her glass hands together with a ghostly chime. 'He won't be for long, in that case. Please remove yourself from the controls. You must not get involved in things you don't understand. Reader you may be, but you are still a child.'

Thumb flapped Majesty near to the Secretary, her tigerish plumage incandescent in the dying sun, as if her wings burnt with inner fire. 'This is my fault, Secretary. The boy was the first Reader to enter Folio, where I found him. He seemed pliable, and a good lure for the others. It was my intention to make him like me, so I told him all sorts of awful things about you and the Unreads – none of them true, of course – in the hope he would return to his world fired up, and bring the others across.' He glanced out of the window at the boy in the armour, holding his head up high, biting his lip in determination. 'I may have gone too far, it seems.'

'What kind of things did you tell him about me, and the

Unreads?' said Jana, unsmiling, her left eye twitching.

'Nonsense!' said Thumb. 'Simple easy lies, which I only said to exacerbate the division between our countries, and to bring the Readers to our aid – in which I succeeded,' he said indignantly, pointing his sword at Evie.

'And what a help she has been,' said Jana. 'Now your lies run rampant all over our world, doing who knows what harm. Have you forgotten the first rule of the Library?'

Thumb smarted. 'No, I have not. But when you chose me as your spy, you made me a liar. I can't change that.'

They seemed to have quite forgotten Evie, the young girl sprawled between them over the Page Turner controls. Now she raised her head up, red and raw from crying, pushing back her hair that had become lank and greasy after too long in the overheated, oppressive artificial air of the Statecraft.

'I hate you both!' she said. 'You lied to a little boy who didn't know any better. You lied to me. You don't believe in anything, apart from yourselves! I don't want to play this game any more.'

'Too late,' snapped Jana, and clicked her fingers. Two Silver Soldiers jerked to attention, and, wheezing upright, lurched over to Evie, clamping their metal hands around her arms.

214

'No, no!' she screamed. 'He's my brother! You can't!'

Jana cocked her head, numbers pulsing. 'I warned you, dear Reader, that the road to revolution would not be smooth, didn't I?'

She reached past Thumb, grabbed the lever of the ink gun and slammed it down. As before, the giant weapon began to tremble. Evie struggled uselessly in the steel grip of the Secretary's robot servants.

'I thought we agreed, Reader, that change could never happen without sacrifice? Change you wanted?' She gestured to the other silver robots in the main cabin below, the wireless operators, navigators and engineers, busy with their duties.

'But not my own brother!' Evie was sobbing so hard; her words were jolting and breathless. 'He's just a little boy,' she gasped.

The Page Turner shuddered and began to fill with ink.

Jana came to her, and cradled Evie's cheek. Her breath smelt like engine oil.

'I know this is painful. And I promise you that when this war is done, we shall build a monument to him. The tallest monument in the City of the Unreads. A memorial made of diamonds, glittering in the sun, and purely to his memory. We shall retell his story, as a war hero! He was not fighting for the Reads, but had been captured by them, a prisoner of war, whom tragically we were not able to rescue amidst the heavy fighting. My people will adore you both. What do you think of that?'

'I think you are a monster!' said Evie. 'Larry isn't just a story! He's my brother – flesh and blood. A human being!' As if to prove that she was the same, she kicked Jana in the stomach, hard. It was like kicking a glass door.

Nevertheless, the Secretary staggered away in shock. 'Fire the Page Turner!' she snarled. 'Fire it at all of them! Destroy the old stories! I want to see every last one expire. And the other Readers too!'

Evie couldn't believe what was happening. Wrestling free of the surprised soldiers, she ran to the cockpit windscreen and slammed her hands against the glass. There was Larry riding on his unicorn, in rainbow colours, his teddy bear resting on the pommel of the saddle. He looked so proud, and happy, and suddenly, she realised, with a blow to her own gut, so very grown up.

'Run, Larry!' she screamed, slapping the glass again and again till it hurt, but he didn't even look up, even as the Statecraft lowered, casting its monolithic shadow over the assembled fairy tales. 'Please, it's Evie! Run!'

Still screaming as the soldiers once more dragged her

away, she could hear nothing but the Page Turner filling and gurgling with lethal ink, muttered confirmations from Thumb that the target was locked and engaged. Evie closed her eyes, and put her hands over her ears.

She couldn't bear to watch or hear a single second more, but there was no escape.

War had found her again.

CHAPTER 19
Say the Name

Simon and Patricia stared for a moment at the statue in the cave, and the inscription – which had flashed briefly but was now dark again, like a cold fire – waited in expectation, as if the Never Reads might suddenly burst out of the base itself, perhaps in a geyser-like explosion of masonry, letters and papers. The only light was a pale blankness that flickered in from the mouth of the cave, rippled and pinched by the cawing desert winds outside.

It wasn't clear whether everything had happened or whether this was just the beginning.

'The one who knows nothing,' said Simon. 'That doesn't sound like our Librarian.'

'No,' said Patricia. 'Don't you think . . . that it might be who the Bears were talking about? The one we might

summon if we said the name?'

'And what if he's the one who took our Librarian? Our magician?'

Patricia didn't have the energy to reply; she just arched an eyebrow at Simon, who grunted. 'You seem very certain of everything, Patti.'

She snorted. 'I wish I was.'

'Come on then, help me out. You keep solving everything. Where do you think we're going to find the Librarian? Or magician? Whatever he is.'

Patricia stared at the grey rock around them, the desert beyond. She had never been more certain of anything in her life. 'Whatever he is, he's not here.'

'But the Bears said—'

'They didn't know! They were just guessing!'

'What about the statue, the runes, the book—'

His sister turned on him. Simon was like a young puppy sometimes. You just had to be firm otherwise he would keep on scrapping till he broke something. 'He was here once, I agree. He must have been. There is no life here, though, Si. It's more like a mausoleum than a library. It gives me the shivers. Professor Kelly said Crowne was the first man to ever know everything. So the one who knows nothing must be at least his opposite, if not his enemy.'

Simon slowly shook his head. 'But what if they are still here? What if the . . . one . . . has our Librarian prisoner?'

'What, we call in the RAF? Throw a grenade in through a window and go in, all guns blazing? Like those thugs who smashed their way into Barfield? You watch too many war pictures.'

'Oh, for goodness' sake! I may not share your obsession with books but I'm not a baby, you know. Why don't we just say the name and see what happens? What do we have left to lose?'

A spiral of dust crumbled down from the cave roof with a clatter on the ground behind, and they both started.

'What if we truly aren't meant to say it?' she said.

'I don't care what you think,' said Simon. She was troubled by his glazed and faraway look. 'The Librarian must be the most powerful force in Folio. If we can't find him, perhaps if we summon his nemesis instead, that will smoke our man out.'

Yet Patricia was more convinced now of the opposite than ever before. This was a truly terrible idea.

'I don't think we should try and summon *anyone*. We don't know what could happen.'

'Have you lost your nerve?'

'No! I wish you would stop saying that every time

someone disagrees with you. It's this place. It's so . . . horrid. Writing in blood, the burning letters, the broken statue . . . it frightens me, Simon. I see now why this land is . . . called what it is. Why the Bears don't even dare say the name. We shouldn't have come here. Wherever the Librarian has got to, I don't think this is it.'

She started to make her way back down the cave, but Simon seized her shoulders and pressed her against the wall.

'Now listen to me, Patti.' His voice was level, even, and his gaze distant, as if he was seeing right through her. 'You're not thinking straight. Trust in old Si. I've got you this far, haven't I?'

Patricia shook her head, blinking away tears. 'Can't you see? The Librarian! It's just something they say. Like "thank God" or "by Jove"! Hoping he might be here was . . . I don't know . . . something to believe in. If he is the Professor's magician, then he disappeared hundreds of years ago. He's probably rotting under a floorboard in Barfield for all we know.'

They were both hot and tense, panting in the dank mouth of the cave.

'No, you're right,' said Simon, releasing her and stepping back. The shadows began to swallow him up, there was just a faint sweaty sheen from his cheekbones, a fixed glimmer in his eye. 'I'm sorry. It is just something they say, something to believe in. How silly of us all to have spent the whole war *believing* that one day we might just defeat Hitler.'

But Patti knew her brother almost better than she knew herself. She knew that tone when she heard it, that tone he used with their mother just before he blatantly disregarded even the most modest request, the tone he used with a policeman once, while holding the man's helmet behind his back with one hand. *No, officer, I haven't seen your hat.*

'Simon. What are you doing?'

'What's the matter, sis? If the Librarian is just a saying, if it doesn't mean anything, if he's dead after all—'

'That's not quite what I said—'

'Then it won't matter if I say this, will it? I'll do it quietly, just in case.' And he held his hands aloft, mockingly, and so gently whispered the words. 'The Land of the Never Reads! The Land of the Never Reads! Never Reads! Never Read!'

Simon spoke so softly that Patricia only just heard him, amplified a little by the walls of the cave.

They both held their breath. Another slew of grit spiralled down from the ceiling somewhere, making a scattering noise, and the pair flinched.

Then silence again, which somehow seemed more deafening than before.

Nothing else happened. No one came, no one called.

Eventually, Patricia let her shoulders sink, and exhaled deeply.

'You see!' said Simon triumphantly. 'Maybe I should do it louder next time. Just some words. Harmless!'

Then he took a step towards her.

As he did so, the ground began to crack beneath his feet. The sound was sickening.

A hairline fracture, nothing more, but one which moved at dizzying speed over the dry earth, branching off into a thousand fractures till the floor of the cave resembled a ruined mosiac.

The first crack tore away from them towards the remains of the statue. It smashed into the base, which in turn spawned a million mini cracks of its own, which reduced the block of solid granite to a pile of fragments. The statue shuddered once, then twice, then toppled, smashing on to the floor in clouds of white masonry dust, flattening the Green Man's book out of existence.

Simon and Patricia, too startled to even scream, began to run.

The walls began to crumble around them, as if the cave

itself was giving pursuit. A roaring, rumbling sound rose up as if the mountain was bellowing, and the roof showered stones upon their heads. They could no longer see, the dust and smoke was so great, blinding their eyes and stuffing their throats. Simon clutched Patricia as they threw themselves free of the cave. The entrance collapsed behind them, leaving just a pile of boulders and one final exhalation of dust.

Patricia shouted something at Simon, which he didn't hear. The desert winds of the Land of Never Reads were whipping about their faces, ripping at their hair, flinging grit into their eyes. She was still on her knees, trying to pull herself to her feet, constantly thwarted by side punches from the storm, at enormous speed, in every direction. She cried again to Simon for help, but he wasn't listening.

Just on his own feet, he had seen something, in the undulating clouds of sand ahead.

Now it was his turn to shout something at Patricia, which she didn't hear.

'He's come! You see. It worked. He's come!'

What had come was a distant figure, its lines and features obscured by swirling debris. A figure that was neither quite man or beast, although it walked upon two legs. As the storm grew heavier and thicker, the new arrival was in danger of fading into just a furry shadow. Yet it stopped. Turning, it looked at Simon and, extending a terrible claw, beckoned him to follow.

His nostrils flared, and his heart leaped. He felt the call. Turning away from his sister, he marched into the winds, shielding his face with his arm against their bite. They swallowed him up, as they had the creature.

'Where are you going?' screamed Patricia. 'Simon! Come back!'

But her cries were swept away, lost in the howling gale.

Far down below, on the battlefield, Larry looked up in shock. There had been a flash and a crack from the mountains. Perhaps thunder, or lightning, or something worse. Whatever it was, it had slammed right into the side of the Statecraft, punching a hole in the fuselage. Now the ship swung drunkenly across the sky, spouting ink uselessly into the air, smoke billowing out from the rear engines.

Things had happened much faster than Larry had expected. The river had been nice and quiet, lazy almost. After much persuasion, Roderick had let him clamber on to his filthy back, before wading irritably over to the far shore. There, the army, which had looked so splendid from a distance, was noisy and hectic. Everyone was so busy, poring over their own plans, or sharpening their axes, or strapping on their armour, that no one paid any attention to a boy on a unicorn, even a rainbow-coloured one.

Then, suddenly, before he could ask anyone what to do, they had started to charge, roaring across the field.

And now, a crashing spaceship.

The battles he played at home were so organised. Not this chaos.

'What was that?' he said. 'Was it a spaceship?'

Roderick the Unicorn looked up and stared at it with his bloodshot eyes. 'How in the blazes should I know?' he said. 'I never said I knew *everything*. Ask a horse, if you think they're so clever.'

'I didn't say—' Larry sighed.

Knights on horseback, giants and wolves galloped past them, in pursuit of the careering airship. A large dragon thundering up behind the pair thumped the ground with his tail and blew a celebratory blast of dragon-flame into the air.

Striking out between the larger creatures, a young man rode up alongside them, brandishing a shepherd's crook, cheering. He was clad in sheepskin all patched with leather and rough thread, wearing a woollen cap tied tight round his head. His ratty face was feverish with excitement.

'That's the Statecraft! Head ship of the Unreads and all that. They just took out some witches. But now look at 'em.'

They watched as the battleship started emitting an alarming mechanical bellow, like a wounded whale, and dived lower and lower in the sky, towards some dark woods on the other side of the plain, below the mountains where the thunderstorm had begun.

'What happened?' said Larry.

'Got struck by lightning, didn't it?' said the shepherd. 'And now the whole lot of 'em are going to cop it! Jana too! It came from beyond the mountains!'

Larry hated the idea of anyone dying, even if they were awful. He just hoped Thumb would be pleased, wherever he was.

'Why should we believe you?' snorted Roderick.

The shepherd snapped. 'Who asked you? Yer just a unicorn! An unfinished story.'

'Why *shouldn't* I believe you?' asked Larry, who always liked to believe people, if he possibly could. Not believing people meant not agreeing with them, which could mean not liking them, and then they might not like you back. He shivered.

Some dwarves charged past, cheering, whirling hatchets around their head.

The boy muttered something, but he couldn't catch it.

'Ha! Typical! Won't admit it,' said the unicorn. 'Lying is in his nature.'

'Why? Who are you?' said Larry.

'I'm the Boy Who Cried Wolf,' sighed the Boy Who Cried Wolf.

'Exactly,' said Roderick. 'Can't trust a word he says.'

Larry looked around for something he could trust. His brother or sisters. His parents. A paved London street. Black railings, a red pillar box, a policeman offering directions to some passers-by. Instead he saw a once green plain churned up by hooves, feet and claws, silver robots engaged in hand-to-hand combat with elves and goblins. Smoke and sparks choked the air, and there was a dull, echoing thump as the large spaceship finally ploughed into the trees on the other side, a heavy black cloud pumping into the sky above. There was a muted cheer from the Reads, but still the soldiers kept scything their way through them.

Larry pulled on Roderick's mane, and they took a careful step back from the fray.

'I know I've been wrong before, but I promise yer, with all me 'eart, that I'm right,' said the Boy.

'About what?' said Larry.

The Boy pointed to the mountains. Black thunderclouds devoured their peaks, spitting out veins of lightning, while showers of molten sparks erupted from time to time, hissing down the mountainside.

Larry looked up, shielding his eyes. Is that where Simon and Patti had gone with the Bears? He suddenly felt very alone.

'See fer yerself,' the Boy said. 'Someone 'as called 'em. They said the name. Now I can say it too. The Never Reads are rising.'

CHAPTER 20
Stories and Magic

Simon unrolled his sleeves, putting his arm over his mouth so he wasn't inhaling lungfuls of grit every time he moved. The grey figure lurched ahead of him, never quite in reach, never moving far away enough to be out of mind. What was out of mind was all thoughts of anyone else. He didn't know where Patti was any more, and didn't care why she hadn't come. She could look after herself. Better than he could, he had to admit, but then she was missing out on the most exciting part of the adventure so far. As for the others, Evie and Larry, well, they were bound to fall on their feet, weren't they? The young and adorable usually did, in his limited experience.

'Hey!' he tried to call to the figure, but only got a mouth of sand for his efforts.

They began to ascend a slope. Simon clenched his teeth, and swore mildly. He did not have the energy for another mountain. But the rise was gentle and, as they climbed, the winds began to quieten. In place of their shrieking and howling was a total, deathly stillness. He strained his eyes to see more of his quarry, now the worst of the sandstorm was behind them, but the figure remained wreathed in shadow. What was clearer to see was the outline of a building at the top of the hill.

A dark tower, jutting out against the dangerous red sky.

Always just ahead, the figure passed inside, silently.

When Simon reached the base of the building, he found a door which was warm to the touch. There were no beautiful Library carvings, only a few ragged planks coarsely bolted together.

It swung open.

As Simon stepped in, he nearly gagged. The inside smelt of the country in high summer and of manure. *Perhaps this is one of those old buildings where they used to keep farm animals*, he thought, like in that strange painting of Barfield they had found before the door appeared, with cows and ducks and geese wandering about inside. A painting that came very strongly to mind, suddenly. So vividly, so precisely – the mullioned glass twinkling in the sun, the briar wrapped around the doorway, the fellow with the ruff – that for a moment he thought he might be in that house, and stumbled in the dark.

No, he was definitely in a tower. There were no books or shelves or chandeliers. Instead, in the lurid desert light streaking through the half open door, he could see that he had arrived at the foot of some stairs. In plain, soft stone, they wound upwards, lit by a chain of burning braziers on the wall.

Simon paused on the bottom step, uncertain. 'Hello?' he called out, his voice echoing emptily around the walls. There was no reply, but he did hear some faint music coming from what he presumed were the upper floors.

So he began to climb the stairs. They reminded him of the crooked, spiral steps to the Professor's study in Barfield. On and on they went. As he climbed, the music grew louder. It was some kind of old music, perhaps, he couldn't be sure – played on what sounded like a church organ. Whatever the music was, and he wished he had paid more attention to all that stuff at school, it was compelling and drew him on. The music grew louder and louder, becoming so deafening that he felt he was in the bellows and pipes of the organ itself.

Finally, the steps stopped at the entrance to a grand,

vaulted hall. The ancient oak floorboards shuddered with the reverberations of the music, and there were lots of candles. Hundred of the things, on sconces sticking out from the wall, sitting in waxy puddles on the floor, standing crookedly in rusted candelabra that hung low from the ceiling, and lined in a jagged jaw of battlements atop the organ in the middle of the room. There were so many candles that the room almost felt on fire, and Simon began to sweat. He stepped inside, but the heat was so fierce he had to turn back.

'Come in, Simon. They won't burn you.'

'Hello? Who is that?' Simon took two more steps in, but the flames were too scorching for him to go further. The scent of the farmyard was overwhelmingly ripe in the rising temperature, and he had to block his nose with his sleeve.

There was no reply, but more music. There was no single tune that Simon recognised, more a jarring cacophony of every kind of song, from playground chants to barrel organ medleys, old church hymns mangled up with the smoky jazz his parents sometimes liked dancing to. It was awful and made his ears hurt.

Yet underneath it all, he could detect a more mysterious music still, unlike any other he had ever heard before, driving a deep and sunless harmony, a melody straight from the bottom of the ocean, bubbling up to the surface in the dead of night.

'Who are you?' he said, again, trying to see through the heat waffle of candle flame to what lurked in the shadows of the vaulted hall.

'Well, I certainly know all the best tunes, don't I?' said the voice. Whoever it was chuckled, and then stopped playing. Simon heard the hollow clunk of the keyboard lid slamming down. Somehow, the end of the music made it easier to see, as if one sense had released another, and Simon could now make out a reddish pair of eyes and a beard. The man, if it was a man, seemed to be wearing a kind of fur coat. He must have been sweltering. And was that, as he turned his head, some extraordinary form of helmet? Almost like bone, rather than metal, canine-yellow and twisted.

'Are you . . . the Librarian?' He winced, and took another step further into the room.

'I am the Librarian's worst nightmare. Yours too, I suspect.'

'So you aren't . . . the fellow from Barfield, Nicholas Crowne? The magician?'

'That fool thought he could defeat me, and he was wrong.'

'You mean that they are the same person? The Professor's missing magician . . . and the Librarian?'

'His magic created the Library, but he was not powerful enough to control the world he made.'

The speaker rose from behind the organ, and began to pace up and down in the darkness beyond. His boots made a clopping noise on the wooden floor, and as he turned, his coat swished so much that it could have almost been a tail.

The candles flickered in his wake. Simon felt sick as well as hot. He had had enough of this shadowy musician and his riddles. 'Why am I here?'

The speaker stepped forward, and for the first time Simon glimpsed a flash of white, shining teeth. 'You were the one that summoned. You tell me.'

'I . . . I thought I might find the Magician.'

'You have come here in search of what he also desired to know, the final frontier of his understanding. The flames burning around us now.' He stepped into the light, and Simon gasped at what he saw, staggering back. 'The eternal flames of ignorance. They destroyed him and they will destroy you.'

Evie didn't know where she was. She hoped she was still alive. Everything was dark. What had happened? There had been that burst of light, and a sharp swerve. She couldn't remember anything after that, or make a guess as to how long ago that had been.

At first, she thought she had to be back in the one place she never wanted to see again. The school, on Maguire Street. Toxic smoke had swallowed all the air, and she struggled to breathe. In the impenetrable murk, there were faint cries coming from all around. Her legs and arms were sore, but nothing – miraculously – seemed to be broken. She was lying face down on something smooth and shiny. Half-opening one swollen eye, she could see silver leather stained with soot and spotted with blood.

Daring to raise her head, she caught sight of torn fragments of seat and twisted metal struts. There were no metal struts in Maguire Street though, just timber, brick, plaster and glass. Squinting, she looked up, and saw only a circle of tree tops, regarding her in a severe and godlike way. This was not London.

The top half of Captain MAG R-1 whirred and spluttered ahead of her, his head hanging low, molten and irreparably damaged, before falling silent. Evie wondered if perhaps the best thing to do would be to go back to sleep.

The silver leather chair, quite shorn of its moorings, seemed to have cushioned her from the worst of the impact.

And remained comfortable, in a way. She laid her head down on the smooth padding. She was just, suddenly, so very very tired. Six long years of war and now this strange adventure. All Jana's talk of revolution and the future had evaporated into clear air, like the Secretary herself, and was like nothing more than a distant, airy dream. Perhaps it would be easier, and far, far better, just to rest here a while.

Her eyes fluttered shut.

All the horror began to flood away, washed out by the balm of deep sleep. Even the aching all over her body faded to a dull pang.

Then there was a sharp point stabbing at the back of her neck.

'Wake up!' said a voice.

She murmured drowsily at the voice to go away.

It wouldn't. 'Reader Evie! Wake up! We have to go – now!'

Evie rolled over, blinking awake. A tiny fairy hovered inches above her nose, perched on a tiger-striped butterfly, slicing his sword through the after-smoke of the crash.

'Thumb! Majesty!'

They both bowed their heads, mid-air.

'But where is everybody . . . How did you survive? What happened?'

Thumb batted her questions away with his sword impatiently.

'I don't know. An explosion of some kind. Enemy attack, a lightning strike, I'm not sure. Possibly the Librarian himself. You saw the thunderclouds. But we must leave now. There are fires and spilt fuel everywhere. It could all go up in a moment.'

Everything Thumb was saying implied moving quickly and suddenly. Evie sank back on to her chair. 'I don't know if I can walk,' she said.

Thumb buzzed down to her eye level. 'But, Evie, my dear, you have to.'

'Why?' She felt tearful now. 'What's the point? The Secretary's dead, isn't she? Now I've lost everyone – Patti, Si, Lall – everyone! What was the point?' Evie roared this last at Thumb and Majesty, with a sudden bellow of pain that she didn't know was in her. 'All the killing and fighting and destruction! What was the point of any of it?'

Thumb looked as sorry and contrite as she had seen him. His voice softened.

'I don't know any more, myself. It's true.' The fairy shook his spiky head sadly. 'I do know one thing, though.'

'What?' said Evie morosely.

He pointed with his sword though the blackened trees

ahead. 'That down there a battle is still going on. A war without end. A fight for supremacy between information and stories. Each side believes that only they can command the truth. Yet the truth is, well . . . And if one side doesn't declare victory soon, trust me, there are far darker, more terrifying forces who will.'

'I don't care any more,' said Evie, and found to her surprise that she was sobbing.

'You must care,' said the knight. 'You must! Even if not for any of those reasons. They are problems for our world, I see that. But also down there, somewhere, is a boy with his bear. A boy who . . . I know . . . should not be amongst all this . . .' He gestured at the smouldering wreckage around them. 'And it is both our fault. So I am imploring you, Evie. I know you hurt, I know this is frightening, but please – help me rescue your brother.'

CHAPTER 21
Learning to Fly

Larry certainly felt like he knew nothing. He couldn't see or hear. In fact, he could barely breathe. He was clinging on to Roderick for dear life, but the unicorn was also struggling for air. As the Statecraft had slammed into the hillside, the Reads had surged forwards in one great crowd.

He had been borne upwards by a mighty wave of beasts and people and robots, and then smashed right down into the seething mass of battle. He thought he heard Roderick cry out something about preferring sums, but then they were torn apart by the surging crowd.

Everywhere Larry tried to turn, he found his way blocked – here by the awkward bulk of a wolf, skidding furiously, or squashed between two hefty trolls trying to swing their clubs, but trapped by the force of bodies

pushing in on them from all sides. If he tried to stick his head up above the sea of inky paper sheets, gusts of blistering smoke from the now blazing Statecraft stung his eyes and choked his throat, so he took his chances with the kicking, lashing parade below.

He hated games, and this was the worst nightmare ever – a colossal rugby scrum without end. Yet trying to dodge a random hoof that swung in his direction, taking the brunt of repeated kicks in the back, even just missing the crushing thump of a dragon's foot, was nothing as to the noise.

The air was filled with sound, deafening and terrible. The Silver Soldiers buzzed as their circuits overheated. Every time they fired a blast of numbers, dispatching a story character into inky letters, there was a whistling drawl, followed by the muted scream and shattering explosion. And in return they were met with roars, cries and cackles. Knights' horses brayed, giants thundered and bears growled – for the Bears had joined the fray, unable to watch from the forest and do nothing.

It was such a cacophony of sound as Larry had never heard in his life. He had heard bombs fall from the sky, heralded by the alien birdsong of the air raid siren, then the shriek, the dull thump, the explosions, the wailing bells of ambulances. He had walked along the city's busy streets, hiding behind his mother's skirts, listening to market stall holders bellowing to advertise their wares, the rackety rumble of motor cars, omnibuses and the distant Underground, shop bells ringing, high heels clicking on stone pavements . . . Nothing came close to what he could hear now. It was an endless, raucous, overwhelming babble and row that seemed like it would never end.

Fearing for his life, Larry crawled between the stampeding legs and feet, muddied, bruised and gasping for what little breaths he could. He was only a little boy of eight, still clutching his grey bear tight, but even though he could not quite understand why, deep down in his heart, Larry knew that whoever triumphed in this battle, it was a war that could never be won.

Then he could see, at last, what he had been crawling towards all this time.

The muddy but unmistakeable flanks of a magical horse with a horn.

As he grasped the dragging wings, and hauled himself back on top of Roderick, Larry remembered the first rule of the Library and (for the first time in his life hoping that a rule was true) whispered into the soft, warm ears:

'Roderick, you can fly. I know you can, because I believe

you can. Please, Roderick, please, you must listen to me. I know you can fly, you can use your wings, now you have to. I am sorry for anything wrong I have ever done, but please, please, you have to believe me, I know you can fly!'

He could not say any more, with the wind punched out of his stomach, as either side of him two huge, dirty wings stiffly unfolded into the air. With deep, unrelenting power Roderick began to beat his wings, pushing past the battle-wearied heads and faltering arms, and up through the oily rings of smoke, into the empty blue sky, flying towards the burning sun beyond.

Patricia ran, and didn't look back. Tumbling into the mountain pass, her sandal slipped off but she ran on wearing only one shoe, the rough ground scourging her foot.

It didn't matter.

She didn't flinch once in the gloom. Instead, she thought of her younger brother and sister, her own flesh and blood, whom she had let wander off in this strange land without so much as a word of love or guidance. Patricia was not the kind to waste time chastising herself, but she was cross – with so many people, beginning with Simon for egging her on in this hopeless quest. Tears ran freely down her face as she remembered how they had all been there for one another during the war. Holding each other tight under the kitchen table while the building shook and the city wailed around them. Laughing as they danced around the sprays from the fire engines, still putting out the flames from the night before. Tucked up in bed, their hair brushed and shiny, smelling damp yet clean after all sharing a warm bath, while Mother sat on the end of her bed and read them all a story.

Patricia didn't know then that stories could die.

She hadn't ever thought that they would have to battle against information. If you made things up, surely it was just a game? Yet none of this felt like a game. Couldn't you believe in facts, like the times of sunrise and sunset, without having to give up believing stories? Then, she saw what she had done.

Patricia had believed in stories, without ever realising that she had.

The pass behind her, she skidded down the slope of ash. She fell once, then twice, and on the third time gave up completely, sailing down on her behind in plumes of dust, not caring any more about the damage to her clothes or herself. It was terrifying and exhilarating at the same time. Stumbling to her feet, as she slid towards the treeline in a shower of tiny pebbles, Patricia began to feel less scared and more determined.

She tore through the Forgotten Forest. As before, the mist began to swirl around her ankles, and her mind felt confused all over again, but she clenched the Green Man's threads, crunched up in a ball into her palm, so as not to forget who she was, or where she was.

And why she was there.

But the limp threads did not burst into fire or reveal any hidden letters.

At last, faint from hunger, her mind loose and disconnected, she found the wrinkled old tree standing in the clearing. The skirt of oak leaves hung down low around as before, and as she embraced the trunk, flinging both her arms around it, the bark was as dry and scaly as she remembered. But there was no crack of limbs, and when she looked up into the floating ceiling of green above, there was no wise old face, no spark of life.

It was just a gnarled old tree, in the middle of a wood.

Except Patricia knew it wasn't. This tree was a man who had given her the long threads sewn into card that she clutched in her hand. A guardian of a Library that was a door to a magical world. A world where story characters lived for real, undiscovered facts battled to gain attention, words caused earthquakes and books set themselves on fire.

'Please, Green Man, I know you're there.' She beat her fists against the unforgiving trunk. 'You have to help me. I know you gave me these . . . threads, but I don't know what to to do with them. It isn't as easy as just opening a book.'

The wind ruffled the branches above, and some leaves tumbled softly on to her head.

'Please! Why won't you listen?'

But it was no use. The wood was impassive as rock. There were only the roots coiling and snaking into the ground, the breeze blowing through the leaves and the silent forest beyond. Patricia slid down to the ground, her back against the trunk, legs splayed apart. Uselessly, she picked at the fraying ends of a root stem.

'I know you're there,' she said quietly. 'But if you won't listen, then that's up to you. I thought you were the guardian of this Library. You gave us presents to help, after all. Surely you can see that this world is in terrible danger? The Reads and the Unreads tearing themselves apart. The Librarian still missing, and now I think Simon has summoned something truly terrible.'

She sighed. Maybe the Green Man had never talked, or even been? Had she made it all up, had it been a strange dream?

'The thing is I don't want your help for any of that.'

Perhaps it was her imagination, but the bark behind her gave the gentlest ripple.

'I know Larry is a silly daydreamer. That Evie can be, well, stubborn. And of course Si is a total ass sometimes. Maybe it's worse to be those kinds of people in this world. Maybe it would be better to be a hero out of a fairy tale, or a perfect piece of hard scientific fact, but they're not.'

Now, the tree began to crack and shake. Startled, Patricia leaped up, standing back in alarm.

Softly, the leaves parted, and there was the vein- and vine-wreathed face of the ancient Green Man.

'Then what are they?' he said gently, in his rasping voice.

'They're my brothers and my sister,' Patricia said. 'They're your Readers, I suppose. But most of all, we're humans. They're not perfect, none of us are. We can't help it. And I think I—' She paused, biting on her thumb. Then she looked up at the soft, round head in the leaves. Her eyes pricked, and her throat flushed. 'Yes,' she said. 'I don't care if you think me foolish. It's the truth, anyhow. I love them. All of them, very much. So if you could help me, then . . .'

'Then would that not be the best reason for helping someone?'

With a resounding crack, one great wooden tree arm swung down, and the sprouting fingers of the whorled hand stiffly unfolded. Carefully, Patricia stepped into the dry palm.

'Love?' she said.

'Humans,' he replied, shaking his head sadly, and Patricia could not tell if he agreed with her or meant something else. There was little time to wonder, as, clutching her tight, the Green Man swung her up to treetop height and, with an almighty ripping and tearing, pulled his root-twined legs out of the earth, shaking soil everywhere, and strode off through the other trees.

'Wait!' cried out Patricia. 'You're going the wrong way. The battle is down there, on the plain – we saw it from the mountain.'

The Green Man did not miss a stride, or even glance at her as he smashed his way through the Forgotten Forest.

'I know where the fight is,' he said. 'But it is not one we shall meet alone.'

CHAPTER 22
Endings

On the rough wooded slopes above the Plain of Meaning, Evie and Thumb fought their way through the smoke, which made their eyes water, trying to wish away the blistering heat, following no map other than the imprint of instinct in their minds. They sought only daylight, open space and freedom. The fire ignited by the explosive crash landing of the Statecraft had set the trunks, bark and undergrowth alight, and the flames hungrily trawled the air trying to slake their unquenchable thirst.

Evie was limping along, bruised, her clothes shredded by the impact and her hasty exit from the wreckage. She had been here before, of course; she knew the drill. The memory of that earlier explosion on Maguire Street now felt, as never before, like a comfort. It was war,

it was horror, but she had survived it once and it gave her strength to believe she would survive it again. She picked her way over charred logs, coughing at the plumes of acrid smoke which sprung up at the base of every tree, like ghostly weeds. Thumb and Majesty hovered ever close at her shoulder.

'Nearly there, Reader!' Thumb said, with a fixed smile.

Evie nodded but did not reply. It was funny how the simplest questions could be so difficult to ask sometimes. Finally, she spoke. 'Why did you do it, Thumb?'

'Do what? Rescue you? Good question.'

'No. You know what I mean. Why did you betray and spy on your own people? We call people like that traitors. In the olden days, we used to chop their heads off.'

'I might ask you the same question. Why did you betray your own brothers and sister?'

Evie's eyes stung, and this time it wasn't the smoke. It was as if they were all there suddenly, ghostly figures all around her. Patricia peering over her glasses, Simon mussing her hair, Larry picking some dirt out of Grey Bear's head. They wavered in the smog, and then, smiling, looked up at her. Was this a hallucination – or were they dead, and come to haunt her?

If they were dead, then . . . how would she explain it to

her parents? The already tottering pile of feelings in her heart came down with an almighty crash, washing a tidal wave of tears up through her core.

'I didn't mean to . . . Jana tricked me.'

Even Majesty shook her noble, elegant head in disbelief at this.

Thumb laughed, but not unkindly. 'You chose the shelf of the Unreads. You made a deal with Jana. Admit it. You fell in love with her dream of a better world.'

Still tearful, she kicked the smouldering end of a log, which collapsed in a shower of red hot sparks and ash. 'So what if I did? I do believe in facts. They're the truth, aren't they? We can't do anything without the right information. I just didn't realise she wanted to destroy all the older stories as well.'

'But there's something else too, isn't there? Admit it.'

'What?'

'You felt out of place, like me. Your world, your family – you didn't fit in?'

'No.'

They stopped as they at last came to the edge of the forest, the trees thinning, the smoke drifting, the air opening up . . . and as her blurry vision began to slowly sharpen, Evie had to blink twice. She could not believe

251

what she was looking at.

The Plain of Meaning was now a field of devastation. A smear of carnage spread out between the trees and the mountains, sucking in the light from the sky. Piles of paper toppled and slithered into one another, smeared with oil and trampled into the mud. Heaps of crumpled robots gave off an oily tang in the heat of the day. And everything was drenched, stained not with blood but running rivers of ink. Flies hovered over the destruction and, averting her gaze, Evie looked up towards the sun. What was that circling in the sky?

Thumb whispered in her ear. 'You did this. You wanted to change the old stories. You wanted to make a world where you belonged. You wanted to prove you were right.'

'That's not true!'

'That's exactly what you were doing. It's what I was doing as well. But perhaps we both underestimated the price we were willing to pay.'

Evie faced him, reddening with rage, and in the same instant the tiny fairy exploded. Not quickly, but slowly, his acorn hat, gossamer wings and mouse-skin slippers disintegrating before her eyes into a buzzing swarm of letters and pages that one by one fell to the ground at her feet. She cried out, and knelt, trying to put the story back together, but it only left her hands black with ink. Slowly, she stood up and turned around.

There behind her, leaning against a singed tree for support, was the Secretary. Her glass robot shell was dented and smashed in places, and her head was at a strange angle, the mouth chattering more than usual. Smiling, Jana lowered her arm, still glowing from the beam she had just fired at Thumb.

'Poor fairy. He did indeed pay the ultimate price. If you are going to be a traitor, it's always best to keep the treachery on one side.' Hauling herself upright, she staggered towards Evie, hissing and steaming slightly, and laid an automated hand on her shoulder. 'Now, Reader – come with me, and we shall complete the work you have begun.'

High in the sky, circling above, Larry could – at a squint – see everything unfolding beneath him. Yet he was powerless to do anything about it. For now Larry had persuaded Roderick he could fly, there was just one small problem.

'I told you,' said the unicorn. 'I can't.'

'What do you mean, you can't land?' said Larry in disbelief. 'You flew up into the air, surely you can come down again?'

'Why do you keep making all these assumptions about me?' snapped Roderick, executing a flawless loop for about the tenth time. 'You hardly know me. Just because I can fly, that doesn't mean I can land.'

Larry was only eight. He knew he didn't know much. But he thought of birds flapping off trees, bombers returning home after missions, the balls he found in the ruins and threw at broken windows to finish them off. He thought of gravity. And he definitely knew one thing.

'Yes,' he said. 'Yes, it does mean you can land.'

'No, no, no!'

'Please,' said Larry.

'NO!' said Roderick. 'Why are you always trying to stop me having fun?'

'But I saved your life. I got you to believe in your wings . . . you're flying for the first time ever!'

'Oh, it's all your doing is it now? I see. Nothing to do with unicorns, naturally. It never is.'

Larry briefly considered jumping off. 'I didn't say that!'

'That's not what it sounded like. You want me to fly down so you can get off and walk away. Just like all the others.'

'I want to rescue my sister! I want to end this stupid battle; it isn't fun any more.'

Roderick flew on through another storm cloud, showering them both in dust and water. Larry wiped his eyes and brushed himself and Grey Bear down, gazing with longing at the green fields and trees miles below, the tiny bright dots that he believed to be his sister and possibly Tom Thumb. He needed to help them. What would his father say if he didn't? Larry wasn't a pansy. He meant, when he thought that to himself, that he wasn't any old pansy. He was the brightest, bravest and most glorious pansy on a flying rainbow unicorn, and he was going to show them all.

'I order you to land yourself, Roderick the Unicorn!' he cried in his most commanding voice.

The unicorn kept on flying in circles, above the wreck of the Statecraft, surrounded by bent and broken trees.

Larry tried again.

'I command you! I imagined you could fly, and you flew. It was the first rule of the Library. If you can imagine it—'

Roderick shook his mane with fury. 'I know the first rule of the Library!'

'Then why can't you do it? Why *won't* you do it?'

The wings almost drooped in mid-air, but the unicorn kept on flying. Somehow, though, Larry felt everything sink in Roderick's body, with a great, sad sigh.

'It's not that I won't, if you'd actually listen to me,' he said. 'It's not in my story.'

Larry hoped Grey Bear wouldn't mind if he used him to whack the unicorn's flanks in encouragement. 'But nothing's in your story! Your story is half finished. Meeting me, joining the battle, using your wings . . . none of these things were in your story! We imagined them! They happened – don't you see, Roderick, we could do anything?'

There were faint cries below. Maybe they had been spotted.

They kept on circling. But Larry could feel the unicorn tiring; the circles were getting smaller, his wings flapping more slowly and weakly, his breath becoming faster and shorter.

'Come on,' he said, softly now. 'You need to land. You can't stay up here for ever.'

'But don't you understand?' said Roderick sadly, and now Larry could see two large tears sliding down behind the pince-nez. 'I can't see what will happen if I do.'

'You'll land! I can help my sister! What else is there to understand?'

Roderick's voice faltered. 'I'm an unfinished story, remember? Whoever started me never finished.' He swooped down above the warring armies. 'Those characters down there . . . that toad in that car, those children in a sailing boat, that gang of detectives . . . their stories are told, complete. They know what the ends of their stories are. Unlike them, I have never known what mine is.' He turned his big, bleary unicorn eyes to Larry. 'And now I am not sure I want to.'

The Magician Project – Extract 22
(KV 1/1569-12)

1st Intelligence, Surveillance and Reconnaissance Brigade

HQ Company, Ashford

18th September 1945, 21:30pm

Author REDACTED/CLASSIFIED

INTERROGATION OF PROFESSOR DIANA KELLY (EXTRACT)

CAPTAIN (REDACTED): For the tenth time, Professor, what have you done with those children? It will be better for you to tell us now.

PROFESSOR: For the tenth time, Captain, I haven't done anything with them.

CAPTAIN: Then where are they?

PROFESSOR: If I knew, I would tell you. This is what I'm trying to find out, what this whole experiment is about, if your thugs hadn't arrived at the worst possible time –

CAPTAIN: You're telling me that four children, aged between 8 and 14, just disappeared into thin air?

PROFESSOR: If you'd only listen for a moment, I'm trying to tell you. There's something about that house, Barfield Hall, it has a power we don't yet fully understand.

CAPTAIN: What kind of power?

PROFESSOR: You'll only ridicule me.

CAPTAIN: No I won't.

PROFESSOR: A magic power.

CAPTAIN: May I remind you, Professor, that I am looking for some children? That doesn't mean I am one.

PROFESSOR: You see! I told you! And all the while you keep me locked up here, answering pointless questions, they might be in terrible danger.

CAPTAIN: In danger? From what?

PROFESSOR: Horrors that a fool such as you cannot begin to imagine, not even in your worst nightmares.

CHAPTER 23
King of the Never Reads

Simon did not know whether to stand still, or to run, to attack, or to raise his arms in defence. He only knew that he was looking at a form of horror, an indelible image, that once seen would not depart the imagination lightly. He had not been in that school on Maguire Street, like poor Evie, bombed in the middle of the day, full of children. Their parents had tried to protect them from the worst of it, but they could tell by her face, her fear, her bewilderment. She couldn't even speak for several weeks after. Even Larry had seen things, foraging in the rubble for treasure, that he would not tell his own brother about. For Simon, it had felt more like an adventure. The siren in the middle of the night, the charge for cover to the shelter, the nocturnal score of ack-ack guns punctuated

by distant explosions. He had never been hurt, never been hit, only once showered by plaster dust from a crack in the ceiling.

The war had often felt like an exciting story happening to someone else.

He now knew that awful things could be real.

Before him, reeking all fetid and rotten, stood a giant of a man, yet it was not wholly a man. A monstrous kind of a goat, in flowing scarlet robes, with huge curling horns, a swishing tail and hands that were part hoof, part claw. In one such claw he clutched a mirror, a simple round disc. It was unlike any mirror Simon had seen before, because even from a distance he could see it was not made of glass. This mirror was made of some kind of black stone. Deep, shining, glossy, impenetrable black – and yet it reflected his own perspiring and frightened face back to him.

'Please,' Simon whispered, more in hope than anything else, his mouth so dry he could hardly speak. 'Where is the magician?'

'Gone!' the creature snapped, showing his teeth. He held up the black mirror in triumph, like a shield. Now, Simon no longer saw his face, or the many candles burning around them. He saw another picture entirely, something not in the room. The Hastings family did not own a television set but he had seen one in a shop window, a crowd peering around to watch. The screen was small, and the image flickered constantly, appearing to fluctuate between programmes.

This mirror had the same effect, never quite remaining one thing or the other. But through the jagged lines of interference, he could make out a person. A figure they had seen hanging on the walls at Barfield, the pale, high-cheeked man with a widow's peak and a beard, wearing a ruff and a scholar's gown. He sat at a desk, somewhere gloomy – then the monster turned the mirror away.

There was no mistaking who it had been, though. Nicholas Crowne.

The lost magician. The Librarian of Folio.

'What have you done with him?'

'Banished him to some dejected corner of this world, where he will remain, as long as I rule.'

'But who are you?'

'The one who knows nothing. And proud of it. The King of the Never Reads!'

Simon was still blinded by the halo of light that flared out from behind the King, and he cowered. His lips felt stuck together, but somehow he found the power of speech.

'Who are the Never Reads?'

He could sense the answer coming, and already wanted it to be different. Whatever his struggles, he was not . . . this horror. He wasn't, and never would be.

The King studied the magician trapped inside his mirror for a moment, and then appeared to swipe the picture away with his hoof. 'The Land of the Never Reads is filled by what happens when people never *read*. That is my kingdom.' Even from his great height, the King could clearly sense Simon's bewilderment. 'Let me show you,' he said, and tapped the mirror.

At once, a mighty draught blew in, slamming the door behind Simon and making him jump. The candles shivered and went out, with a little sigh. In the darkness, the King held up the black disc, and a story began to unfold upon it. It was like being back at the pictures, though no one was smoking, or shouting, or throwing things as they often did when he went at home.

'Your kind have always sought knowledge as a means to power.'

The film, if that's what it was, played out very quickly. Simon watched moving pictures that were quite unlike anything he had seen in a cinema. There was a man and a woman, naked, in a garden. Then a snake, and an apple tree. The woman took a bite from an apple.

'I know that story!' said Simon.

'One of the first, and one of the oldest,' said the King. 'Not long after, mankind had so many stories they began to write them down and store them. Not just stories, but records too.'

Now Simon gazed on pictures of scribes carving letters in clay tablets, using the funny kind of stick letters he had seen in the Librarian's cave. The scribes were wearing more clothes than Adam and Eve but not much. They piled the tablets up in rows in a large room. The picture moved on, and now the tablets had been replaced by scrolls, and the scribes were wearing even more clothes, and the building looked very grand, like a museum. Then the scrolls became sheaves of paper bound together, and books, and there were scribes and monks poring over them in dark libraries of wood. As time sped on, there were more and more scrolls, sheaves and books, and some of them looked so precious that they were chained to the desk.

'A library was a store of knowledge for man, with which he slowly conquered the world around him. A library was a source of power. Destroy it, and you destroy his power.'

Simon recoiled as the mirror seemed to explode in flame,

and he watched a grand and elaborate ancient building burn to the ground. Another library, he assumed. People tried to carry the contents out, but the flames licked after them, and they burned too.

'Without your precious books, your knowledge, you are just beasts fit for the bonfire,' said the King. 'One man saw this power and tried to take it all for himself.'

The fire disappeared as the glass started to show pictures of Crowne building his collection.

There was a real room, in the roof space of Barfield, exactly where Larry had discovered the door. There were chandeliers full of candles, and shelf after shelf of books. Messengers on horseback delivered more books, and some arrived in crates by cart. Crowne read them all, feverishly turning pages, sitting by windows, using every hour of light that the day gave to read.

'The first Librarian of this Library sat down to own and read every book ever written in his own time.'

As Crowne set about his task, his hair grew longer and unkempt. His beard and nails were left untrimmed. Barfield looked more and more dilapidated, with broken windows, missing chunks of thatch in the roof, weeds rocketing up in the yard. Crowne grew pale and hunched, turning the same colour as the milky pages that he was buried in.

266

'Why?' said Simon.

The King waved a hoof, and the picture disappeared. The candles woozily spluttered back into life. Simon ran a finger around his collar, as the temperature once more rose to furnace-like levels. Then it was just the two of them, Simon sprawled on the floor, the King of the Never Reads standing tall above him.

'He wanted to understand magic.'

'You mean . . . the magic which made Folio?'

'Yes. In this case, the most powerful, most coveted, and most dangerous magic in the entire universe.'

Simon hadn't believed that any kind of magic was real, but this adventure was forcing him to think again. 'What kind of magic is that?'

The King shook his shaggy beast of a head, the horns quite golden in the candlelight. 'You still don't know? After everything!'

Simon felt like such a little boy, in front of the headmaster. He had been hauled in front of some scary headmasters, but none quite as scary as this Beelzebub.

'No, I don't,' he said in a small voice.

'The magic of reading. The magic that allows you to be here in the first place.'

Simon remembered Larry opening the book of fairy

tales, the blinding flash of light . . .

'But why do you care? I thought you were the King of the Never Reads?'

'Every magic has a weakness, no matter how strong its spell. Every magician has a nemesis, no matter how powerful he is. And Reader Simon, Nicholas Crowne, Reads *and* Unreads, I am your nemesis. For I thrive on a world where people *never* read . . . Their weakness gives me power.'

'Why would people want to never read?' said Simon. It wasn't like *he* didn't want to read. Far from it. It was just so difficult to make the words behave sometimes. That didn't stop him from enjoying stories, or discovering things.

'So they can be free from the chains of knowledge! Look!'

The King gave his most wolfish, frightening smile, and flung his hooves open wide. And he began to laugh. At first, Simon smiled too, thinking maybe it had all been a joke. But the King of the Never Reads continued to laugh in great echoing peals, throwing his horned, goaty head back.

Simon stopped smiling.

The laughter continued, and now it was so menacing and violent that Simon put his hands over his ears. The

King's body was convulsing, his jaw shaking so much it almost seemed to detach from his head, and Simon could not tear his eyes away from the endless darkness of his gullet, his hooves trembling with ecstasy. It became too disturbing to watch, and with great effort Simon shifted his gaze to the candles all around, in their saucers, in their candlesticks, sconces, lanterns and pots. One by one, as the demonic laughter cascaded through the air, they transformed.

No longer were they bright, burning lights in the darkness.

They became creatures. Pale-eyed, skeletal ghouls. One by one, the unhappy subjects of the goat King revealed themselves, and, turning their baleful gaze upon Simon, began to laugh too. A joyless, mirthless cackle. They were saying words too, and Simon tried to work out what they were. Yet the more he listened, the less sense they made, until he realised they were not even words, at least none that he recognised. It was all just noise – terrifying and yet quite without meaning.

A babbling, shapeless noise that filled the room in clouds of nonsense, like a poisonous gas, sucking the air out of the room. He found it harder and harder to breathe, clawing at his neck, his chest squeezing . . .

Simon gasped for air, resolving that he would find a way, he would not be defeated by these ghouls, or by words, ever again. First, though, he had to escape. As he felt the skin blister on his back, and his hair scorch, he scooped up his bag and managed to feel his way to the door through the heat and the haze and ran as fast as he could down the crooked stairs.

There was a noise behind him, and he jerked his head around to see the tower exploding in the air around him. Fragments of stone and shards of wood were smashed aside by the monstrosity that now rapidly bloomed from the ruins of the building. The King of the Never Reads had swelled in size, a colossal god of darkness, rolling after Simon in black, horned clouds. The demon goat bestrode the wreckage, and flung his ragged arms out wide as Simon tumbled to the ground.

'You cannot escape me! The magician himself could not and neither will you!' he roared, and as he twisted his hoof-claws towards the boy, the land began to rise up beneath them, dragged up by some invisible, irresistible magnetic force. 'Ignorance is a bottomless pit! Sooner or later it will suck you in!'

'No! Help!' screamed Simon hoarsely, even though he knew no one could hear.

'Take me to your siblings! Take me to your precious battle. For that is where I will thrive. While the Unreads and the Reads are locked in self-destruction, the Never Reads will triumph and rise. Not just in this world, but in yours too.'

Then there was a strange riffling noise in the air. A noise he had heard in Barfield, by the painting, and in the Library. He had heard it in the crags as Patricia and he approached the Never Reads, and inside the tower. But now it was so loud, deafening him, like a vast iron fan in some steaming factory, the size of a whole wall, stirring the air, making it turn faster and faster around him . . .

Everything began to shake – the air itself, rising up and down in heavy liquid blankets, the rocks and dead trees of Folio's horizon fracturing into different planes, vibrating with the force and energy of a combustion engine.

Simon looked down at his fingers, his feet—

Shimmering, beginning to tremble and disappear before his very eyes.

In his ears, laughter, echoing so loudly he could not think.

And – suddenly – an explosion of light, then the darkness of nothing.

CHAPTER 24

Better Magic Still

On the Plain of Meaning, it had started to rain.

'Where are we going now?' asked Evie, as Jana pushed her down the hillside towards the battlefield, the robot's still warm arm stump pressing in between her shoulder blades. Even the once mighty Secretary was beginning to stumble, her glass body twitching, her head jerking from side to side in a way which she appeared unable to control. The cries of those left fighting were faint and far apart. Otherwise, the scene was eerily quiet, punctuated by the odd flutter of paper or robotic whirr.

'I told you, Reader, to finish the task. We have defeated the Reads, now we must completely cleanse our world of the old stories. No more made-up nonsense, just the facts.'

Evie muttered something under her breath.

The Secretary jabbed her. 'What was that, dear Reader?'

'It looks like they have defeated a lot of you as well.'

'Robots are replaceable.'

'Including you?'

'You are very rude for a girl your age. You ask too many questions.'

Everyone always said this to Evie, and, in a curious way, it made her feel happier and safer. She knew where she stood now. Jana had just revealed herself as no more perfect than so many grown-ups, parents and teachers. She didn't have an answer. The Empress of Information didn't have an answer to her simple question. Perhaps there wasn't an answer to everything?

'What are you going to make me do?'

But before Jana could reply, they stopped, both looking out over the battlefield.

The faint cries had become more urgent, sharper. They were now shouts, loud and insistent, aimed in their direction. Three figures clambering over the piles of the injured and destroyed, leaping in strides towards them. Two larger, and a smaller one.

Bears.

Even though they had not parted on the best possible terms, or, in fact, no terms at all, Evie was pleased to see them. She started to yell and scream as Jana grabbed her wrists and held her tight.

'What are you doing, child? Are you trying to get us both killed?'

Evie kicked and struggled. 'Let go of me! Let go!'

Father Bear's muzzle was scorched by number rays. Mother Bear's fur was ripped and bloodstained. Even Baby Bear seemed to have lost his customary bounce. They lurched towards them on all fours, till they reached the foot of the hill. As they drew closer, the other surviving soldiers of the Reads limped into line behind the Bears. Evie searched in vain for a small boy on a unicorn, but there was no sign.

She looked at her former hosts as they drew close, expecting them to spring to her rescue, or to lob a honey pot at the Secretary. But as Evie kicked and beat her fists uselessly against the robot leader, a feeling of dread flowed through her veins. For she was looking again at the Bears as they faced her a few feet away.

Their eyes were hard, their features set, their expressions grim.

There was not one flicker of friendliness or recognition.

And, at last, Evie understood.

They were not here to rescue her.

Then before she could speak, Jana clamped a glass hand over her mouth and addressed the Bears.

'Fairy-tale characters. The war is over. Surrender now and I shall release your Reader friend. Then we shall make peace on favourable terms.'

Evie dropped her head in despair. Before she had merely feared it, now she *knew* her outlook was hopeless. Father Bear snarled his lip up to reveal some dripping teeth.

'She is not our friend,' he growled.

Mother Bear stared at Evie so hard that she had to look away. 'We saved you from these robots once before. We took you in and fed you. And you left without so much as a thank you or goodbye. Where did you go, Reader?'

'She came straight to me!' cackled Jana. 'She told me *everything*. Naturally, I immediately sent a squadron of Silver Soldiers to destroy your house. Thanks to this brave little girl, your squalid little fairy tale is at last coming to an end, Bears.'

'No!' Bears don't swear, but Father Bear sounded like he just had. 'We wait for the other children. Only the Readers can rule. There were four. They cannot all be lost.'

For a moment Jana was silenced. Then, slowly, she removed her hand from Evie's mouth, who began to breathe easier. The Secretary's glowing eyes and chattering lips seemed to soften, and for a moment they almost appeared kind.

'Yes! A reader will rule. Reader Evie. You remain as loyal a servant as you ever were. We stand and fight. Then I shall make you Secretary of all of Folio – Reader and Ruler supreme!'

Now, on the plain ahead, silver limbs and heads rose up jerkily from the smouldering carnage. The Silver Soldiers remaining on the field still outnumbered the Reads.

There was only one way to decide, Evie realised. She had to ask the Bears one question. She *had to*. 'If your story is so perfect, then tell me, what really happened to Goldilocks? Why was her dress on your bed?'

Father Bear stood his ground.

'Like many stories, it is more complicated than you think.'

Clanking, a troop of battered robots now dragged themselves into a pincer position, surrounding the remains of the Read army.

'I knew it!' said Jana. 'Never trust a story. They are worse than lies! Silver Soldiers, prepare to fire.'

One by one, shining arms raised in the Bears' direction.

Mother Bear looked down, fussing for a moment with some briars tangled up in her fur. When she looked up again, her eyes were wet. 'Goldilocks didn't know it was a bears' house she had wandered into. We came home . . . and we scared her.'

Evie remembered the first time she had met the Bears, their sharp claws and sour breath.

'So she panicked, and tried to jump out of the window. But she was clumsy – she'd already managed to break one of our chairs – and as she threw herself out, she banged her head on the low windowsill beam in the rush. We couldn't get her to wake up again. No matter how hard we tried.'

Evie looked up. She thought about all the times she had tripped and fallen over in a hurry to get somewhere. Or to get out of somewhere, like a burning school.

'I kept the dress, because I wanted something to remember her by,' Mother Bear said slowly. 'It was our fault. We scared her. She was only a little girl . . . I'm so sorry, please forgive me . . .' She turned to Father Bear, who put a reassuring paw around her as she shuddered with sobs into his chest.

Evie had been told a lot of stories during the last few years. She had been told why people dropped bombs, and why it was all right for us to do it, but not for others. She had been told people were alive, when they were in fact dead. She had been told the war would be over by Christmas, then by next Christmas, and on and on. Evie knew when people were lying and when they were telling the truth, because she had learned the hard way.

'What are you going to do to the Bears?' she asked Jana.

'Send them back where they came from, of course. Then we can begin to build a better world.'

Evie shook her head. She knew now this wasn't the answer. 'No. Because my better world still has the Three Bears in it.'

'Sorry, little girl,' said Jana. 'This isn't your world. I know all that there is to know. Every piece of information in the world is stored on my internal computer, from the temperature of your hand to that of the sun in the sky. I know everything. That puts me in charge.'

'But you don't *know* me,' said Evie. 'You may know what my temperature is, or my height or my weight, but you know nothing about me. The real me, inside my head.'

'You are a little girl way out of her depth, who has served a useful purpose. What else do I need to know?'

Jana's graceful swanlike neck curved this way and that, her mouth chattering. The sun emerged from behind the storm clouds, shining straight through the rain, through her glass body, and for a moment she was quite transparent.

Evie was transfixed by her sinews and muscles of many coloured wires, all twisted tight together. She understood, now, what Thumb had been talking about.

The price of things. The price of power, the price of betrayal, the price of survival.

She had betrayed the Bears, her brothers and sister, and – worst of all, she felt – she had betrayed herself. This robot no more wanted a better world than Evie wanted another war. Jana may have known everything, but she believed and cared for nothing other than herself. Evie looked out across the horizon, through the driving rain and brooding clouds, and stiffened at what she saw there.

The most extraordinary silhouette, striding towards them.

Almost impossible to describe, she had never seen anything like it before.

Then she realised.

And, like blood returning to warm frozen hands, she felt a new feeling flow through her, under the skin.

'What else do you need to know?' Evie repeated the Secretary's question back to her. 'Well, firstly, that you are wrong about me. I am not just a little girl. My name is Evie Hastings. I want to change the world, but for *everyone*. And, more importantly, I have an incredible sister who is going to change it with me.'

Jana cocked her head in confusion, and then recoiled, flinging Evie to the ground, as the Green Man, bearing Patricia aloft in his twiggy crow's nest of a fist, strode right between the two armies.

He kicked a dragon out of the way, who rolled on to its side, spluttering fire in fury. Three Silver Soldiers tried to clamber up his other rooted foot, but he shook them off as easily as if they were ants. Unfurling a veiny arm, he pursed his lips and blew a ball of lime-green phosphorescence into the pouring sky, where it exploded into a thousand emerald stars.

'You warring armies!' he cried in his reedy voice. 'Reads *and* Unreads! I am the guardian of Folio, carved of the same ancient wood as the Library itself, one of the oldest stories amongst you, sent here by the Librarian to protect his work. I am constrained by his magic. I cannot fight for you. I will do my best to protect you from what is coming. But first you must look.'

As the stars slowly sank over the battlefield, they lit it up like flares, and both armies could see that they were no longer alone. Patricia and the Green Man brought with them a third army, and the rules of the game had changed in an instant.

Rank after rank of ghostly figures hovered silently over the mounds of busted robots and pages. They were translucent, and shimmered, hard to see in the driving rain, but gained sides and angles from the Green Man's fireballs. All the characters destroyed by the Unreads were there, from the pixies to Tom Thumb himself, looking more made of cobwebs than ever, hovering on a spectral Majesty.

To Evie's surprise, marching alongside the phantom Thumb, there were also ghostly Silver Soldiers, drifting over the ground, led by the phantom of Captain MAG-R1, still missing body parts after the crash of the Statecraft.

Of course. When the Unreads were defeated on the battlefield, they were sent to the Forgotten Forest too.

A whole army's worth. The Forgotten army.

Or History. Or We Have Been Here Before, Evie thought, her heart gladdening at the sight of the spooky legion. Not so much reinforcements, perhaps, as a warning. Forces to learn from rather than be reckoned with. The losses of the past ranged out across the muddy furrows, as immovable as a thousand grey headstones on a Flanders field.

Perhaps, she realised, you couldn't kill stories or facts.

They just faded out of sight for a while. But they were always there, shadows lengthening under the trees in the forest, waiting for the light to find them again.

Patricia stood tall in the Green Man's broad palm. Her wet hair was plastered across her face by the wind, full of twigs and leaves, and her cracked glasses perched lopsided over her nose. *Truly*, Evie thought, *I have never ever seen my sister looking so handsome.*

Then her handsome sister spoke, and everyone was listening to the war-torn girl standing in the walking tree. The different armies all listened, because the ghosts were following her, and both Read and Unread alike wanted to know what their intentions were.

'I know you want to fight, and that you both want to win, but please . . . hear me out. The Librarian is still missing.' The Bears sighed, their shoulders sinking.

'But we found what looks like his cave—'

At this angry shouting broke out, from all sides.

'You found the Librarian's cave? Where? Did you find the Librarian?'

'Patti? What happened to Simon? Where is he?'

Jana spluttered with disbelief. 'The Librarian does not exist! You are making this up!'

Patricia silenced them all with a wave of her hand. 'Oh he exists all right, but is still lost . . . for now. And I think I know why. It still scares me, very much, when I see you still fighting because that wasn't what the Librarian created Folio for. There's still so much we don't know about his plan.'

'We know everything,' sneered Jana.

'There's still so much we *don't* know,' Patricia repeated. 'Where the Librarian is remains a mystery. But I do know what he discovered.'

The sky was clearing now, the rain clouds brushed away by scudding white airy fleeces, and a cold wind blew through the grass. What smoke remained from the fire of the spaceship wreck was drifting to nothing, the last of the smouldering piles burning itself out. Patricia could feel machine and story character alike yearning for answers, but, most of all, she could feel Evie watching and waiting. She strongly felt the presence of Larry too, wherever he was . . . and Simon. They could have been on the edge of a battlefield; they could have been waiting for a bus in the rain or sitting by the hearth at home.

It was them who mattered the most. Humans. Her humans.

'The Librarian put you all – Unreads and Reads – in Folio, to work and live together. Facts may be the true answers to so many questions, but without stories to make us care about those answers, they have no power. And he discovered that the one we should all fear most is the one who knows nothing.'

'Who's that?' said Evie.

Before Patricia could reply, there was a sound in the air that made every soul put their hands or paws to their ears, clutching their heads in agony. It was riffling, as if a fan had been turned on. The noise the children had all heard in the Library before, only now the sound was not just mysterious, but epic. How, perhaps, the earth might sound when it cracked apart in an earthquake, or the aftershock of the biggest bomb ever invented.

'I think,' said Patricia, rolling up her sleeves, 'we are about to find out.'

CHAPTER 25
The Power of Nothing

They did not have to wait long. Steering his cloud of darkness like a vast dreadnought, the King ploughed through their first line of defence – the army of Forgotten stories – so smoothly that he hardly seemed aware of their existence in the first place. The ghostly figures were trampled underfoot before they even had time to mount an attack.

Evie wanted to close her eyes, but knew she had to face whatever was coming. She hoped that it was not her imagination making her see a phantom Tom Thumb spirit out of the way just in time, floating up into the sky on a shimmering Majesty. Scrambling for safety, she ran to the Green Man, where Patricia helped haul her into his curled palm. Perhaps one giant would protect them against another.

But with a single roar of rotten breath, the King extinguished the glowing fireballs of the Green Man, and rolled on, his shadow now long enough to cast the children into shade.

'Army of the Reads! On my command – close ranks!' Father Bear bounded up and down the line of his forces, barking orders. 'One! Two! Re-ady!' he shouted.

Feet stamped, shields locked, spears shook. The story characters exchanged nervous glances behind their helmets as the titanic monster rumbled ever nearer. In his filthy wake, the pallid ghouls Simon had seen at the tower shrieked and jabbered, spilling out of the King's folds, baring crooked fangs and flexing sharp talons. As they drew closer, they leaped down on to the battlefield with war cries of naked rage, swinging scythes and axes around their heads, charging for the Reads.

'Hold your line,' urged Father Bear, trying to keep his voice steady.

Baby Bear cowered behind him, clutching at his legs.

The Green Man took two steps back. Patricia and Evie tried not to flinch as they felt his woody grip tighten around them. Even from the great height of their position, they could feel the ground tremble down below. They watched the dragons lower their necks, tails flicking, as they prepared to breathe fire. And the ogres, male and female, swinging their clubs nervously from massive hand to massive hand, hunkering down, ready for the onslaught. Princes and princesses drew their finely wrought swords, glinting in the sun, beads of sweat forming across their brows.

But no giant, or dragon or creature alive in the Library was ready for the onslaught of the Never Reads. There was simply an ever-growing mass of hate approaching, blotting out the light.

Evie jumped at a piercing shriek from a ghoul—

Then came a belch of full-bellied laughter and a bone-shattering crunch as the King smashed into the Army of the Reads. Her sister clutched her hand tighter, both of them trying not to watch as an ogre came crashing to the ground just yards away, her club disintegrating in an explosion of dust.

There was so much chaos and confusion, it was hard to know where to look. Hordes of screeching Never Reads ripped their way through a glittering host of fairy-tale characters with psychopathic glee. The Green Man stepped further and further behind the front line, faster and faster until his walk almost became a run. Patricia tried to spy where the Bears had got to, but they were lost in a haze of dragon smoke and clouds of dust.

Next, Jana and the Silver Soldiers of the Unreads stepped forward to take on the invaders. For a moment, they seemed more disciplined than the stories, moving seamlessly in shining formation. The robots were incapable of feeling or showing fear as the rabble surged towards them.

But as they trained the full force of their number beams on the impending apocalypse, rather than blasting the King and his forces, the fiery rays were sucked into the dark morass of his folds, followed by the soldiers themselves. Powerless to resist, one by one the soldiers of truth hurtled rocket-like through the air, which was already swirling with flying foliage and earth, disappearing into the irresistible black hole of the King's cloak.

Floored, Jana struggled upright. The number stream beneath her skin looked on fire, flashing with rage. Her once mighty silver robots crawled around at her feet, others lying in jagged pieces, their wires still twitching.

'You cannot exist,' she stuttered, raising her smouldering arm at the King. 'You defy logic and reason. You will destroy everything.'

'Yes, I will!' said the King, and, with a gargantuan hoof, crushed her into a disc the size of a dustbin lid, which fizzed and spun for a moment before disintegrating into a small mound of metallic dust. The pile lay on the ground for a moment, before a gust of wind tossed it into the air, and the Secretary of the Unreads – or what remained of her – was scattered in the air, nothing more than millions of pulverised atoms. As the storm winds spread them far and wide across Folio, for the briefest of nanoseconds she had dominion over the land she once sought to conquer, and then she was nothing.

That was it. She had been killed just like that. There was no negotiation, no second chance, no final battle. This incredible robot, with all her knowledge, technology and power, had been obliterated in a single second, quicker even than the electric currents which once powered her.

Evie stumbled, clutching her sister's hand. Jana hadn't just been forgotten, but completely erased. That was new. The Secretary had been a warmongering tyrant, but deep down, Evie knew that she had not deserved this end.

Two wrongs did not make a right.

'Patti,' she whispered. 'When is it all right for me to say that I'm frightened?'

'Now,' said Patricia, bracing herself. 'Now would definitely be a good time.'

* * *

Trapped high above the clouds, Larry was clutching Grey Bear tight as the unicorn listlessly circled around and around. They were all drenched by the rain, although Grey Bear wasn't shivering as much as Larry. Roderick's flanks and wings were matted, heavy and dense with moisture.

Larry couldn't remember the last time either of them had spoken.

He wanted to land, and help his sisters down below, and find his brother, wherever he now was.

Roderick refused to, uncertain of what his story had in store for him.

Grey Bear had not been able to say anything (at all) that might have broken the deadlock, and so the unicorn had executed every other possible aeronautical manoeuvre apart from landing. He had dived, very fast, towards the trees and battlefield below. Then just before his hooves could graze the tree tops, he would soar up again, flapping his magnificent wings with such strength and ease that it was very hard to tell he had only taken up flying that morning.

As Larry grabbed on to his mane for dear life, and tried not to scream, Roderick did figures of eight, loop the loop, death spirals – moves that would have given even the bravest fighter pilot in the Battle of Britain cause for respect. Larry had to gulp ice cold air when he could to keep breathing, and after a while, his head began to spin, sparks flying in his eyes.

The horrid monster beneath them, whatever it was, was destroying everything. Larry had watched through closed fingers as it laid waste to the wonderful world of Folio. The magic world through the Library door was crumbling right in front of him and there was nothing he could do to stop it. And if it destroyed Folio, then what would happen to him and Evie, and Patricia, and Simon?

He felt sick. He couldn't think. Dizziness rang in his ears, and he clutched at the unicorn's mane to stop himself sliding off.

There was only one person who could save them, and save Folio.

Unfortunately that person was miles above the action, flying around and around on a grumpy unicorn that couldn't land. Larry felt sick because he wasn't sure he could be that hero. He would never be as brave as his father, with a strip of medals as long as his arm. He was going to spend the rest of his short life on a rainbow unicorn, until the monster ate them or Roderick finally ran out of energy, plummeting to the earth. And there did not appear to be a parachute of any kind on board.

Larry's head sank, his shoulders drooped, and a tiny,

ghostly fairy rose up from the clouds below, floating into view.

A fairy riding a butterfly.

'Mr Thumb,' said Larry, trying not to let his voice crack.

The fairy bowed his transparent, phantom head.

'You're a ghost. Are you dead? Am I dead too?'

Majesty fluttered and drew up alongside Roderick, close enough for Thumb to whisper in his ear. His voice was different to before, echoing and distant, like someone speaking faintly from the bottom of a well.

'You will be if you don't do something.'

Larry was so tight and tense, he could barely speak. 'But what, though?'

Thumb was buffeted by a storm gust, briefly knocking him adrift, but he slowly glided back. 'Do you remember what I gave you?'

Larry fumbled in his pocket, and pulled out the ring, laying it flat in his palm. The polished wood was grubby, but as they watched, the soft rain slowly rinsed the grime away.

'I'm sorry,' said Larry. 'I promised I would help you. I've failed, haven't I?'

The fairy knight drew in closer. 'Not yet,' he said softly.

'What it does it say on the inside, there?'

Larry shook his head, and mumbled. *'If you can imagine it, it must exist. Somewhere.* But that's not true. I never imagined any of this, and now Roderick can't land, because no one finished imagining him either.'

'I can hear you both, you know,' snapped Roderick. 'Not all unicorns are deaf, actually!'

'Is that really true, though, Larry?' said Thumb.

Screams and explosions rang out from below. A sickly burning stench filled the air.

Larry blinked. He began to remember something, an image . . .

'What was the last thing you imagined? Before you came to Folio?' Thumb was insistent, urging him on.

'I can't remember! It was so long ago. The end of term.'

'And what were you doing at the end of term?'

Larry squeezed Grey Bear so tight he thought his arms might fly off. 'I don't know . . . a sports day . . . there was a prize-giving . . . I can't really remember!'

Beneath him, Roderick had stopped flying. His head drooped and his wings folded against his sides. 'I am so terribly tired,' he said.

Then it began. They started falling, spiralling down through the clouds.

Larry looked at Thumb, floating down alongside them. He clenched the ring tight in his hand, even as they fell.

'I remember!' he said, with a little gasp.

Thumb grabbed his wrist. 'Go on!'

'I was writing a story,' Larry said, glancing at the tumbling rainbow unicorn, and now remembering exactly why Roderick had seemed so familiar. 'About a unicorn. But I . . . never finished it. I never had the time.'

'Well there you go,' yelled Thumb, through the roaring air. 'No time like the present!'

On the Plain of Meaning, only the Green Man now stood between Larry's sisters and total annihilation.

'Can't you do something?' Patrica begged him.

'I am only a guardian! I can defend, but not attack.'

With that, the tree god blew another ball of emerald fire into the air, which showered seeds into the earth at his feet. The seeds sprung into saplings, which swelled into trunks, forming a towering stockade around him and the children.

But the reprieve was momentary, as a black-clawed foot came splintering through the newgrown fence, followed by a hoof-claw hand and a pair of red, demonic eyes, glittering with laughter. More wood was rent apart, and in the monster's other hand, raised high in the sky, she saw a flash of something she recognised.

'Patti!' called down a voice. 'Get away from here!'

'Simon!' she cried.

Her brother hung limp in the demon King's hairy fist, his hair streaked with blood, his face swollen, one eye bruised shut. But in the other eye there was still a glimmer of defiance. He pushed feebly at the talons clutching him, yet still they held tight.

Patricia and Evie desperately searched around for help or reinforcements, where minutes ago there had been not just one but three armies, allied together. Now there was only dusty chaos and bodies and moans. Sparks danced in the air. A riderless horse juddered past them, braying, before being dragged to the ground by jabbering Never Reads, disappearing under the mob with a sickening whinny.

At last, the King of the Never Reads loomed above the sisters in all his horror. Any attempt at maintaining a recognisable human form had been discarded, and the two girls found themselves staring up at a colossal blackened goat skull with blood-red eyes that blocked out the sun, reduced to a thin corona behind his twisting horns. Jaws dripping with venom, he leered down at the two children hiding in the branches of the tree. Globules of saliva fell on the leaves, shrivelling them like acid.

His voice was so loud and reverberant, it made their ears sing with pain.

'Don't worry. I'm not going to harm your precious guardian. I can't.'

With a single claw, he tapped the Green Man's trunk, which bubbled and blistered, but neither creature moved their ground.

'The one who knows nothing,' Patricia said, reeling from the stink of his breath. 'What do you want?'

'Nothing!' he said. 'Nothing you can ever give me. I am just not interested.'

She nodded. 'Yes. Your total lack of curiosity is the most objectionable thing about you.'

The red eyes squinted at her, not comprehending.

'It is of no matter. I shall destroy you, just as I have the others. And I shall start with your brother here.' He squeezed Simon, who cried out with pain. The King of the Never Reads smiled. 'Making you watch, of course. That's half the fun.'

Simon kicked and punched the demon's claws as best he could. He could barely breathe, but with every gasp he swore that – even if it was the last thing he ever did – he would destroy this monster.

All around her, Patricia could see, taste and hear the devastation he had wrought. She knew that the time she had to avert a similar fate for her and her siblings was so short as to be hardly worth counting. Her mind shook like a steam engine in full tilt, screaming, ready to explode. She found it almost impossible to speak, her voice trembling more than the leafy hair of the Green Man. Where was the knowledge that could save them now? What story could possibly comfort them at this final, unforgiving hour?

'Can't you save us . . . can't you do something? I thought everyone joining forces together would work. We're only children, you see.'

The Green Man shook his head sadly. 'His powers are too great for me. But remember: Readers Rule.'

'Well, it doesn't ruddy feel like it!' snapped Evie.

At this the King in the sky above roared, and millions of gabbling Never Reads scampered up the folds of his cloak, licking their lipless mouths as they gawped at the two girls like a pack of grinning hyenas. One jumped on to the tree, but the Green Man shook him off. Then another, who Evie kicked aside. And another, wrestling with Patricia till she kneed him in the belly and he tumbled off with a yelp.

Scrambling to her feet, she wiped some blood off her lip, which she had bitten into with fear.

'This isn't working, Evie. We're fighting, not ruling.'

Hanging limp in the King's fist high above their head, barely conscious, Simon muttered something. 'Patti . . . your gift . . .'

'We can't hear you!' said Evie.

'Your gift!' he cried out again, gasping for life. 'We were both given one. Use yours, Patti . . . and promise me . . .' His head sank again.

'What? Promise you what?' yelled Patricia.

'That you will tell father I was brave. That I tried—'

'Enough!' said the King of the Never Reads, and, opening his bottomless, cavernous mouth, raised the poor boy, head-first, towards his gaping jaws.

CHAPTER 26
Turning Over

'I'm sorry,' whispered Larry into Roderick's ear as they tumbled through the clouds, the air whistling past. 'I'm so sorry, Roderick.'

'Why?' whispered Roderick. He was trembling, but his wings were just beginning to flap. Thumb, with one final wave, was flung away by the force of the air as the boy and unicorn plummeted towards the ground.

'Because I just remembered how your story ends.' Larry tucked Grey Bear into his waistband, and grabbed Roderick's mane. His throat choked but he got the words out all the same. 'You help me become a hero.'

Roderick tensed, and his great white wings raised once more into the air. He shook his head and the gold pince-nez flew free into the clouds, far out of sight.

'What did you do that for?' said Larry.

'I don't need those any more, now, do I?' replied the unicorn grimly, and with a most un-unicorn-like roar he spread his great white wings wide for one last time, and dived towards the demon below.

Cowering in the Green Man's palm, barely able to breathe through the gritty haze of burning wood sparking around her, Evie watched through her hands in disbelief. As a rainbow unicorn, ridden by her little brother, waving his toy bear in the air like a knight might whirl a mace, flew straight into the King's left eye.

The beast howled with pain as black blood sprayed out of his eye socket in pulsing spurts, and, writhing, trying to yank the invaders free, he flung Simon free into the air.

For a split second, her brother hung in the sky, as if caught by an invisible hand, before dropping with sickening speed straight to the ground, landing with a dull thump. He lay where he fell, not stirring.

With one last extra flap of wings, now dripping with demon mucus, Roderick and Larry clumsily reversed out of the monster's eye and began to circle around his head. Half blinded, the King lashed after them as if he was trying to swat a buzzing fly. The pair looped and looped, but it was clear that the unicorn was losing power rapidly. Then a hoof-claw clipped his rear leg, and the boy and the unicorn came rocketing past the girls, Larry screaming as the pair ploughed into the thicket of trees at their rear. There was the sound of snapping branches, a muffled cry and then silence.

Patricia hardly noticed. One brother lying motionless on the ground, the other crashed in the trees behind her. She shut her emotions down and forced herself to focus. The war had taught her some useful tricks after all. In her mind, as she stared at the rampaging King, consumed with hatred and revenge, just three words played over and over again, a record jumping back to the same groove repeatedly. Simon's advice.

Use your gift.

Never taking her eyes off their enemy, her hand closed around a bundle of threads in her pocket, tied to a strip of card. She pulled it out and held it up by the card, the colourful threads catching the light. So lightweight – a nothing, it seemed.

The King stared at her and it, uncomprehendingly.

Patricia didn't care. She knew what it was now. She hadn't seen before, but now realised it was just a question of looking at things in a different way. It always had been.

In her hand was not just a useless strip of card, but a bookmark.

For keeping your place. For finding your place again.

For reminding you where you were, when all seems lost.

Darkness fell across her face.

'Now for you two,' said the King of the Never Reads, still roaring with obscene laughter despite the leaking hole in his eye. 'I have been waiting for this for such a long time. Readers rule? No one rules here but me! Oh, to see the look on that magician's face. I have destroyed his precious Folio for ever!'

He put his two claws together and raised them as one huge balled fist, the size of a battleship.

Patricia didn't look up, despite the colossal shadows descending on her head. She looked down at the bookmark in her hand. And saw now how old it was. The fine threads were frayed, the card stained and warped. Of course. It wasn't just any old bookmark that the Green Man had given her. This bookmark was hundreds of years old. It had been placed in every book in the Library, and – once upon a time – every book ever read.

It had touched the words of everything ever written. It had lain across all the knowledge, every story in the world.

The magician's bookmark.

Impossible. A thing of cloth and card. It could be torn apart in a second.

Could it be magic still? Could it be powerful?

She closed her eyes and held it up towards the monster of ignorance . . .

Such a flimsy thing.

But the threads began to flutter in the breeze. And as they fluttered, they miraculously grew, stretching into long ribbons . . .

'What is this foolery?' said the King, pausing for a moment as the ribbons unfurled rapidly into the air, wrapping themselves tight about his arms and claws. He tried to snap them, writhing with fury, but could not and instead, kicked out at the Green Man with a heavy hoof.

The ancient tree had withstood worse storms, but with a splintering groan, he reeled from the blow, tipping the girls out of his palm on to the exposed field.

'How long will the ribbons hold him?' shouted Evie to her sister. She scrambled to her feet just as a colossal hoof slammed down inches away, spraying clods of mud into the air with the force of an exploding shell.

'I don't know!' called back Patricia, as she too frantically sought cover.

'Should we run away?'

Patricia grabbed her sister's arm, hauling her to safety as another hoof thumped down, making the ground shudder. They spread their backs flat against the Green Man's battered trunk, cowering in terror.

For a moment, Patricia found herself quite incapable of speech.

Then she found her voice. It sounded very fragile compared to the King's bellows and savage blows. But it was her voice.

'Evelyn Hastings,' she said as quietly and calmly as she could. 'Our city was once bombed for fifty six days and nights in a row. Did we run away then?'

Evie's bottom lip trembled and she shook her head. 'So what do we do instead?'

The King gave a roar so shatteringly loud that a crack appeared in the Green Man's trunk, and the ribbons binding the demon's claws began to fray. A hoof plunged down again, this time missing the girls under the tree by a whisker. It was only a matter of time before their foe found his target.

And right that second, more than ever before, Patrica wished that she and Simon had found the magician, that the Librarian had returned after all.

As she wished this, the card part of the bookmark in her

hand, that the magician had once so carefully held, began to glow. It burned with an inner fire, yet it did not hurt. A fire that radiated out from the card in rippling waves of heat and light. The waves encircled the King, and all the children where they stood or lay, in a bright shimmering sphere.

For a moment, in that globe of fire, Patricia and Evie thought they saw a giant face, a bit like the face Evie sometimes saw in the moon. And although elements of the face perhaps seemed familiar from a painting in the Professor's study, it was somehow different at the same time. It was neither quite male or female, of any particular colour, nor old or young.

The face was not friendly or unfriendly, smiling or frowning.

But it was unmistakeably one thing.

Human.

'Are you . . . the magician?' Patricia dared to whisper. 'The Librarian?'

The huge head, translucent, glowing and filling the air, turned to her. The eyes closed, the lips parted, and the lost magician – oblivious to the furious cries of the demon king – blew upon them.

A gentle, warm breath, a soft wind, that felt as old as the woods and hills.

'Remember what you know,' said a voice in the wind.

The strangest thing was, that the more the breeze washed over the children, the more Patricia felt an urge to close her eyes. She found herself remembering where she had been and what she had done. So did Evie, who grabbed her free hand, standing close by. As did Larry, wrenching free from the two branches he was stuck between, dazed but very much still alive. Suddenly he remembered too. Along with Simon, rolling gingerly on to his back where he now lay, badly injured but breathing.

As the light from the Librarian's bookmark shone out over them, the children didn't think about the King of the Never Reads any more, or his ignorance and hatred, but instead, remembered everything they knew.

They thought of the stories they loved – of heroes fighting adversity with honour and courage. Tales of love, kindness and compassion. Legends, myths, folk tales, nursery rhymes, plays and novels scrolled through their minds, at a dizzying pace. Of course they had also learned about evil, greed, ignorance and selfishness, everything embodied by the monster now flailing above them. But there was always resilience, and goodness and decency too. Like stories and facts, those things never ever went away either, just sometimes disappeared further into the shade.

But most of all, they remembered who they were and what they had done. Evie, her eyelids shut and flickering, saw again with a blazing clarity that day on Maguire Street. Only this time she didn't just see the classroom above collapse in a downwards explosion of timber and masonry before her eyes, or the bodies she had to step over, but also, outstretched, the hand of her friend Lillian, in the gloom and clouds of dust, that she had clutched and hauled to shivering safety.

Patricia, feeling Evie's nails dig into her palm, remembered a miserable grey, wet excuse of a day in February. She had come into the kitchen and found her mother sobbing over the sink. It didn't matter what about, or what for. Her mother had apologised to her for crying, saying again and again as she wiped her eyes, 'I'm sorry, I'm so so sorry. I'm trying as hard as I can to be strong for you all, but sometimes, I just—'

She never finished the sentence, because Patricia had wrapped her thin arms around her mother's neck, and they had held each other as the rain slid down the window.

Larry thought about the conversation with his father again, about the bullies at school, who called him a pansy. His brave father, who had helped rescue all those people at Dunkirk. But when he got back home, he was going to tell his war hero father it didn't matter if he, Larry, was a pansy. He loved him, but what in fact did his father know about pansies, or even unicorns, for that matter?

Simon, wounded and exhausted, clutching his side, could not put reading out of his head. Of all the moments! So what, he couldn't read, not very easily at least. That was too bad. He found it hard. So hard, sometimes, that it hurt and made him feel ill, and made him hate everything to do with books and reading. Who wouldn't? But, groaning again with pain, rolling around in the shadow of this monster, he remembered through gritted teeth the other stories. The bulletins they had gathered around the wireless in silence to listen to every morning during the war, the rumours and gossip that swept around the school during the day, and the tales his mother had often made up for him at bedtime. Stories which were not in any book, but which were now his only comfort as he closed his eyes and tried to make the pain disappear.

But they chiefly, in this fantastical world, remembered the most powerful knowledge of all. That they were, each and every one, human beings, who loved each other, who would always have more in common than they didn't. Like the long summer they had just shared. Exploring Barfield, running from the soldiers, breakfast with the Bears – all their hopes, fears and dreams, as individual and peculiar as they were. As the children remembered all these things, good and bad, just as the Librarian had always intended, a new power began to take shape for the first time in Folio.

For as the King struggled under his bonds, something else began to rise out of the ground beneath his giant, stamping hooves.

Pushing through the green turf, rutted with mud and dust, oil and ink—

Soil crumbling from its top, breaking through all the piles of bodies and machines. The Green Man edged back towards the wood and the wreckage of the Statecraft as the land beneath his feet peeled away as easily as a layer of onion.

'No!' howled the King of Never Reads, trying to stamp the turf back down as if he was dancing on hot tin. But he could do nothing, powerless, as the Plain of Meaning tore up high into the sky.

It looked like an uprooted tree trunk, all roots and soil and worms.

Except this trunk kept on rising. A whole battlefield became a ramp, and then the prow of a battleship and, finally, a pointed steeple rising high, high into the sky.

As the ground raised up, the King and his army fell

over, sliding on to their backs, their legs in the air. Even the gargantuan demon looked foolish, tied and kicking.

At first, it was all the children could do not to laugh. The Never Reads, whimpering, began to scuttle back towards their home of darkness, ignoring the thunderous protestations of their leader as he lay writhing on his cloak, shrinking in size with every moment, until very soon nothing more remained of him than a tiny, miserable smear of mud.

The Hastings children gazed up at what they had imagined into being, that had cast all the carnage and monsters asunder. It was so glorious and blinding that they as one put their hands up over their eyes.

Far ahead of them, rippling like the finest cream as it covered the land, all the way to the mountains of the Never Reads, gorgeous and pure, was their everlasting gift to Folio. A sea of all their hopes, infinite with possibility, stretched out before them, both magnificent and terrifying – the place the magician's bookmark had returned them to. The beginning of every new and better story.

A single, endless, blank page.

CHAPTER 27
Another Adventure Begins

Now at last the great war in Folio between the Reads and the Unreads, that had lasted for so many years, was over. The storm clouds were swept away by a sharp new easterly wind, and the jagged peaks of the Never Reads – which had appeared so savage and cruel from the Bears' kitchen – now sparkled with freshly fallen snow.

Whatever, whoever, the face in the fire had in fact been, they were also blown away by the wind, without another word.

The two sisters turned to each other. Patricia, her hair matted with black grease and blood, her glasses cracked and her shirt hanging in ribbons. Evie, pale and bruised, but still in one piece. Clutching hands, they ran to Simon, who lay shivering on the edge of the blank page.

'Si!' Patricia fell to her knees and embraced him.

'Please don't do that – it hurts,' he managed to say, with the ghost of a smile. But his skin was ice cold, and blood bubbled at the corners of his lips. He seemed to be gazing into the clear sky beyond them, with a glassy stare.

'Please! Can't someone help us?' Evie called out, her words echoing across the virgin expanse of paper.

'You've had a bad fall,' said Patricia, because she knew Simon hated being lied to. 'But we'll do what we can.'

They scanned the new plain, desperately searching for someone who could help. All around them, the surviving members of the Forgotten army were reforming into story characters and robots, only somehow brighter and sharper than they had been before, on this dazzling white page.

A voice came over from a newly reformed group of story characters. 'Perhaps I might be able to help?'

Evie turned and saw the portly old gentleman she had spied from the Statecraft, along with his pipe-smoking friend in a deerstalker hat. At the time she had thought they looked like war correspondents. The older man, in a top hat and long coat, and carrying a distinctive black leather bag, broke off from his friend and walked towards her.

'Doctor John Watson,' he said, a smile cracking across his ruddy face as he doffed his top hat with a little bow.

He marched over the blank page, which was already beginning to fill up with new tracks and prints. 'What seems to be the problem?'

The girls explained, and as they did, the doctor listened and nodded. He laid his hand on Simon's brow, and put a stethoscope to his chest, and felt his pulse. Gently, expertly, he examined the boy, speaking softly to him all the while, and listening intently to what he said.

Then he stood up, and spoke to the girls.

'I'm afraid your brother is very gravely injured.'

'Can you do anything?'

'You have to help him!' They both spoke at once, over one another.

He shook his head. 'I'm afraid the damage he has sustained is quite out of the reach of my medical knowledge.'

'There must be something you can do,' said Patricia feverishly.

'I can alleviate his pain, I can see where the injuries are, but on my own, without nurses or the relevant instruments . . .' Doctor Watson shrugged. 'I'm so sorry.'

'Except you're not on your own,' said Evie.

'I don't understand,' said the doctor, frowning, but she was already racing across the page to a huddle of Silver Soldiers, reforming from the Forgotten army. As she approached, they turned and whirred, their immobile faces staring at her, number arms raised. But Evie simply smiled, and said, 'How would you like to use your knowledge to do some real good for a change?'

Which was how Simon became the first ever patient treated by the Silver Soldiers, followed shortly by Larry, Evie dragging more robots towards him, grabbing their heavy metal wrists and pulling them along so that they nearly tripped over each other. She was no longer afraid of them, though, neither Unreads or Reads, facts or stories.

She would never feel afraid of either of them ever again.

Larry lay slumped over Roderick, in a jagged mess of sheared branches and bristling leaves. Evie pointed to him.

'There,' she said. 'Perhaps at least something of what Jana learned in her experiments will be able to make him better too.'

She was right. For what the number rays could destroy, they could also heal. The gleaming robots bent over the two boys, at Doctor Watson's direction, gently touching them, while their arms glowed and pulsed. Patricia could not believe her eyes as colour returned to her brothers' faces, and they began to sit up, ignoring the doctor's commands. 'Do you think we'll ever be able to treat people the same way at home one day?' she asked Evie.

'I am sure of it,' her sister replied, with a gleam in her eye. 'Maybe not in our lifetime. But one day.'

Unfortunately, even the healing powers of the robots had their limits.

Roderick, the bravest unicorn who ever flew, died in active service helping defeat the King of the Unreads. His wounds were too severe for him to reform, but his ghost happily retreated to the Forgotten Forest, and immediately began to castigate the toadstools and weeds he found there for not taking a sufficient interest in geometry.

After watching the action unfold from the clouds, a certain tiny fairy knight decided it was safe enough to float back down to earth and reassume his place amongst the Reads.

'We ought to try you for treason,' growled Father Bear, towering over him, Mother Bear and Baby Bear still at his side, bloody but unbowed.

'And I ought to try you for manslaughter of an innocent young girl!' Thumb countered.

'You are all still stupid made-up stories!' muttered one of the Silver Soldiers tending to Simon. It stood up, and raised a gleaming arm, which began to glow. 'We ought to try you for war crimes to machines and facts.'

'We could say the same of you!'

The Bears dropped to all fours, growling, and Majesty reared in the air, Thumb brandishing his sword.

Then, calmly, Patricia stepped in between them all. She placed one hand on Father Bear's chest, and the other on the robot's. 'No more fighting. You're on the same side now.'

'But he is a traitor!'

'They are murderers!'

'Stories aren't real!'

'We are not asking you to change your stories, or make up information,' said Patricia. 'But you did say that one day Readers would rule.'

'Maybe. We didn't mean anything like this, though,' spluttered Father Bear. 'We wanted you to take charge, and pick a side!'

'Readers rule,' Evie reminded them. 'You all said it. That means you have to do what we say, surely?'

The Silver Soldier turned to the story characters. 'The children are right, Bear. Folio is their land now. They fought for it, and must make it theirs. That is the logical outcome. Readers rule.'

There was a pause, and much scratching of furry chins and bristling of fairy eyebrows, then, at last:

'Very well,' said the Bears and Thumb as one. 'Readers

316

rule. Command Folio for us.'

But the four Readers – Larry leaning on Evie for support, Grey Bear battered and bent, but still in his waistband, Simon, lying on the ground, Patricia standing beside him – all shook their heads.

'We can't stay here to boss you lot around,' said Patricia. 'We are Readers, but before we are Readers, we are something else.'

'Stupid children?' muttered Baby Bear.

Patricia laughed. 'Not just children . . . but human children. So, as humans and readers, we will leave you with a rule instead. A Readers' rule, for you all to live by.'

'A new rule for the Library,' said Larry weakly. 'You said there might be more, Mr Thumb, after all.'

'Very well,' snapped the fairy. 'What is it?'

Patricia glanced at her siblings as if for approval, but she did not require it. Somehow, they all knew at once exactly what was needed. Because it was now so obvious to each and every one of them.

'Well, your only rule so far is, "If you can imagine it, it exists somewhere."' Simon said quietly from the ground.

'Now here is another one.' Patricia drew a breath. 'From the Librarian himself. You must promise that you will always . . . remember what you know.'

317

Her words fell like fresh snow across the new page. And they brought with them a wintry hush, as every single Read and Unread stopped what they were doing, broke off their conversations, paused in their repairs or nursing of injuries and turned towards the four Readers.

At first, the inhabitants of Folio were as one, as never before. A perfect picture of outrage, disbelief and bewilderment. Then after what seemed like an eternity, slowly, quietly, Baby Bear repeated Patricia's words back to her, in a dreamy murmur. 'Remember what you know!' He nodded in the direction of the Silver Soldiers. 'Does that mean I need to know about them too?'

'Of course,' said Patricia, 'and they you.'

The little bear screwed up his face for moment, and then loudly declared, to everyone's relief, 'I like that!'

Father and Mother Bear repeated the words after him, followed by Thumb, then the Silver Soldier, and the murmur became a whisper, which became a ripple of conversation and recognition and laughter. Fairy-tale princes stood alongside computerised machines, and together, they raised their arms in the air, to give a resounding cheer.

'Remember what you know!'

Then, it was time to feast. As more and more stories and facts reformed, they worked together, building great banqueting tables, covering them with embroidered cloths, and laying them with gold plates, crystal glasses and silverware. The previously warring armies' camp kitchens were commandeered, to serve up platter after platter of the most delicious food the children had ever tasted.

The eating and drinking went on until sundown, accompanied by enchanted songbirds alongside dancing robots, and the laughter and cries of joy rose up into the summer afternoon sky so incessantly, it seemed they would never end.

'Well I never,' said Tom Thumb to Patricia, dabbing his lip for crumbs with the smallest white handkerchief in the world. 'Perhaps you do not need to stay here to rule us after all. But where will you go instead?' he asked.

Patricia looked out at the rolling green dales of the Land of the Reads. The sun shone brightly into her eyes, and she squinted.

'I think,' she said, 'we were sent here for another reason. For something even more important than ruling. To find a missing magician. Whom you call your Librarian.'

Far away, on a distant horizon, there was the faintest rumble of thunder.

Simon started uneasily in his seat, grabbing his side in pain. He had seen him. In the black mirror clutched by

319

the King of the Never Reads, he had seen the Magician. It had nearly cost him his life. Wincing, he staggered to his feet.

'Simon!' said Patricia in alarm, but grimacing he shook his head and looked directly at Thumb.

'Librarian. Magician. He exists. I saw him. His knowledge helped save us all. But if I have learned anything, it is that there is so much we still don't know.' He paused, catching his breath. 'We have to find the Magician. He helped us bring peace – perhaps he can help us do the same in our own world, too. For good, this time.'

'But do you truly believe you can find him?' said Thumb, looking away, twirling his neat hands. 'He's been gone for so long after all . . .'

'You know as well as I that full order will not be restored until he returns, fairy knight,' warned Father Bear.

'We also think he's the magician our Professor's looking for,' said Larry. 'And we think that's why she's in trouble. Why we ran into the Library in the first place, and how we ended up in Folio.'

'If we find him, then perhaps things will return to normal at home as well,' said Patricia, and she didn't know whether she was trying to convince herself or the others more.

Thumb looked grave. 'You know there are many, many other lands in Folio? And who knows what other worlds you can access through the Library? As you have discovered, not all of them are as friendly as this one . . . There are many we do not even know of. There may be even some that are twice as dangerous as . . .'

He cast an anxious glance towards the sharp peaks of the Never Reads, which for now remained serene against the evening sky.

'That sounds like our kind of adventure!' said Simon, with a wince of a grin.

'Shush,' said Patricia. 'There may even be some that are twice as wonderful, of course.'

'Quite, quite,' said Tom Thumb, who suddenly remembered how much he hated farewells. 'Well, don't let us detain you . . .'

And with that, the children got up from the table and made their excuses. There were hugs and embraces, none quite so deep or long as the one Larry gave the little knight, so much that the others feared he might crush the life out of him. Then the Hastings children were on their way once more.

'Until the Librarian returns!' cried Thumb, doffing his cap as he and Majesty began to soar back into the open sky.

'As he surely will!' replied the Bears, and the Silver Soliders, as they waved their Readers off for one last time, waving and waving, until they had quite disappeared from view over the horizon of the new page.

The four adventurers set off towards the setting sun as it slowly disappeared behind the trees, to continue their search for the lost magician.

Over time, they discovered stories they had never heard of before, stories of people and countries and ideas quite unlike any other they had ever encountered. But Patricia, Simon, Evie and Larry did their very best to navigate all the many lands of Folio with the same curiosity and excitement which had led Larry to open the Library door in the first place.

As for the Librarian – they followed so many clues, trails, rumours and false leads. But wherever the King of the Never Reads had dispatched him to, they could not find it, no matter how hard they tried. Yet the more they searched, they more determined they became to find the infamous magician. Their wandering lasted so long that everything they thought they knew – blackouts, Big Ben, bowler hats – began to feel further and further away, until it was quite hard to tell if any of that had ever been real or just a very vivid dream of another distant magical world.

One day, after so many journeys they could hardly tell any more which way was left, and which was right, the children found themselves in a dense and tangled forest. The canopy of leaves was so low and heavy that not much light could get through. Thick roots snaked about their feet as they edged their way along the winding path in the gloom.

'I know this sounds odd,' said Simon, who now had a scruffy beard, very much like an explorer from a picture book, 'but have we been here before?'

'It does feel familiar,' agreed Patricia, looking like a stronger and more golden version of her mother, as she unpicked brambles from her sleeve.

A low grey mist began to sweep around their ankles.

'I don't recognise it,' said Evie, peering around at the shadows, before getting out her notebook – which, incidentally, was what she now did wherever she went.

'Me neither,' said Larry, and the others still blinked at his deep voice and square jaw.

They were all silent for a moment. The mist got deeper and whiter, rising to their waists like a sea.

'Hang on,' said Simon to Larry, 'who the blazes are you?'

'I was going to ask you exactly the same question!' said Larry.

This was the moment Evie tripped. At first she thought it was another wretched root or thorny bush blocking her way, but bravely reaching her hand down into the wispy fog, she found herself clutching not a branch, but the leather spine of a book, half buried in the ground, covered with dead leaves, overgrown with roots. With some effort, she pulled it out and studied it, frowning. It was a very old thing, with leather covers, and crinkled pages, and some embossed writing on the front.

'*The Golden Fairy Tale Treasury,*' Simon read out over her shoulder, pronouncing each word slowly. Where had he heard them before?

'Hey!' said Larry, and then forgot why he had. For some reason, he wanted to yell, 'That's mine!', even though he knew it couldn't be, whatever it was.

The four children found a shaft of warm light that had sneaked through the trees, and gathered underneath it, looking over Evie's shoulders at the strange object. None of them knew any longer who they were, or why they were there, because in all that time, the Forgotten Forest had lost none of its power. If they had looked around just a bit more, they might have seen something to remind them: a tall, grey oak tree, with just the faintest outline of a mouth in the bark. The trace of a smile.

But they didn't. Instead, they watched as Evie slowly opened the cover of a book which they had lost so long ago. And it might surprise you to learn that there were no fairy tales inside, no pictures of wizards and monsters, but a series of short handwritten passages, in an elegant, sloping hand, with the date at the top of each one.

'*The Diary of Professor Diana Kelly*,' read Patricia.

They all looked at each other, and shrugged in confusion.

'There's a note at the start,' said Patricia, and started to read, but Simon interrupted.

'Here, let me . . .'

The others looked at him uncertainly, but Patricia passed him the book anyway, and he began to read it out again from the beginning. He was hesitant at first, and stumbled over a couple of words, but as he read his voice grew stronger and clearer.

Dear children, if you are reading this, then you have succeeded where I once tried and failed. But it also means my experiment has only just begun, and that, I'm sorry to say, I am in danger. Which means you are too. It's time to come home.

When he stopped and looked up, Simon no longer had a beard, but only the grimy, floppy hair of many years ago. Evie had no notebook, only a familiar frown, and Larry was back in shorts, clutching a small grey bear. They all stared at each other in disbelief, and then were hugging and laughing as the memory of everything came flooding back. Then they realised where they were. The wooden shelves, the rows of books, the creaking floorboards beneath their feet.

'We're back,' said Larry softly.

And that was how their next adventure began, where the best adventures have always and will always begin.

In the Library.

The Magician Project – Extract 35
(KV 1/1577-8)

CLOSING REPORT

1st Intelligence, Surveillance and Reconnaissance Brigade

HQ Company, Ashford

29 September 1945

Author REDACTED/CLASSIFIED

CONCLUSION

After our soldiers stormed Barfield Hall and arrested Professor Kelly, she refused to reveal the whereabouts of the missing children, even under extreme interrogation.

Eventually, after an exhaustive search of Barfield Hall, the children were discovered. We believe that aided by her housekeeper, Mrs Martin,

Professor Kelly had secreted them in what appeared to be a walled-up attic. Our men finally accessed the space by using sonar equipment to detect a void, and then breaking down the wall.

They uncovered the children in some kind of disused library in the roof eaves. Ancient and rotting shelves lined the walls, and a dilapidated chandelier hung from the ceiling. There were only a handful of books, all very old and falling apart.

The children appeared confused, almost as if some trance or spell had been broken, full of strange stories about fairies and robots, asking our men if they had seen a magician.

(This ties in with what the Professor has told us under interrogation, hence the name of this file.)

It thus remains our contention that Professor Kelly was conducting an illegal, unauthorised and highly dangerous psychological experiment using young minors, that was not in this country's best interest, or indeed theirs.

That experiment has now been shut down. Barfield Hall is closed and we recommend that the government secure it permanently. The Professor will be detained and charged, along with the housekeeper, and the children kept in for clinical observation before being debriefed. They will of course be required to sign the Official Secrets Act.

Only one last matter remains outstanding. After our officers had overseen the medical evacuation of the children, they also arranged for the removal of all the Professor's notes and files, to be placed in this archive.

As they were locking the old house up for the very last time, at the end of a long day, placing box after box of papers into their truck, the captain in charge became convinced someone was watching them from within. This was quite impossible, because the entire building had been swept by trained soldiers and declared clear. Yet this experienced officer swore on his life that a figure was watching them from an upper window.

A man with a pale face, piercing eyes and a dark
beard.

But it was probably just a trick of the light.

STATUS: FILE CLOSED. CLASSIFIED FOR 70 YEARS.

The Magician Project - Extract 35

(KV 2/1589-2)

Simon Hastings School Report
(Michaelmas Term 1945)

CITY OF LONDON EDUCATION COMMITTEE

ST. THOMAS'S SCHOOL

Report on the work of *Simon Hastings* Standard *III*
for *Michaelmas Term* ended *Dec 23rd* 19*45*

Subject	Maximum No. of Marks Possible	Marks Earned	Report
READING	*10*	*9*	*Extraordinary improvement*
WRITING	*10*	*8*	*Unrecognisably good*
ARITHMETIC - Mental			
ARITHMETIC - Written	*30*	*20*	

ENGLISH (a) Composition	10	8	*What has happened?*
(b) Grammar & English Exercises	44	37	*Not bad at all*
(c) Spelling	10	9	*I can't believe it*
(d) Recitation	10	8	
(e) Literature	10	7	
GEOGRAPHY	10	4	*Very strange ideas.* *Folio?*
HISTORY	10	6	*Prepared a project on* *Elizabethan scholar* *Nicholas Crowne.* *Impressed!*
SCIENCE	10	8	*More like science* *fiction! Silver soldiers* *indeed.*
ART (including Drawing)	10	7	
MUSIC			
PHYSICAL TRAINING	10	8	*Where did he learn to* *run so fast?*

CRAFTWORK (a) Wood	10	8	
(b) Metal	10	7	
(c) Needlecraft			
(d) Housecraft			
(e) Other crafts			
Total:	204	154	

Position in class: 2 Number in class: 17

Attendance possible: 75

Times Absent: 2   Times late: 1

Conduct and General Remarks: *Simon has made considerable and frankly inexplicable improvement in his reading and written work and yet ... he seems distant and unhappy. Like he would rather be somewhere else. Is everything all right at home?*

D. Kirke

Class Teacher

The Magician Project – Extract 34
(KV 1/1634-8)

Letter, Evelyn Hastings to Professor Diana Kelly (17/2/46)

58 Colville House
Waterloo Estate
London E2
Sunday 17 February 1946

Dear Professor,

I am writing to say how sorry we all are that you have gone to prison.
I promise that we didn't tell them anything that helped or put the blame on you.

We are all right. Larry is obsessed by unicorns. He can't stop drawing or writing about them. They all involve Roderick, and some of them are very funny! One even won a prize at school. Simon is doing miles better at school too. His teachers say they don't recognise him when it comes to reading. Father and Mother are so proud!

Patricia and I spend as much of our free time as we can in the local library, which reopened after Christmas. As you can imagine, we open more books than we read. I know that our library wasn't founded by Nicholas Crowne and isn't in Barfield, but we keep hoping ... you know. Patricia has become mad keen on maps. I think she's trying to find out if 'you know where' is a real place.

We hope you are OK and being looked after. Are we allowed to visit and bring you cake?

Just one more question.

What happened last summer? Really, though, what happened? What did you do to us?

Yours sincerely

Evelyn Hastings

The Magician Project – Extract 37
(KV 2/1594-2)

Newpaper Article, Kenneth Halliday, 1946

DAILY HERALD
MONDAY DECEMBER 2nd 1946

'MAGICIAN PROJECT' CHILDREN FACE FIRST CHRISTMAS TOGETHER WITH DIGNITY AND PRIDE

This newspaper has been granted exclusive access to the children from the now notorious Barfield Hall chemical weapons experiment, first reported by our Special Investigations Correspondent, KENNETH HALLIDAY, this autumn. The Hastings children are facing their first Christmas back at home after their horrendous ordeal, and the War Office invited Mr. Halliday along to see how they were doing.

The Hastings children are bright and cheery at first, just as children their age should be, especially at the start of Advent. We are not meeting at their new home, for security reasons, but in a regular café near the War Office. Larry Hastings, now aged nine, has red cheeks from the bitter cold, and is full of tales of his first Nativity play, where he took the part of Joseph. And you could not hope to meet two more well brought up young ladies than his sisters Evelyn and Patricia. Unlike their boisterous younger brother, they sit in polite silence until it is their turn to answer a question. We are sure their mother must be very proud! It is only their older brother Simon who seems to bristle at some of my remarks, but isn't that typical of most boys his age? And after all, he's been through a lot – they all have.

Regular readers will be aware of their role in the sensational story this reporter broke earlier this year, of the highly regarded scientist Professor Diana Kelly, who until the end of the War, worked on a top-secret programme at the War Office research facility in Porton Down, near Salisbury. It is still unclear what happened, but it appears that Professor Kelly had a nervous breakdown, yet again raising questions in some quarters about women's suitability for the difficult roles the War thrust them into.

The true facts of the case remain classified military secrets, but what is clear is that under the pretence of a free summer holiday for the children of an old school friend, the Professor lured and coerced the children to take part in a dangerous psychiatric experiment that nearly cost them their minds.

Their father, Frank Hastings, is a decorated war hero who saw action at Dunkirk, so it is not surprising that this honourable man takes his share of the blame. 'It was a rotten mistake of ours to send the nippers there in the first place. Diana Kelly was a pal of my wife. All I knew was she worked for the government. Hush hush, for sure, but our government. What harm could come from that?'

Evelyn pipes up, her eyes bright in the twinkling Christmas lights of the corner house. 'But there was no harm, Father. It was wonderful! I wish you could have come with us.

We want to go back. I'll take you if you like!
You could meet—'

Mr. Hastings looks very uncomfortable,
fingering his collar, and the representative
from the Ministry steps in to remind the
children that they are forbidden by the
Official Secrets Act from mentioning any
details of their experience. I'm afraid that
readers of this paper will have to wait until
that information is declassified in 2018 to find
out more.

But it certainly leaves your reporter curious ...

The Magician Project – Extract 43
(KV 3/1587–14)

Funeral Order of Service for Professor Diana Kelly, 8th March 1954

THE ORDER OF SERVICE
For the Funeral of
PROFESSOR DIANA KELLY
29th November 1898 - 5th March 1954

In the Church of St. Mary's
Dunstall, Suffolk
Monday 8th March 1954

WELCOME and INTRODUCTION
Reverend Hugh Hamilton

BIDDING PRAYER

HYMN no. 89
'There is a Land of Pure Delight'
(Isaac Watts, 1709)

READING
Deuteronomy, 30:1-8
DUNCAN KELLY

EULOGY

JANET MCLEITH-STEWARD,

Parliamentary Secretary to the Ministry of Defence

READING

'All Hushed and Still Within the House'

(Emily Brontë)

EVELYN HASTINGS

All hushed and still within the house;
Without - all wind and driving rain;
But something whispers to my mind,
Through rain and through the wailing wind,
Never again.
Never again? Why not again?
Memory has power as real as thine.

HYMN no. 23

'Were You There?' (American spiritual)

ADDRESS

Reverend Hugh Hamilton

HYMN no. 106

'Ride On, Ride On in Majesty'

(Henry Hart Milman, 1827)

PRAYERS AND COLLECTION

There will be a collection on behalf of the
Suffolk Library Service

BLESSING

The Magician Project – Extract 45
(KV 4/1999-14)

Magazine Article, Barfield House Sale, 1961

COUNTRY LIFE
WEDNESDAY JULY 19th 1961

Upon instructions from HM Government, Wadley and Wools will Sell by Auction the residual contents of Barfield Hall, Barfield, nr Salisbury, Wiltshire in a marquee on the premises.

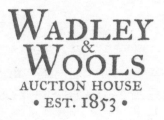

WADLEY & WOOLS
AUCTION HOUSE
• EST. 1853 •

The contents have been temporarily removed to The Wadley and Wools Auction Rooms in Salisbury for cataloguing, photography and security, together with other surplus lots removed from temporary government storage facilities.

Furnishings include Art Deco Marcel Charreau sofa and lounge chairs (1928), artworks include Victor Lakovsky 'Meditations On' series (I-VIII, oils),

'Still Life of Hounds with Game' (J. Masterson, 1797) and 'The British Navy engage the Dutch Fleet' (1673) and a 16th-century portrait in oils of Sir Nicholas Crowne, the notorious early modern magus and scholar, artist unknown.

Other notable entries in this sale include a 1945 Armstrong Siddeley Lancaster, matching numbers, pre-select gearbox, in excellent order throughout, one previous careful owner, includes original bill of sale from dealer in Salisbury.

But perhaps the most extraordinary lot in this auction is an unrivalled collection of over 90,000 books, manuscripts and ephemera, making up Nicholas Crowne's renowned collection, once reputed to be the most extensive private library in Europe, dating back to the sixteenth century. Regrettably, owing to the size of the collection, and following strict instructions from HMG that it be broken up, this is only available for purchase in separate lots. Any items not sold will be disposed of for security reasons.

The Magician Project — Extract 45
(KV 2/1589-2)

Larry Hastings Dissertation Cover

**THE BOARD OF RESEARCH STUDIES REJECT THIS
DISSERTATION FOR PH.D 1ST APRIL 1965**

WHY UNICORNS EXIST

by Larry Hastings,
King's College

Thesis presented for the degree of PH.D
at the University of Cambridge

INTRODUCTION

It is my contention in this paper to suggest that
the unicorn, once believed to be mythical, is a
real animal which does exist. Furthermore, that
unicorns are some of the noblest, bravest and
kindest creatures to be found on this earth.

The Magician Project — Extract 89

(KV 3/2601-2)

Diary of Professor Patricia Hastings, extract

Monday October 2nd 1972

My new students arrive today. I enjoy watching them drifting around Newcastle in a bit of a daze. There are so many new buildings going up so fast and yet still so much of the old city - markets, slums, bomb sites - increasingly look something from another era. Still, as future geographers, it's all good material for them!

Wednesday October 4th 1972

Simon called. Still no word from Evie. She has been out of contact for over a week now. It's silly to worry, I know. Simon is quite sure she's just taken herself off for a holiday to a Greek island or something, but it is so unlike her not to call or even send a postcard. I even wondered if she had gone to New York to see Larry... I rang and rang till eventually I got hold of his roommate, Ricardo (?), who said that Larry was out and that there was no sign of Evie. Larry seems to be out whenever I ring. I just hope he's having fun and taking care of himself, whatever he's doing.

I do worry about Evie the most, because out of us all, she took the longest to adjust after...all that business. Evie was the hardest hit by the Professor's death. We all were. But her obsession, that there was some government conspiracy, that to honour the Professor's legacy we all had to go back to...it doesn't bear thinking about. The last time I saw her, she looked terrible. Pale, hair too long, didn't look like she had been eating properly, ranting and raving about some book the Professor had sent her, and a secret clue which would explain everything.

I told her. It can't be explained.

It was a dream. Drug-induced, hypnosis, call it what you will. We read some fairy tales and the Professor tricked us into believing it was real.

But it wasn't. It still pains me, all these years on, that it wasn't, but Folio wasn't real. It can't be. If only there was a way of making Evie understand that.

Thursday October 5th 1972

I am so shaken I can barely write these words.

All our worst fears have been realised.

A hammering at my door late last night. It was raining so hard, I barely recognised her. She looked so deathly, my first impulse was to call for an ambulance, but she shrieked at the very idea.

Then I saw what she was carrying with her. And she told me everything.

Oh God, Evie, what have you done? WHAT HAVE YOU DONE?

DON'T MISS
THE NEXT
ENTHRALLING
ADVENTURE IN
FOLIO...

THE
FROZEN
SEA

COMING SOON

ACKNOWLEDGEMENTS

'Some day you will be old enough to start reading
fairy tales again.'
C. S. Lewis

If you've got this far, then it is perhaps clear to you that both I and this book owe an enormous debt to another author: C. S. Lewis. Readers ask me one question more than any other. 'What was your favourite book as a child?' It's almost impossible to make a choice but, unbidden, the same story comes to my mind every time. I remember lying in bed, aged eight, reading *The Lion, The Witch and the Wardrobe*. The wonder of it filled my dreams. A wardrobe that led to another world. A battle between good and dark magic. Victory achieved by heroic children equipped with special gifts. In 2017, I decided to revisit the work that opened my eyes to the human potential of story-telling. What you have just read is in part a homage to one of the all-time classics of children's literature, and in part my attempt to reimagine a similar kind of story from a modern perspective. I'm hugely grateful to C. S. Lewis for the gift of his Narnia series, my gateway to the magical world of reading, as they have been and remain for countless others.

I would not have got this far without my editor at Quercus Children's, Sarah Lambert, and would like to thank her for not thinking I was mad when I first suggested this project to her, and I would also like to thank her cover Kate Agar for also not thinking I was mad when I finally finished and delivered this story to her. I am grateful to them both for their support, rigorous scrutiny and invaluable advice, and in particular Kate for taking a project on midway with such generosity and sensitivity.

Thanks also to Becca Allen, for making sure that everything in this library was correct as well as magical with her scrupulous copy-edits, and to proofreader Adele Brimacombe who made sure any new magic laws were confined to the text and not the actual laws of space and time. Thanks also to Ruth Girmatsion for co-ordinating us all.

The cover by Ben Mantle is sensational and would be picked up in any library. I thank him for so embracing the world of Folio and bringing it to life, alongside designer Samuel Perrett at Hachette Children's.

I remain indebted to my agent Clare Conville and all at C&W for the love they give to all my books, as well as to my husband Will Tosh for all the love he gives to me. I would thank Huxley our dog but to be honest he mainly got in the way with this one.

Finally, I would like to thank the many real librarians out there, working in schools, public libraries and freelance, who every day, connecting readers with the right books, remain the selfless guardians of the only true magic there is.

Join Kester on his animal adventures in the bestselling and award-winning

THE LAST WILD
trilogy

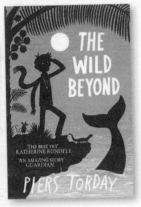

'An amazing story…
deserves to win prizes'
Guardian

'Inventive, with laughs,
tears and cliffhangers'
Sunday Times

'A wonderfully strange
and strangely wonderful book'
Financial Times

'Action-packed'
Daily Mail

'Brings to mind the smarts
and silliness of Roald Dahl'
New York Post

'Written in a vivid, urgent style,
The Last Wild may be as critical to
the new generation as Tarka the Otter'
The Times

On a frozen Christmas Eve, Mouse Mallory
and his family set off across a snow-white valley
to visit his grandparents. But an accident sends
him head-first into a magical quest where
he'll have to face grave dangers . . .

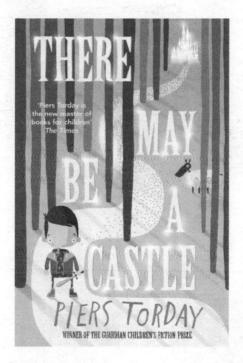

A remarkable story about love, loss
and the power of the imagination.

WWW.PIERSTORDAY.CO.UK

Visit Piers for news,
school visits, events and more!